Head of Falls

—

A NOVEL

EARL H. SMITH

North Country Press
Unity, Maine

While the author has sought to accurately depict the time and place of this novel, the principal characters and their stories are entirely fictional. Where real-life historical or public figures are described, the situations and dialogues related to these people are not intended to recount actual events or to alter the fictional nature of the work. Otherwise, any resemblance to any person, living or dead, is coincidental.

ISBN 978-1-943424-15-3
Library of Congress Control Number: 2016952827

Cover art by Kathy Speight Kraynak
Copy edited by Beth Staples

North Country Press
Unity, Maine

For Emily, my inspiration

Music is well said to be the speech of angels.

–Thomas Carlyle

1954

Everything seems to move faster than ever before. New television stations go on the air every day, and the news arrives the day it happens. Roger Bannister runs the mile in under four minutes, new cars have more pep than drivers can use, and Bill Haley quickens the pace of pop and begins a musical revolution. With the opening of the first shopping mall in Michigan, buying habits begin to change, and a new Florida restaurant named Burger King lets people eat faster, as well.

The Korean War is over, and the Cold War has begun. Communists move into Vietnam, and whole islands are annihilated by hydrogen bomb tests, but Americans pay little attention. After a decade of war, there's catching up to do at home. Senator McCarthy is condemned for his reckless hunt for Reds under beds, the Supreme Court orders desegregation of the nation's schools, and children are at last spared the scourge of polio by a single shot in the arm. To tidy things up, the words "under God" are added to the Pledge of Allegiance.

Wall Street climbs to its highest point since the Depression, and in Waterville, Maine, as in most river towns in New England, thousands labor in the great mills, running three shifts a day to meet the demands of a spending world. Even as the old industries churn on, inventors file for patents at the rate of 200 a day, and new businesses are beginning to reshape the economic face of the nation.

One

I'll be 15 years old next month, and I'm pretty sure I've already learned most of what anybody ever needs to know. Right up there among the important things is that if you want something done you'd better do it yourself, and even then you can't be sure it will turn out right. I've also figured out – the hard way, I might add – that things aren't always as they seem, and it's a big mistake to believe everything you hear. Take weather forecasts, for example. I don't know about other places, but here in Maine the weathermen are entirely untrustworthy, especially when it comes to hurricanes, which get themselves all puffed up and scare you half to death, and then at the last minute, fizzle out or head off to Nova Scotia, or someplace like that.

Reports of a hurricane named Carol have been in the news for days, but nobody paid the least bit of attention until yesterday, when she came roaring ashore in Connecticut, and folks around here woke up and began to scramble for batteries and plywood.

I had no idea who Carol even was until the afternoon, when the manager of the city swimming pool told us lifeguards that the place was closing for the season. The announcement came right out of the blue. The pool was supposed to be open another week, but with the storm coming and school just around the corner, the higher-ups decided to shut down early. Nobody bothered to ask me. I would have inquired how they thought a girl was supposed to make ends meet with the last week's pay snatched out from

1

under her nose just because of a stupid hurricane. Mom needs help with the rent, and I was hoping to squeeze something out of that last $17 check for school supplies, maybe even a couple of records. *Rock Around the Clock* has been at the top of the charts for eight straight weeks, and for the lack of a lousy 50 cents, I still don't have a record with Bill Haley's name on it.

It poured last night, and this morning there was barely a sunrise. I stay up in my room, sitting cross-legged on the floor with the 45-rpm player Margaux gave me when she got a new one with an automatic changer. I love it, and I barely moved all morning, going from tune to tune as I shuffled through my stack of favorites. At the moment, the world is plumb full of terrific new songs, and I'd like to have every one. Al Corey's Music Center, upstairs on Main Street, has lots of sales, and that's when I poke around to find the bargains. Already this summer I've added Kitty Kallen, *Little Things Mean a Lot*; Rosemary Clooney, *Hey There*; and Patti Page, *Cross Over the Bridge*. I got Eddie Fisher's *Oh! My Papa* because I like the music, but for the life of me, I don't understand how anybody can get all that gushy about his father.

Between records, I can't help but hear the howling wind. It's picked up over the last hour, and green leaves, ripped from the trees, are splattering on the windowpanes. The sound is frightening, and I try to block it out by turning up the volume and listening to Perry Como croon *Wanted*, all the while making believe that he wants me. My legs are stiff from sitting, and I decide to wind things up with Tony Bennett, my most favorite crooner of all.

> *Must I forever be a beggar*
> *Whose golden dreams will not come true*
> *Or will I go from rags to riches*
> *My fate is up to you ... up to you ... up to you ... up to you ...*

The needle is stuck in a worn groove, and I give it a gentle nudge to let Tony finish up. When he's done, I hear the wind screech again. It sounds as if a locomotive has jumped the railroad tracks across the street and is headed straight this way, and it makes me nervous. I step across the narrow hallway to peek into Gabe's room, but he's not there. I should have known. These days, my big brother is always off somewhere, anywhere, without a care, leaving me with nothing but the smell of his sweaty sneakers. I'd like to hate him for it, but I can't.

Downstairs, I hear Mom pacing in the front room. Ordinarily she'd be at work up at Jabbur's, the Lebanese restaurant on Hathaway Street where she waits tables and washes dishes through breakfast and lunch. Her customers are mostly mill workers who left home too late to make breakfast or forgot their lunch pails, but nobody with an ounce of sense is going out to eat in the middle of a hurricane. Mr. Jabbur must have let her off early.

I go down and sit with Mom, and we squirm to avoid the broken sofa springs while we listen to the WTVL announcer read storm bulletins, straight from the ticker: the Kennebec River is rising, there's flooding everywhere, trees are down, power is out, streets are unsafe, people should stay home. Mom lets out a tiny gasp after every bulletin, but we don't have much to say. We rarely do. After a day of chatting it up with customers for the sake of tips, she's worn out with the gab, and when we're alone together we tend to talk with our eyes and nods of our heads. The only exception is her endless fretting about all the things that are sure to go wrong. The poor, dear woman can spot tragedy in a bar of soap.

As if she's heard me thinking, she breaks the silence. "Just you wait, Angela," she says, fiddling with the dial on the Crosley to clear the static, "any second now, we're going to be crushed to death by a falling tree."

She sounds a bit too certain to suit me, and I don't answer. Instead, I sit and gaze at her in amazement. Her tall, thin body is frail and tense. Her black hair hangs straight and wispy, and her gray eyes flit about in panic. I study her fingers, red and cracked from endless dishwashing, and wonder what will become of her when I'm old enough to leave home. I'm pretty sure she can't take care of herself, as she's totally clueless about so many things, not the least of which is my father. I'll admit that I'm a little short on knowing a whole lot about love, but I'm not sure I'll ever understand the kind that keeps her loving him. I think she believes he's her salvation, if there is such a thing, but she's dead wrong about that. The man is her very undoing.

I walk to the window just as a truck rumbles by, loaded with cotton bales, headed for the mill. Front Street is flooded, and the tires send a wall of water over the curb and onto the glass. I flinch and step back. "Listen, Mom," I finally say, "there's not a thing to worry about." She's abandoned the radio and is fumbling her overworked rosary beads. "For one thing," I tell her, "there aren't trees around here big enough to crush anything." I also remind her weather forecasters can't be trusted. She's not convinced by any of it, I can tell, and she comes to join me at the window, craning her neck, looking for signs of certain doom.

The daylight – what remains of it – is fading fast, and the wind is hurling rain against the windows, making them chatter in their loose frames. Above the windows, the wallpaper is soggy and dark. The eaves are leaking again, but this time the rain is creeping down the walls in a wide, dark tide. I'm afraid Mom will notice and want to build an ark, and I'm about to distract her when the announcer says in a somewhat shaky voice that winds have reached 80 miles an hour. In that very second the radio goes silent, and I glance up to watch the lone bulb above our heads flicker once, then die as well.

Mom feels her way into the kitchen, looking for candles, she says. I remind her we don't have any, and we end up sitting silently in the gloom for what seems like an age. Finally, about 6:30, the light bulb comes back and the left-on radio lets out a howl. "Well," Mom pipes up, suddenly sounding very sure of herself, "we can certainly be grateful the police station is right down the street or else it would be days before we got the electricity back in this neighborhood." I'm not at all sure how she knows the priorities of Central Maine Power repair crews, but I'm grateful, too, as I don't think I can stand another minute of sitting in the dark, listening to Hail Marys and the screaming wind. I'm about to stick my head outside for a quick look when we hear loud thumps on the porch.

"Baba's back." Mom's voice trembles, and she sucks in her breath. I bristle, not so much at the prospect of my father's return, but because she's used the affectionate Arabic name for father. I haven't called him Baba since I was 10, and I don't plan to, ever again. I call him plain "father," and, if I dared, I'd call him Ashur, like everybody else, but I know I wouldn't get away with it.

Even before we see him, we hear loud curses as he struggles in the darkness to find the broken handle on the screen door. He's obviously spent the afternoon, or the entire day for that matter, with his cronies at Archie's Bar, down and across the road, beyond Temple Street. It's a daily miracle he's able to weave his way home without getting mixed up in traffic.

Mom nods silently and, like a mother hen, she beckons me to follow her into the kitchen. It's a familiar drill. My father's been drinking too much for a long time, but it's gotten worse since July, when he lost his job as a picker at the Wyandotte woolen mill. The supervisor asked him to clean the acid baths, and my father went into a rage and ended up throwing ammonia in the man's face. My father got sacked on the spot. Of course, he has a completely different version of the story, but the real truth came from Bernie Nelson, the neighborhood cop who brought him home.

For weeks, my father has claimed to be out every day looking for a new job. Mom believes him, but I don't. It doesn't matter, in any case. Everybody knows my father's a nasty drunk, and there isn't a mill boss for miles who's foolish enough to hire him.

I feel myself grow tense as he stumbles inside, jamming his shoulder hard against the doorframe to catch his balance. The rain has slicked his stringy, black hair; and his shirt, blotched with stains, hangs over his grimy jeans. His unshaven face is twisted into a frightening snarl. Without so much as a how-de-do, he asks about supper. The word *supper* comes out like *subber*, but it isn't a question, in any case.

"Power's been out, Ashur." Mom is sweet and calm. "It came back just a few minutes ago. I'll make something, right away." It's the wrong answer; I knew it would be.

He starts to rant on about his supper when he suddenly spots the sagging wallpaper above the windows, and his eyes bug out. "What in hell have you been doin'?" He points at Mom. "Sittin' on your ass while the place falls down?" I know I should keep my mouth shut, but I can't help sticking up for her and I try to explain that we'd just this minute seen the damage. I don't get two words out before he cuts me off and starts to come toward us, into the kitchen.

There have been many fights like this before, and I usually block the horror by somehow managing to disappear in my own thoughts, in a kind of trance where I don't see or hear what's going on in front of me. It doesn't work now. He's screaming, and his fists are up. Mom's pleas have become sobs, and she's looking for a place to hide. I crouch near the stove, sick to my stomach, wishing with all my heart Gabe would come through the door. He used to be able to calm things down, but when he got big enough to look my father directly in the face, he got some thrashings of his own. The thought of Gabe gives me an idea, and I decide I'll take my cue from him and simply leave.

I'm almost to the door when my father sees me. He turns and raises his fist. "Just where in hell do you think you're goin', young lady?" I have two choices. I can run or I can stay, and I've already decided not to stay. As evenly as I can, I tell him I'm going next door, to Margaux's. He gives me an odd look, and I know his fogged brain is churning to find a reason why I can't. I don't wait to hear it. Instead, I push the screen door hard against the wind, and step out of one storm and straight into another.

Two

Heavy rain is pelting in from across the river, straight onto the porch. I forgot my jacket, but I'm not going back, and I stand at the top of the steps and let the wind and rain cool my face while I try to decide what to do. I'm not going to Margaux's, that's for sure. I lied about that. She isn't home, and I knew it. I'd desperately like to find Gabe, but I have no idea where he might be. The Boys Club, his favorite haunt, is certainly closed; after that, I have no idea.

Like many of the houses on the narrow lots along Front Street, ours has an apartment tacked on the back. The Mathieus live there, and this morning in the driveway Margaux told me her grandparents were terrified by the coming storm, and she and her parents would be spending the day with them, up town, on Pleasant Street. I didn't think anything about it at the time, but now I curse the luck that has taken her away today, when I need her most.

Margaux is my very best friend. We've always been a pair, like the Bobbsey Twins her mother says. We work together in the summer and chum around after school, hanging out at the Y, poking through the records at Al Corey's, trying on dresses we can't buy at Butler's Department Store, and drooling over the pastries in the windows of Harris Bakery. In another week, we'll both be sophomores at Waterville High.

Right now, what I need most from her is not her companionship as much as some of her spunk. When it comes to courage, she has me beat, and it comes from having polio when she was seven. She got cured all right, but it left her with a hunch in the back, shriveled muscles in her left leg, and a fierce determination. She could feel sorry for herself, but she doesn't. When she falls down, which is actually quite often, she gets right back up on her feet, and God help anybody who tries to give her a hand. At the moment, I could use that kind of guts for myself.

A new blast of wind from the river shakes me back into the moment, and I shudder to realize I've been standing on the porch much too long. If my father sees me, he'll certainly drag me back inside. I'm soaked, and I have to go someplace, anyplace, and quickly. Thoughts of the river make me wonder if the Kennebec is over its banks, and I decide I'll have a look. Gripping my blouse tightly at the neck, I go down the porch steps, cross the crumbling curb, and step into the street, trying to avoid the mammoth puddles.

Down below, at Temple Street, the road crosses over the railroad tracks, but up here at my end of Front Street, the grade is high, and long ago a narrow road was cut under the tracks, leading to the sloping land between the railroad and the river. I've been through this cut a zillion times. It's scary, and I never liked it much. In the dark, I like it even less. Briefly out of the wind, I shiver when I hear my own footsteps echo off the mossy granite walls.

After a dozen nervous steps, I come into the neighborhood called Head of Falls. Looming on my left is the ancient Waterville Iron Works. Up the river and out of sight are the noisy shops of the Maine Central Railroad. Straight ahead, I can see the lone streetlight that marks the corner of Head of Falls Road. Here, wooden tenement houses are bunched together, leading to a line of low, connected warehouses, each one now in darkness, their massive doors firmly closed.

This afternoon, the radio announcer said the Hathaway Shirt Company on nearby Appleton Street was shut down because of the storm, and I'm relieved to find the Wyandotte mill is up and running. The long building protects me from the wind, and I feel strangely comforted by the familiar clattering of the looms and the lights that glow in the windows that line the topmost floor.

Head of Falls Road ends abruptly at Temple Street, and a narrow street continues on the other side, following the railroad tracks as they begin to bend east, toward their own bridge at the falls. I stop in the intersection and turn to look up into town. I can see that the power is still on, and the rain, mixed with the yellow glow of streetlights, makes a shimmering halo over the tops of the tall buildings on Main Street.

From here, it's just a short distance down to the suspension bridge that carries foot traffic to and from the giant Hollingsworth & Whitney paper mill across the river. At this end of the wooden walkway, I can see the light over the tollhouse where the keeper collects the two-cent fare. The shifts won't change until 11, but even now there are a few men hunched against the rain, carrying dinner pails over the swaying span.

This close to the water, I can hear the river boiling as it heads for the falls. Near the tollhouse, buildings are arranged haphazardly on both sides of the road. Mostly tenements, the structures are jammed together, some perched precariously on the last, steep pitch to the river. Lebanese immigrants have lived in this sprawling neighborhood for a half-century, close by the iron works and the woolen mill, not far from the Lockwood cotton mill and the shirt factory, and a short walk across the footbridge to the paper mill with its belching chimney and mountains of cordwood.

I walk down Temple Street far enough to see that water is already lapping the back porches of the houses on the riverbank, and I shudder when I think what might happen to these poor people if the water gets any higher.

The rain suddenly makes another surge, and I start back up the hill, stopping to glance down the tiny street called King Court, hoping to find a place to get out of the wind and rain. Halfway down, on the right, I see a small, white clapboard house standing out oddly in contrast to the unpainted tenements lurking on either side. I've seen this little house before, but I've never been close. Tonight I go that way, following the glow of a single bulb that hangs at the side of the front door.

The house is plain as plain can be. Two small windows flank the entrance, and a tin-roofed canopy barely shelters the thick, granite stoop. I go to the steps and sit down, drawing my knees up to my chin to get out of the rain. A car is parked in the narrow gravel driveway, headed out, and I huddle there, transfixed, watching in the dim light as the rain runs down the shiny, black hood.

I don't move for what seems like a long time, wondering if I can safely return home, wondering where I might go if I don't, wondering what will become of me. My father frightens me. My mother loves me, and I love her, but most of her time is taken up with the work she needs to do to keep things going. My brother has all but given up. I don't know if I have aunts, or uncles, or cousins, but my grandparents are gone. Mom's folks are dead, and my father's family, like so many others, spread out and lost track of each other in the confusion of finding their way in a new country. It's no wonder I sometimes think of running away. In despair, I bury my face in my hands and begin to sob.

The moment of self-pity ends abruptly when I hear the creaking of a door behind me. I brush away the tears and get set to run, but first I turn to have a quick look. An old man is standing there, outlined in the warm light of the doorway. His round face is clean-shaven, and he's wearing the hint of a smile. Plump red cheeks hold up the bottoms of his wire-rimmed glasses. His hair, like mine, is black, thick, and curly, and in the pale light I make out wisps of white.

"Well, hello," the old man says, grinning warmly. "My name's Elias. Can I help you?" Lebanese, I say to myself, like me. "This big girl here is Adagio." He points to a fluffy yellow cat peering from between his legs. "And you?"

"Angela," I say, my voice croaking just a little. "Angela Jamal." He cocks his head. "My mother's Yara," I add, thinking he might know her.

He smiles. "Oh yes, of course. She works at Jabbur's, up on Temple Street. I go there often. Fine woman."

"And, my father's Ashur," I put in, for no reason, except to be complete.

He looks down at the cat and pauses. "I think I know him, too."

"I was out for a walk," I say, feeling foolish the instant the words come out. Again I start to turn to leave, but he holds out both hands.

"Oh, please, don't go," he shakes his head. "You're soaking wet. You'll catch your death of cold. You must come in, at least for a minute, and dry off." He sees me hesitate. "I don't believe your mother would mind, at all."

I know better than to go inside the house of a stranger, but something tells me there is nothing here to fear at all. I glance down at my dungarees. The blue has turned to black from the wet, and the wide, turned-up cuffs are filled with water. I touch my hair. It's wrecked. The curls that hung to my shoulders when I left the house have sprung into tight black knots. It's still pouring, and I'm shivering from the cold. I pause only a moment, and then I nod.

"There you go," he says, smiling as he steps back and holds the door. It's a relief to be out of the horrid weather, and I stand by the doorway for a minute to take it all in. Familiar smells of old linoleum and kerosene are softened by the pleasant fragrance of cooking and Old Spice, and the walls and tables are filled with aging photographs of smiling faces. On the right, a narrow staircase rises to what must be a tiny attic, and beneath it, a wooden table and a pair of chairs make a tiny kitchen. A worn rag rug covers the floor in front of me, and on the left, a padded Morris chair is pulled up near the heater, its metal chimney guarded by a sheet of wrinkled tin on the wall behind.

The last place I look is straight in front of me, and I'm astonished by what I see. Of all things, it's a piano. I blink my eyes once or twice; it can't be true. I've never seen a piano in anybody's house, and I certainly never expected to see one in my neighborhood. The old man chuckles when he sees me stare, and he points to a padded bench squared up in front of the keyboard. "Sit here," he says, "I'll fetch a towel." He disappears behind a door in the corner by the kitchen, and I sit down and turn to gaze. It's the closest I've ever been to a real piano. There are two at school, but Mrs. Bizier protects them like the guard who watches the bank vault at Federal Trust.

The cover is closed over the keyboard, and I'm beginning to wonder if I dare open it just as the old man returns. "Old towels dry the best," he says as he hands me a thin and tattered cloth. I wipe my face and arms, and then begin to ruffle the towel through my hair, stopping to tug at the ends to straighten things out. Adagio comes and makes circles around my legs, purring all the while.

The man has no sooner turned the Morris chair to face me when he trudges off again, headed for the kitchen. "You should have something in your stomach," he announces. I wonder how he knows. The missing supper at home was what caused the fight, and I'm pretty sure there's going to be no supper at all tonight.

He returns with an open box of cookies and a cheese-spread glass filled with milk. "There," he says with a sigh of satisfaction, "now I really must ask how you happen to be out for a walk on a fine evening like this." He laughs at his own joke, a warm belly chuckle that invites me to join in, and I realize that I can't remember when I last laughed about anything at all.

"It's a long story," I answer. "And, you don't want to hear it, Mr. ..." I don't know his name.

"You can call me Mr. M," he says, and then goes on to explain that when he first arrived from Lebanon he got a job at the Wyandotte, where lots of his fellow workers were French-Canadian. "They had a hard time with Moussallem," he explains, laughing again, "just as I did with some of their names. They decided to call me Mr. M, and it stuck. It's fine with me."

"Well then, Mr. M," I say. "Thank you for being so very kind." I bend down to rub Adagio's ears. "I wish I could stay, but it's possible my folks will be wondering where I've gone."

I turn for a last look at the wonderful instrument behind me, and I can tell he's watching me. "Let me tell you something about that piano," he says, before he goes on to explain that he came to Waterville from Lebanon in 1910. "The Turks drove us out," he says. "We are Maronites; they wanted to kill us." He says there were already relatives here who found him a job at the mill and gave him a place to stay until he could save enough to bring his wife and make a home with her.

"Jamilah was a beautiful piano player," he says with pride. "She gave lessons to children in Aleppo, where we lived. I knew she was going to miss her precious piano, especially in a strange, new country, where she didn't know a soul." He explains that a lady up on Burleigh Street bought herself a new piano and posted a notice in the mill, offering the old one for sale. "Sears & Roebuck sold these Beckwiths for $100 new," he says. "I offered $10, a whole week's wage, and she took it. It was in this house the day Jamilah arrived, and it's been here ever since." He goes on to tell me his wife had the tools and knew how to tune it, a skill she taught to him.

I can't help but gush. "What a perfectly beautiful story," I say as I gently place my hands on the lid. "Do you mind?" I ask, even as I slowly lift it up. There on the board behind the keys is the Beckwith name, in gold letters as complete and crisp as they must have been when they were new. I sit in awe, reaching to pass my fingers over the carved wreath of leaves that adorns the front.

"Forgot to tell you," he says as I give Adagio a pat and stand to leave. "Jamilah never stopped teaching the piano. When she came to America, she taught lots of local kids to play, as well. She never charged much, sometimes nothing." The big chuckle comes back. "As a matter of fact, she taught me to play, too, and it didn't cost me a nickel." He sighs. "Before she died, I was good enough for the two of us to be able to play together."

The tale fascinates me, and he knows it. "Tell you what," he says, "if you like, I can teach you to play, too." He pauses. "No charge." I can only bob my head. "If you want to come and learn," he says, "just tell your mother, and we'll make a deal."

Three

There's a loud rap on the front door, and I sit up and squint at the clock by the bed. Eight o'clock. Either the thing ran down last night or it's Margaux, the only one I know who's dumb enough to get up this early on a day with nothing to do. I grab my robe and scramble downstairs in my bare feet. All bright and perky, she looks every bit as if she's off to a dance at the Y. Her red sweater is buttoned up the back; she's wearing a pair of capris, and white socks sag over the tops of her shabby penny loafers. The sun we haven't seen for two days is finally peeking out, and a tiny breeze tosses her floppy ponytail as she reaches out with both hands to give me a hug.

"Let's go up into town," she pipes up right off the bat, eyes positively sparkling. "We can see how the La-Di-Das made out in the hurricane." Margaux calls anyone with more money than we have La-Di-Das, and the way I see it, that includes an awful lot of people.

There's no use trying to go back to sleep now, and so I run to pull on the clothes I draped over a kitchen chair last night to dry, zip in and out of the bathroom, snag a two-day-old doughnut off the counter in the kitchen, and am back by the front door in two minutes. I think about leaving a note, but there's no need. Mom is already at work, and my father is in the same place where I found

16

him when I got back from Mr. M's – flat on his back on the sofa, mouth wide open and gurgling, sleeping it off. When his head clears up and he thinks about going down to Archie's for more job interviews, he won't even notice that I've gone.

Margaux had stepped inside the front room while she waited, and now she's gaping in open-mouthed wonder at the lump on the sofa. I shoo her out the door. "They was a big row last night," I explain when we get to the sidewalk.

"Another one." It isn't a question. "Was Gabe home?"

"Nope."

"Men are turds," she says, out of the blue. "Absolute turds." Margaux's world is arranged somewhat like a garden, where all the women are roses and all the men are cow turds.

"What about *your* father?" I fire back, not sure if I'm being defensive or if I hate thinking she's right.

She shrugs her humped back. "Well of course, there *are* exceptions," she says, dismissively, "and my father is one, but yours, I hate to say, is a genuine turd."

"Margaux!!"

"Well, he is, and so's Gabe. He ought to have been home to look after you."

If she's going to generalize about turds, I'm not letting her include Gabe. "It's not his fault." I shake a finger under her nose. "Life hasn't been very good to him, and my father's only part of the story." I then recite a long story that she's heard before, about how Gabe, barely five-foot-six, got cut from the basketball team the year he entered high school, and what that meant to him in a basketball-crazy town where the Lebanese boys dominated on a New England championship team only ten years before. Even so, I remind her, he never gave up, and since that time he's played on pickup teams at the Club, day after day, night after night. My father has never seen him play, and Mom has been only once or twice. I go when I can to show support, and right now I'm not about to let Margaux call him a turd. Not on your life.

"Well then," she huffs, "maybe Gabe *is* an exception, like my father. But your father stays on the list, along with most other men around here." She pretends to look around. "Take Spike, for example." Spike is not a random choice. He is actually Bill Moufette, a classmate at school. Both handsome and rich, he even has his own car, a new black Ford Crestline with loud glass-pack mufflers and a fake continental kit. The girls at school drool over him – and his car. "Just look at him," Margaux goes on, as if he were standing right in front of us. "Fancy threads, fancy car, and a fancy nose straight up in the air. He's a stupid peacock, if you ask me."

I wag my finger an inch from her nose and smirk. "You know what?"

"What?"

"I think you like him."

She giggles, then promptly goes back to last night's fight. "So, tell me, what did little Miss Angela do when it all began?"

"I took off," I say, flat out.

"In the middle of a hurricane?"

"Yup. Walked down by the river, got soaking wet and, surprise, surprise, met the nicest man you could ever imagine."

She spins around, her weak leg making a long arc on the turn.

"He's a nice old man," I quickly explain. "Name's Elias Moussallem, but I call him Mr. M."

Her eyes grow wide. "I knew his wife," she announces. "Her name was Jamilah. She had just begun to give me piano lessons when I got sick. By the time I got better, she'd upped and died."

I'm relieved that Margaux knows Mr. M, otherwise she'd probably say I'd lost my mind. Instead, I feel free to give her every detail of last night's visit, including, at the end, his offer to teach me to play the piano. "I'm going to do it," I say, leaving no room for doubt, "but here's the problem. He wants me to tell my mother first, and you know what that means. She'll make him out to be a pervert of some kind and come up with all sorts of reasons why I shouldn't."

"So what?" Margaux shrugs. "Just go ahead and tell her. She'll come around, but sweet Jesus, make sure she doesn't blab it to your father."

We've walked as far as Joseph's Market without a pause in the conversation. The Joseph brothers are outside in their white aprons, overseeing the replacing of a plate glass window, and they wave as we step into the street to pass the store. When we come to St. Joseph Church, we both bend a knee. Although my church is Maronite and Margaux's is Roman, we long ago agreed that despite using two separate languages that neither of us can understand, Sacred Heart and St. Joseph are both Catholic and, as such, deserve respect and genuflection.

At Temple Street, we turn up into town, cross Main Street, and keep going. Dakin's Sporting Goods store is closed, a sheet of plywood nailed over the front door, and when we get up to the converted mansion that has become the YMCA, we begin to see that there are limbs down and entire trees uprooted. The ground is littered with torn leaves and bits of soaked debris, and across the street, a giant fallen elm covers the entire walkway in front of the Congo Church.

"I'll tell you something," Margaux proclaims as we gawk, "the name Carol is used up. Done. Kaput." I don't get it, and she goes on to explain that last year, when they first gave women's names to tropical storms, they said the same names would be repeated year after year, except for those that made a big impression. Those names would be retired. This year, both Alice and Barbara conked out before they amounted to much. Carol was on her second trip around.

19

Thoughts about the business of naming hurricanes makes me wonder, and I turn to Margaux. "How come they only use women's names?" I ask her. "A hurricane's not a ship, after all, and certainly not a rose."

"Because," Margaux says promptly, "men are the ones doing the naming and, as I've already tried to explain to you, men are turds." We walk in silence until we come to Elm Street, by the library. Margaux dials her voice way down and nudges me. "Don't look back now," she whispers before I quickly turn to look back. "It's Fergie," she says disgustedly, as if a skunk is following us. I tell her to hush.

There's nothing wrong with Fergie, or at least nothing to keep anyone from liking him. At school, the kids call him a nerd. That's partly because he's both short *and* skinny, and maybe also because his thick, wire-rimmed glasses draw attention to an ever-changing sea of pimples. Nobody will admit it, but the thing that really bugs people about Fergie is that he's scary smart.

I turn around once more, and there he is, advancing at a rapid pace, both arms wildly waving. He must have been in the Y when we went by, and spotted us.

"Be nice," I warn Margaux.

"I will," she says with a great, heaving sigh. "But I'm not going to call him that stupid nickname. What's his real name, anyway?"

"Fergie is for his last name, Ferguson," I say. "His real first name is Clarence."

"Cripes," she says, "No wonder they call him Fergie."

He catches up just as we're perched at the intersection, about to cross into Coburn Park. "Hi, Angela," Fergie says, drawing up a bit too close, as he always does in order to see. "Hi, Margaux."

"Hi," she grunts without enthusiasm.

I try to make up for her rudeness. "Well, my goodness, Fergie. How are you, anyway? Are you all ready for school?"

He nods his head vigorously, and says he can't wait. That makes Margaux groan.

All three of us are about to step into the street when we hear a shout from the other side. It is the patrolman, Bernie Nelson, standing in front of a sawhorse that blocks one of the sidewalks in the park. He cups gloved hands over this mouth. "You stay right there," he yells. "I'm coming."

He stops traffic in both directions, sort of like Moses parting the Red Sea, and I look beyond him, into the park. Trees are down everywhere. Several large elms are laid out straight on the grass, their massive roots reaching upward like creepy hands. One tree has fallen near the Civil War statue, and a big limb has collapsed the iron fence almost to the ground. Across Park Street, another fallen elm has scraped the front of the Baptist Church, tearing off clapboards and making splinters of the notice board on the front lawn.

"Now just where do you kids think you're going?" Bernie smiles as he draws up, hands on his hips.

Margaux doesn't hesitate. "We're up town to see how the La-Di …"

I cut her off. "Just out looking at the damage, Officer Nelson," I say politely.

"Well, I'm afraid this is as far as you can go," he says, flatly. "It's much too dangerous to go beyond here." He proceeds to describe the things we can't see, no doubt hoping to discourage further exploration. "Trees are down all over town," he says to a chorus of chainsaws coming from the park. "Power's still out in lots of places. Pleasant and Gilman streets got it bad. Silver Street is closed. There's a big tree over the road by the bridge, and another one just beyond, near the Meader Farm on the Oakland Road."

I look at Fergie, who is completely enthralled by the report. "This is much bigger than '38," he announces somberly, as if he were around in 1938. "More damage in dollars, anyway. Thirty-four dead in New England already, and there are bound to be more as soon as people get out and start stepping on power lines." He makes it sound like he's hoping for more fatalities.

Margaux ignores Fergie and shakes her head while she takes in the sights before us. "Never mind retiring the name of Carol," she reflects. "Seems to me like they'll have to retire the name of Elm Street, as well; maybe even the name Elm City, along with it."

Fergie slowly shakes his head. "That would require the act of different agencies," he says, annoyingly. Margaux groans, yet again. Fergie pays her no attention, and, out of nowhere, ups and asks the officer if yesterday's Flying Yankee was on time. Since the old steam locomotive, Number 470, made its last run through town in June, Fergie has been obsessed with the sleek new diesel.

"She was over five hours late at the station," Bernie says. "Supposed to arrive at 3:58 in the afternoon. Didn't pull in until after 9:30."

Fergie is writing it all down in a notebook, and Margaux glares at him. "What in hell are you doing, anyway, writing a history book?"

"Look," the officer interrupts, "I've got work to do, and I want you kids to get on home. You understand?"

We nod like the Three Stooges. Fergie excuses himself and heads up toward the post office. His home is on Western Avenue, the other way. Most likely, he's off to collect more storm data. Margaux and I turn to go back when I notice the roof of the fancy Lombard Apartments across the street. Several bow-tie television antennas are bent double, hanging straight down over the eaves.

"Makes me think," I say to Margaux, "how's your marvelous TV?"

"Fine, how's yours?" She's snippy. I should have known. She's sensitive about the subject of her television. When the Mathieus got the first set in the neighborhood last spring, I'd made the mistake of calling her a La-Di-Da, and she didn't like it one bit.

You know I don't have TV," I say. "All we've got is that cheap little radio." Then for good measure, I remind her that the Bakelite is cracked from having abruptly met the wall during one of my father's rampages.

Margaux didn't really mean to be short, I can tell, and she recovers quickly. "We'll check out my TV when we get home. Dad will be there. He's the only one who knows how to tune it in."

When we get back on Front Street, I begin to wonder if I'm the only one in the whole world who hates the thought of going home. If Mom weren't there, I probably wouldn't go at all. Margaux catches on. "Come to my house," she says. "My mother will have something to eat." I nod agreement, but I know I can't hide out forever.

Sure enough, her mother's at the door to greet us. "Hi, girls," she says with a smile. "Come in. You must be famished." Mrs. Mathieu is a wild cook, always fretting that we haven't had enough to eat. Margaux's dad is sitting on a hassock in front of the TV, fiddling with a dial as he gazes in awe and wonder at the test pattern.

Mr. Mathieu still can't believe he has television. He's worn us down with the story of how he got it. The first color sets came out in the spring, and his supervisor at the Hathaway went out and paid some ungodly amount of money to buy one. Mr. Mathieu bought his old 21-inch black-and-white for 25 bucks. It was the beginning of an addiction.

At last, he notices us and gets up for hugs. Margaux clings to him and lets him whirl her around. I hunch my shoulders and twist to the side while he squeezes. "Now, be a dear," he says to Margaux, "go up to your room and turn the antenna just a bit. I'll tell you when to stop." Margaux trots upstairs where her father has installed a bow-tie antenna on the roof, just outside her window.

A flat brown wire runs from the pole through a hole in the bedroom floor and down the wall of the living room where it's connected to the TV.

"I'm going to have to get me an electric rotor," he says to me over his shoulder. "Two new stations are coming on the air this month." Up to now, we've really had only one, Channel 5 in Bangor. Portland's Channel 6 only comes in when the weather's right. Mr. Mathieu says Bangor is adding Channel 2 in a week or so, and a big new station is going on the air by the end of the month. "Can't wait for Channel 8," he says. "Can you believe it, it's coming from the very top of Mount Washington?" It's easy to tell he's in heaven. Right now, he's trying to pull in the Portland channel. "Stop!" he yells up to Margaux. "No, go back. No, too far. That's it. That's it. Don't move." The test pattern is barely visible through a blizzard of snow.

Margaux returns just as her mother brings a plate of peanut butter sandwiches. I eat two, and then sheepishly take another. We all sit and listen to Mr. Mathieu go on about his precious TV. "It has twenty-three tubes and two rectifiers, you know," he says. We nod in faked astonishment. We don't know a thing about tubes and rectifiers.

"*Father Knows Best* is coming on that new channel," Margaux's mother chimes in. I know the program from the radio. It isn't very true to life, but it takes my mind to a place I'd like to be. "And," Mrs. Mathieu adds enthusiastically, "we'll be able to get *Make Room for Daddy* there, as well."

Finally, I can contribute something to the conversation. "Danny Thomas is Lebanese, you know." They don't know. "His real name is Amos Kairouz. He changed it to Danny Thomas, but he ends up being Lebanese, just the same."

I glance at the wall above the TV. It is 2 o'clock. Mom will be home. Half a sandwich is going stale on the plate, and I snag it before I leave. It's gone by the time I take the dozen steps to my own side door.

When I step inside the kitchen, I'm surprised to see Gabe standing there. I haven't seen him for a week, and when I rush to greet him, I get the sudden feeling something's wrong. There's a scowl on his face, and he barely gives me a hug. I glance over his shoulder at Mom. She's slouched at the kitchen table, holding a hand to her head. She looks up, and I see an ugly purple welt on her cheek. Her left eye is swollen shut.

I almost scream. "He hit you, didn't he?" I start to sob. "The mean bastard hit you, I know he did." I've never used that word before, and it feels good.

Mom looks shocked. "Now Angela," she says, "there's no need for dirty talk." I can't believe a woman who carries on about the simplest things in life is calmly sitting there with blood all over her face, correcting my language. I turn to Gabe for help. Mom sees me look. "Listen, you two," she says. "Don't go making a big deal out of this. Baba didn't mean to do it. It'll all be fine."

"Of course it's not fine," I shoot back. "He can't do this. We're not taking it any more. We've had enough." I stop long enough to think about what I've said, and an idea pops into my head. "I'm going to report him to Officer Nelson, this very day. That's *exactly* what I'm going to do."

Gabe nods at me. He plainly agrees. Mom is horrified. "Listen," she says, "you'll do no such thing. It'll only make things worse." She goes on to tell us the fight was all about nothing. My father wanted her tip money; she didn't have much. She told him she needed to save for the rent, and he got angry. "Baba will feel terrible about what he's done, I know he will. Sometimes, he just can't help it. You know he wasn't always like this. Before the war …"

Gabe leaps to his feet and cuts her off. "Bullshit," he yells. "He's nothing but a damn drunk, and you know it. The war's got nothing to do with it. He was a cook's helper at Fort Dix, for God's sake. How could the war have done a thing to him?"

After that outburst, it's scary quiet. My brother and I stare at each other for a long time, silently communicating. There's no point arguing with her, and besides, she looks so sad it wouldn't be right to frighten her any more. Gabe and I can figure things out, with or without her permission.

Finally, we start to talk about other things. Mom wants to know if we have what we need for school. We say we're fine, but I know we're both a little short. She warns Gabe about skipping school, and then says I've got to buckle down. I can't imagine how she knows. She inquires about our sneakers, and we each gauge the length of their remaining lives.

We've chatted for an hour before Gabe ups and announces he's leaving. He has a game at the Boys Club, he says. Mom begs him to stay. "Baba will be home soon," she says. "I just know he's going to be sorry about all of this," she says, pointing to her eye that seems to grow more ugly by the minute, "and I want you to see for yourself." She heaves a sigh and fakes a grin. "It won't happen again, I promise you." I go to the sink, wet a cloth. What my father has done to her makes me sick, and he deserves to rot in hell for it.

With Gabe about to leave, I suddenly remember that I need to tell Mom about my piano lesson plans, and having him around might help in case she sees something wrong with the idea, which she's bound to do. There's no good way to fit the notice into the present conversation, so I hand Mom the wet facecloth and simply blurt it out. "I'm going to take piano lessons."

I'm surprised when Mom just shrugs. "Every girl should know how to play the piano," she says calmly. Mom knows how much I love music, and she knows how disappointed I've been at not being able to find a place for it in high school. I intended to get involved last fall, when I entered, but it didn't work out. When it came to the band, I was a day late and a dollar short. Most members own their own instruments and have been practicing since grade school. The opposite is true for the Glee Club where it's clear no experience or training is necessary. It's gleeful enough, but it's obviously made up of mostly tone-deaf girls who would rather have been cheerleaders. Not for me.

Mom is quickly on board with the idea of lessons, but Gabe isn't so hasty. "You're what? Who's teaching you? How much will it cost?"

I answer his first and last questions, hoping he'll forget the middle one. "I'm taking piano lessons and it won't cost me a thing." I figure I can fill in the details about King Court and Mr. M later on.

Four

There's hardly any traffic, and Front Street is quiet. Margaux and I sit on the front steps in the warm sun, absorbed in our separate thoughts. It's Labor Day. Most families are gathering up for celebrations, with cookouts and all, but we have nothing to do. The Mathieus had their party yesterday and invited me, but Margaux's father has to work today. My family would never think of having a cookout, even if we lived outdoors.

My mind is on the piano, where it's been ever since Mr. M offered to teach me. I wish I'd accepted his invitation, right then and there, but no, I left him dangling. Not only that, but I've also begun to worry about how I'm going to find time to practice. I can't do it at home like a normal person would, because we don't have a piano, and unless a Steinway comes floating down Front Street in the next spring thaw, we're not likely to get one, either. Maybe Mr. M will let me practice on the Beckwith, but I don't know when. School starts tomorrow, and I can't get behind like I did last year. On top of all that there's the after-school job stacking shelves at Cottle's grocery, taking care of Mom, and Lord knows what else.

Margaux is peering into my face, trying to read my mind. I save her the trouble and tell her my worries about leaving Mr. M in the lurch. No surprise, she doesn't see the problem. "Call him up," she shrugs. "Work it out." It sounds simple enough, except we don't have a phone. The company shut it off when my father lost his job and Mom stopped paying the bill. I don't even know if Mr. M has one; I never thought to look.

"Okay," Margaux pipes up, "so what say we take our bikes and go down and see the old man?" I'd thought of doing that, but not with Margaux. Mr. M is *my* friend, not hers, and I don't want her to get in the way, which she surely will if I give her half a chance. Still, I can't leave her by herself on a holiday, so I tell her we can go if she promises to keep her mouth shut. She agrees, but I know right off it won't work.

We haven't used our bikes for more than a week, and when we pull them out from under the porch, we have to brush off a whole lot of mud and debris from the storm. Margaux has a girl's bike, not very old but already dented and scratched from many crashes. My Raleigh is a hand-me-down from Gabe. Threads show through the rubber on the back tire, and the top tube of the boy's frame requires me to wear trousers. I take a couple of rubber bands off the handlebar, snap them to the bottoms of my pant legs, and we're set to go.

I let Margaux ride on ahead so I can keep away from her tire spray, and when we reach the corner at Temple Street, she has to stop and wait. "What say we run the bridge?" she says, eyes sparkling. I know what she means. She wants us to race straight through the tollhouse without stopping, just to save two cents. I raise a hand in protest, but she's already zipping down the hill, feet off the pedals, making all the speed her weight will give her. I'm still way behind, and as she zooms past the tollhouse I begin to wish I'd kept up.

The toll keeper must have seen Margaux flash by, for she comes out of the shack in a second, carrying a broom by its head. She yells something and waggles the handle at Margaux, then turns and aims the thing at me as I approach at full speed, out of control.

I just know she means to cram it in my spokes, and at the last second, I jam on the rear handbrake, skid sideways the final ten feet, and fall off within an inch of her feet.

As I scramble upright, I notice my knees are bleeding, and I can see Margaux, mid-way across the swaying bridge, straddling her bike and bent double over the handlebars, laughing. The angry keeper gives me a foul look and shoves her free hand under my nose. I fish in my pocket, find a lone nickel, and give it to her. She returns a penny. "Tell your smart-alecky friend to never pull that stunt again." She owes me more change, but I'm not about to argue with an old woman carrying a broom, and I smile sweetly, straighten up the bike, and pedal off to Margaux, who now is sitting on the boardwalk, holding her sides.

"It's not funny," I say, shaking a finger and sounding a little like my mother as I list the various things that could have resulted from her foolishness, including serious injury and jail time. "And, by the way," I tack on at the end, "you owe me two cents."

There's no way we're about to go back over the footbridge and face the witch again, so we take the long way to Mr. M's by walking our bikes up the hill into Winslow. When we reach Benton Avenue, we get on and coast down the sidewalk alongside a chain link fence. Margaux points to the mountain of pulp near the Hollingsworth mill. "Too bad they've gone and put a fence up here," she says. "I'll bet we could ride our bikes all the way to the top." I don't bother to tell her that's the reason they have a fence.

I'm still steaming about the tollgate episode, and don't speak to her all the way down the hill, or as we dodge traffic over the big bridge, or as we pedal back up Front Street. I don't say a single word until we arrive at Mr. M's on King Court and I notice that his car, although freshly cleaned of clutter from the storm, is still parked in the same place, nose toward the road. "I don't think he gets out much," I whisper to Margaux as I gently rap on the door.

"My goodness," Mr. M says when he appears. "Now, there are two."

"I've come to arrange piano lessons, and my mother knows I'm doing it," I say, straight out, still catching my breath. "This here's my friend Margaux. She says she knows you."

He studies her face. "Well, I'll be," he says. "Margaux Mathieu. Yes, of course, I remember you. Jamilah gave you lessons. It must have been almost ten years ago." He beckons us in, and I head straight for the piano bench. Adagio is curled up there, and I gently nudge her over to make a place to sit. Margaux goes for the sofa. Mr. M turns the Morris chair away from the stove and faces us.

"We worried about you when you were sick," he says to Margaux. "We kept track through your mom. You recovered well?"

Margaux adjusts her left leg to line it up properly with the right one. "Good as new," she huffs. He offers us cookies. I say there's no need. Margaux says it seems like a very good idea, and he goes off to the kitchen, returning with a fresh box of Oreos. Margaux takes two.

Mr. M sits back and folds his hands over his belly. "So," he says, "you start school tomorrow. Tell me all about it." He's in no hurry to negotiate piano lessons; he wants to talk.

Margaux takes the bait and chatters on in some detail about subjects and teachers, making it clear she intends to be prepared for most anything. I explain I have no college plans, but I'm taking the right courses, just because. He nods approvingly. Margaux grabs another cookie. "Do you get out much?" she asks. I choke on a bite. She's being far too brassy, and I shoot daggers with my eyes.

Mr. M doesn't seem to mind at all. "Not much," he admits. "We got the Buick Special new in 1941, just before I retired. We used to go lots of places, even as far as the coast on a weekend, but I haven't used it much since Jamilah died. These days, I go to Mass at St. Joseph on Sundays, make a couple of trips to the market during the week, and sometimes treat myself to lunch at Jabbur's."

"What did you do in Lebanon?" Margaux is either being very kind or very nosy, and I think I know which.

Fortunately, Mr. M still isn't rattled. "Interesting you'd ask," he says. "People think the Syrians were all peddlers, but the truth is lots of us were silk makers. I knew how to weave, and that's why I came here." He seems proud when he tells us it didn't take him long to become a weaver at the Wyandotte. "Sometimes I ran five looms at once," he says. "In those days I'd come home looking like a snowman, year round. Jamilah made me shake off as much lint as I could before I came into the house, but I couldn't do much about the oil on my feet. I just left my boots on the stoop, year round."

"Did Mrs. M work at the mill?" Margaux simply will not let go.

"Back home," he says, "they didn't approve of women working in factories. The Maronite Church said it was immoral. Over here, things are different. The women outnumber the men in the mills, but the Church was slow to accept the change."

Margaux nods vigorously. "Just like eating fish on Fridays," she says, as if the ban on Friday meat and women working in factories was even close to the same thing.

Mr. M looks puzzled, and it's little wonder. "Anyway," he says, "when she came here we decided it was better for her to teach piano, and I'm glad she did."

At last we're on the subject of pianos, and I jump in quickly to keep Margaux from taking us somewhere else. "About those lessons," I say.

"Yes, yes," he says, getting up and coming over to the bench. "Why don't we start, right now?" I hadn't thought about beginning lessons today, certainly not with Margaux around. I just wanted to arrange them.

"You got a TV?" Margaux has gone beyond annoying, and she's dead wrong if she thinks she's going to watch *The Guiding Light* while I learn the piano.

"Hardly anybody here has a TV," Mr. M says, "but one of these days I mean to get one." He gestures toward a big glass jar on the kitchen table. It's less than half full of coins. "It'll take about two hundred dollars," he says with a grin. "As you can see, I've got a long ways to go."

I give Margaux another "shut up" look, and Mr. M flips open a book that stands on the shelf above the keys. "All of Jamilah's lesson books were under the bench," he says, pointing to where I sit. "This is Number One." He points to the first page, covered with tiny colored stars and pencil marks.

"It's not as hard as you might think," he says. "Once you get the hang of it, you just keep getting better and better. Sort of like weaving," he says.

"Or riding a bike." Margaux thinks she's being helpful. I turn to give her a dirty look, and she's grinning ear-to-ear. Tiny bits of brown cookie are stuck between her teeth.

Mr. M sits next to me and uses his right thumb to strike a white key in the middle of the keyboard. "It all begins here," he says. "Good old Mr. Middle C. Whenever you sit down at the piano, you start by squaring up your belly button with this key. You need to find it every time, without looking. Now, sit tall, shoulders back, arms like this." He demonstrates, then walks his fingers up the keyboard. "C, D, E." He does it again: "Do, Re, Mi." And again: "One, two, three." Then I do it myself, copying him, calling out the notes. It's simply wonderful.

We sit for a half-hour or more, expanding the range, adding the low notes with the left hand and putting the pinky on the C instead of the thumb. I love every minute, and I'm eager to go on. Mr. M is very patient, gently insisting I fix one thing in my head before I move to another. After awhile, I'm able to name the notes of the keys I'm striking, with either hand. He tests me by calling out random notes, and I get most of them right.

Never mind the mysterious black notes or the pedals near my feet, I haven't even begun to figure out how to read the notes as they appear on the music sheet, on and between the lines on the scales. I turn to Mr. M. "When can we start reading the notes and playing a song?"

He smiles. "Next time," he says, cocking his head. "And when, pray tell, will that be?" I tell him I have to work after school on Monday, Wednesday and Friday, and four hours in the afternoon on Sunday. We agree I'll come for lessons on Tuesdays and Thursdays, right after school. "In between," he says, "you're going to need to practice." The thought is no more than out of his mouth when he stops and scratches his chin. "Here's a plan," he says. "Tomorrow at school, you go and talk with Mrs. Bizier. I know her. Ask her if there's a convenient time when you might be able to practice on one of the school pianos. They've got two, an upright and a grand. You don't need the grand. Ask her if you can use the upright when her students aren't scheduled. I'm sure she'll think it's fine."

I'm not anywhere near as sure as he is, but I agree to ask, and then my mind goes back to the things I've just learned. "Do you think it might be possible for me to play just one actual song before I go?"

He starts to chuckle in the way I'm getting used to, a way that makes you want to laugh along with him. "Well, I suppose it is," he says as he closes the lesson book and begins to pencil notes on the back cover, BA GA BBB, AAA BDD, and more. "Okay," he says, "don't look at your hands, just strike the notes."

I do as he says, and my heart almost leaps out of my chest as I recognize what I'm playing. "Oh, my goodness," I blurt out. It's *Mary Had a Little Lamb*.

Margaux, whose mouth has been kept shut by the Oreos throughout the entire session, breaks her silence. "Well, I'll be damned!" she exclaims, clapping her hands, "if you've not become a regular Liberace!"

Five

On the way to school, I do my best to annoy Margaux by singing scales and silly children's songs. At the corner of Gilman Street at Sacred Heart Church there's a bunch of students waiting to hitch rides up Mayflower Hill to the college, and as we pass them I sing *Mary Had a Little Lamb* at the top of my lungs. It's payback for her idiotic intrusions during yesterday's piano lesson, and it's working.

"Oh, for God's sake, will you ever shut up?" Margaux pleads when we've gotten by, "You're embarrassing me." The very thought of *me* embarrassing *her* is ridiculous. The millennium must have arrived. I tell her my singing is no more stupid than the silly poodle skirt she's got on, but all the while I wish I had one of my own.

I keep my mouth shut for the last two blocks up to school, but in my heart I'm still humming, and why not? Life is getting better all the time. For one thing, I am now an exalted sophomore, and can go to school without knots in my stomach. Then too, there's my busy schedule that keeps me away from my father, and best of all, there's the discovery of Mr. M and the prospect of learning to play the piano. All I need to do is convince Mrs. Bizier to let me use a school piano for practice, and I'll be set up for total and complete happiness.

The day is warm and sunny, and students are scattered over the school lawns and up the granite steps, waiting for the first bell. Spike Moufette has pulled his fancy Ford up to the curb out front, and the Crew Cuts are belting their new song, *Sh-Boom*, out his open windows. My brother and his friends are down there with him, cheering at the God-awful racket that comes from his twin tailpipes when he revs the engine. The ground shakes.

Nearby on the sidewalk, a number of girls are milling around, laughing and singing with the music, making perfect idiots out of themselves. Margaux lopes off in that direction, and I'm thinking about joining her when I hear my name shouted from the very top of the steps. It's Fergie. His face is flushed with excitement and, just when it looks like he might come down to say hello, the bell rings and he abruptly turns and fights his way to the front so he can be first through the door.

Two paper signs – A-L, M-Z – have been hung behind tables in the corridor outside the principal's office, and students are lined up by name for homeroom assignments. The terrified freshmen are easy to spot. Several are cowering up against the wall under a new giant mural of *St. George and the Dragon*, a gift from last year's exceptionally talented art students. I recognize one of the girls, Pamela, standing directly under the sword and looking a lot like the bewildered dragon. I strut over and offer to help. She's looking for her homeroom, number 210. "Upstairs," I say brightly, "first on your left." She couldn't be more gratified if I'd saved her from drowning.

I'm not standing in either line because I already know where I'm going. My homeroom teacher is Mrs. Aldrich, down the hall on the right, and I head off that way, breathing deeply to take in the oddly pleasant smell of the freshly oiled wood floors, which very nearly overwhelms the stink of sweat and sneakers wafting up from the gym.

I have no more than selected a desk in the very front when Mrs. Aldrich walks over and whispers in my ear. "I must talk with you when we're finished here," she says without the least explanation, making me wait nervously through the next half-hour as she goes over the usual opening-of-school rules. When she asks if we know the location of our nearest air raid shelter everybody nods. Then she says there's no need to practice the duck-and-cover air raid drill because we already know it, although I suspect the real reason is that we no longer fit under our desks. Finally, she finishes her list by reminding us that the water bubblers are not to be used for spitting gum, and then dismisses the class with one hand while calling me up to her desk with the other.

"We've been going over your record," she says right off. She doesn't say who "we" are, but I know I'm in trouble. "You didn't do especially well in your courses last year," she says somberly. She's right about that. Nobody knows about the troubles at home, and I'm not telling. I barely passed geometry and had a lot of trouble with French. Margaux tried to help me, but it didn't work. "We're thinking," Mrs. Aldrich says, continuing with the royal *we*, "perhaps you'd be better off if you reduced your load a bit by, let's say, taking home economics instead of algebra."

It doesn't take a genius to figure out where she's going with this, and it makes me bristle. Nobody talks much about it, but there's a certain division between those students preparing for college and those who aren't, and everybody knows who's on what side of that fence. It doesn't have a whole lot to do with your interests or, for that matter, your abilities. Instead, it seems to be about how much money you have. I'm pretty sure I won't be going to college, but I have absolutely no interest in home economics. I've been cooking my own meals since I was 12, and the skirt I'm wearing is ample proof I know how to sew, because I've had to let the damned thing out three times in the past year.

I jump in before Mrs. Aldrich can make her full case. "I had some troubles last year," I truthfully confess before I spring a lie. "But now, they've all been fixed. I'm sure I'll do much better. You just watch and see." I give her the most pathetic and pleading look anybody could imagine.

The excuse sounds weak, even to me, and for an instant I'm afraid I might be licked when, for some strange reason, she cracks a kindly grin. "Okay, fine," she says as if she'd rather not have had this conversation in the first place, "we'll just wait and see how things go."

Having narrowly escaped a lifetime sentence of making cakes and aprons, I take a deep breath and head off to classes. In French, we begin a review of what we learned last year and forgot over the summer. The English teacher, Miss Klarity, assigns us to read *A Tale of Two Cities*, which is fine with me, because I've already read it. It was hard going at first, but when I began to think of myself as Lucie Manette, I couldn't put it down.

I just know biology is going to give me trouble. Just the smell of the place is enough to make you gag, but I adore Mr. Seale in civics, because he talks about interesting things, and he's such a nice man. I often feel sorry for him. The word around school is that he's "shell-shocked" from the war, but not everybody is sympathetic. Some of the yahoos in class like to drop their books on purpose, just to watch the poor man jump.

The last class of the day is algebra, and I can tell the minute Mrs. Good opens her mouth that I'm in over my head. She rants on about constants, variables, and polynomials, just as if she was speaking English. Maybe Gabe can help, at least until he graduates.

With classes at last finished, I'm ready to find Mrs. Bizier and pop the question. Just the thought of asking her makes me nervous. There's an important matter at stake, and I'm not especially good at talking with teachers. Fergie has his hand in the air all the time, always with the right answers. Teachers have begun to look right through him and invite some dummy, like me, to answer instead. Spike cracks jokes without being called on, just to make the girls laugh; and Margaux specializes in distraction. She knows the right buttons to push to get teachers off track and forget to make assignments. She does it to Mr. Seale all the time. I generally try to make myself invisible and keep my mouth shut.

The music room is cluttered with instruments and music stands, and the route to Mrs. Bizier's tiny office in the back is an obstacle course. As I pick my way, I take a close look at the upright piano, pushed up against the wall outside her door. It suffers from a hard life. Deep scratches mar the finish, and entire chunks of wood are missing from its stubby legs. I doubt the thing is even in tune. I could tell for sure if I played a scale, but now is not the time. Besides, the lid is down over the keys, fastened with a padlock that looks menacing and very much out of place.

I rap meekly on the door, then push it open when I hear a grunt on the other side. Mrs. Bizier is bent over her desk, working at something, and she doesn't even look up. I stand there and wait, fidgeting with my hands while I gawk. She is, to put it kindly, a large woman and, as usual, she's all dolled up. Large red earrings jump out the sides of her head, and an assortment of cheap bracelets dangle from her wrists. Remarkably large breasts rise like twin moons above her brightly flowered dress.

She finally puts aside whatever she's been doing and looks at me without trying to hide her impatience. "Yes?"

I've rehearsed. "My name is Angela Jamal," I say. "I'm a sophomore, and I would like to know if it would be possible for me to find time to practice on the upright piano when it is not being used by any of your students."

One look at her and you'd think I'd asked for a date with her husband. "Certainly not," she barks before she suddenly calms her voice and begins to talk at me like I'm five years old. "You see, my dear, the pianos are for music students only. They're not toys, you know." I tell her that I am a music student, even though I'm not one of hers. "Well then, who's teaching you?" she asks.

"Elias Moussallem."

"Elias Moussallem?" She actually smirks. "His late wife Jamilah taught beginners for awhile, but he's no piano teacher. He's a mill weaver. People who haven't been trained should definitely not be allowed to teach." I have the urge to tell her that there are trained people who shouldn't be teaching, either. In fact, I'm prepared to give her an immediate example, but I hold my tongue. Instead, I explain that Mr. Moussallem's wife taught him to play and that he's actually very good. She waves both hands, and the clanking bracelets drown me out. "Perhaps you can find some other place to practice," she suggests. "A church, maybe?" *Really? I'm supposed to march into Sacred Heart and ask Father McGillicuddy to play the church organ? Fat chance.*

I'm set to further plead my case, but I can tell it's no use. It won't do any good to make her angry. Instead, I take a deep breath and struggle to hold back tears. *If I can't practice, I'll never be able to learn. I can't go down to Mr. M's every day; there isn't time. What will I do?* I won't let her see my disappointment, and I thank her with faked politeness and back slowly out the door.

Margaux has been waiting on the front steps, just where I put her when I told her she couldn't come with me. She sees me coming and, as usual, props herself on all fours before struggling to her feet. "What did Mrs. Brassiere have to say?" She uses Mrs. Bizier's student nickname as she brushes off her poodle skirt. "Are you all set?"

"She said no."

"Bitch!" The word rings loudly off the granite steps, and I look around to see who might have heard. I'm about to scold, but I know she's only trying to be supportive and I simply push her on ahead.

41

We're halfway home before I give Margaux the details, and I've only started when I'm interrupted by the sound of running footsteps behind us. It's Gabe. Margaux blurts out the story the instant he catches up. I shake my head to stop her, but it's too late. My brother knows about the piano lessons, but he doesn't know a thing about Mr. M, and he's not going to like it. Despite his high rate of absenteeism, he's always kept a close eye, behaving like my mother by coming up with bad things to say about every male person I've ever mentioned except, of course, his friend Spike, who he thinks walks on water.

"Mr. M? Who's Mr. M?" Sure enough, Gabe is suspicious. I tell him all about the man and explain there's nothing to worry about, that I very much want to learn. I'm not sure why, but he doesn't say another word and promptly turns his attention to Mrs. Bizier.

"Well, I'm just going to march in and see her," he says, flat out. "It's a *public* high school, for God's sake. We all own a piece of that old, wretched piano." I remind him he doesn't even know the woman, he's never shown an ounce of interest in music, and he and his friends would die before they joined the chorus. "Well then," he says, "I'll just go see Mr. Fallon." Mr. Fallon is the assistant principal, in charge of discipline, and Gabe knows him quite well. Even so, I tell him to never mind, that I'll work it out, and we change the subject.

When we cross Upper Main Street, I'm just beginning to think it would be nice if Gabe came on home with me, when he turns left and drops down the tiny side street to the Boys Club. "Catch you later," he says over his shoulder. "We'll get this all figured out. Don't worry." I feel a pinch of fear and sadness as I watch him disappear.

I stop in at Margaux's apartment long enough to grab a couple of cookies from Mrs. Mathieu's kitchen table jar, then walk slowly to my own side door. The second I enter, I can tell something is very wrong. God has been playing tricks on me all day long. What now?

My father is sitting at the kitchen table. He is shaved. His hair is combed, and his dungarees are clean. There's even a tiny grin on his face. I'm about to go back outdoors to check the street address when Mom pipes up from in front of the kitchen sink. "Oh, Angela," she says, "you are simply not going to believe this." The bruise on her cheek has turned a pale yellow, and she's wearing the biggest smile I've seen for months. "Baba has a job."

She comes and throws her arms around me. I let out a squeak, and the questions tumble out. "Doing what? Where?"

"I'm going to go to work tomorrow at the Lockwood," my father answers for himself, sober as a judge. "A friend of mine at Archie's got me the job. It's in the warehouse. Nights. It only pays 75¢ an hour, but there's opportunity to move up." I nod in amazement, taking it all in. He stands up to give me a hug, and I quickly dodge under his arm and race upstairs.

Six

I think Mr. M is the calmest, sweetest man I've ever known, and I'm stunned by his reaction to the news that Mrs. Bizier has declared me ineligible to use a school piano. His face turns crimson, and he begins to bang his fists on the arms of his chair. "Just who in hell does that woman think she is?" The outburst makes me jump, and Adagio bolts from his lap in fright. "In case you don't know it," he says as he glares at me, "that woman was a Maroon long before she was a Bizier." He stops to let the thought register. "She and her people lived right down here on King Court." He points out the window. "There's a lot of sinful things you can do in life," he says, "but one of the very worst is to forget where you came from." I know where he's headed with all of this. If Margaux were here, she'd save him the trip by instantly proclaiming Mrs. Bizier a first-rate La-Di-Da.

The dear man then bends close to me and launches into a recitation of the history of Waterville's immigrants, in time order. I already know the story, but I can tell it won't do any good to interrupt, and I listen politely. He begins with the French, who began to trickle down from Canada more than a hundred years ago, settling here on the few acres between the railroad and the river. They called the place Tête de Chutes, he tells me, which translated nicely into English without any need for a "the." It wasn't long, he explains, before the French began to outgrow Head

44

of Falls and built a new community a half-mile downriver, on a flat sweep above the river called The Plains.

"We began to come here at the turn of the century," he tells me, "when we were still Syrians, before Lebanon broke off. There weren't many of us, and this neighborhood was perfect – nearby the mills, close to the shops in town, a short walk for everything we needed." He pauses to remind me there were other enclaves in the city as well: a small number of Russian Jews in the north end, Irish nearer the center of town. "Around here, we all live and pray separately," he says, "but when we get together, we get along just fine. Always have."

The last thought easily takes him back to Mrs. Bizier, as he's not ready to let go. "And, we don't need people like Nadine Maroon Bizier screwing things up. So what if she moved out? People do it all the time, but most of them don't forget where they started." The thought of moving anywhere has never even come up in my house, but I know some who have. Just last spring, Spike Moufette's lawyer father took his clan off The Plains and into one of those fine new homes on Mayflower Hill, up near the college. In fact, the college itself is the best moving example of all. It's taken 20 years, but a couple of years ago Colby pulled its last stakes near the river and is now completely settled up the hill.

Mr. M is stuck on the subject of moving. "Of course, everybody wants to better themselves," he says, "and more power to 'em, I say, but when they forget where they come from, they might just as well slap their grandparents in their faces." I'd never really thought about it that way, but then I don't have any grandparents, either.

Finally, he heaves a big sigh, beckons Adagio back onto his lap, and we get down to the business of solving the mystery of where I can practice. First, we take inventory of the pianos we know, but pianos don't hang around with their keyboards yawning open, waiting for somebody to walk up and play. The very idea is hopeless. Most churches have one or two, but like at school, they're locked up and guarded. We know there are pianos in some of the fancy houses around town, but nobody's about to let you waltz into their living room to sit down and play. Besides, Mr. M says most of these parlor pianos are for show, covered in dust, doilies and photographs, and probably have cracked soundboards, as well. We end up where we began, with no solution at all, and decide I'll simply have to come to his house between lessons and practice on the Beckwith.

It takes a few weeks to get adjusted to the new schedule. On weekdays I go to school, stock shelves at Cottle's on scheduled days, run home to make something to eat, then go off to Mr. M's for an hour or two, and finally back home to fall into bed, exhausted. Weekends are the same, except I swap the school time for extra sleep and adventures with Margaux. Everything gets done but the homework. There's never time for homework, and it's piling up. I'm not sure what I'll do about it, but two things are certain: I'm not going to stay up all day *and* all night, and I'm definitely not going to give up a single minute with the piano.

~

My birthday is coming up, and the closer the day gets, the more I realize I'm expecting too much. All we ever hear around the halls at school this year is *Sweet 16* this and *Sweet 16* that, with lots of whispers, giggles and chatter about over-the-top parties with frosted cakes, tons of gifts, and fancy dresses. Frankly, both Margaux and I are sick of it, and it's not only because we're not invited.

When my big day arrives, I'm pretty much convinced that any real glamour attached to being Sweet 16 is reserved for fairy princesses and movie stars. In the morning, I get a tiny peck on the cheek at school from my brother, who first wants to compare notes on my father's behavior, and then he congratulates me and promises a gift. I'm not holding my breath. After work, I find a card from my mother on the sideboard, along with a scribbled note saying she's off to play Bingo at St. Joseph. My father, no surprise, has forgotten about my birthday altogether, and it's fine with me. In his case, I prefer his neglect. It's good enough that Archie's is closed when he gets off the night shift and that he's so tired that he sleeps all day. The only problem is that he falls off the wagon every weekend, but at least his predictable routine gives time to plan escapes.

By the end of the day, I've worked my way into a sour mood, and decide I'm not going to spend my birthday night all by myself. Instead, I decide I'll go down to Mr. M's for a visit, maybe even an extra practice. He doesn't know it's my birthday, and I didn't tell him because he'd think he had to get me something, and I don't want him robbing his mayonnaise jar for me. The TV fund is growing slowly enough, as it is.

I'm just heading out when Margaux pokes her head through the kitchen door, whoops a greeting, and invites me for dinner. She didn't say a word about my birthday all day, and I thought she'd forgotten. I don't know why, but I start to cry as I rush to give her a big hug, forget about her withered leg, and send her sprawling on the kitchen floor. She rolls once and pops up onto her knees in an instant, all the while managing to keep a grip on a tiny package. "Here," she says, shoving it up to me like a prayer offering. "It's for you. Open it before we go."

From the shape I can tell right off that it's a 45-rpm record but, for Margaux's sake I ooh and ah as I fumble with the paper. Sure enough, it's Nat King Cole singing *Darling, Je Vous Aime Beaucoup*. Yuck! I don't especially like the song; it's barely on the charts. The flip side has *The Sand and The Sea*. Double yuck! I would have much preferred Perry singing *Papa Loves Mambo*, but I wasn't expecting any gift at all, and so I don't complain.

Margaux goes to some length to explain that she picked the song with great care, in order to help me with my French. As a

47

bona fide French girl, she has taken it upon herself to instruct me in the language. She took a seat directly behind me on the first day in class, and her frequent whispering in my ear has been a great help all year long. Her finest contribution came when she finally figured out we had been speaking Canuck French all along, when Mademoiselle Vachon wants Parisian. Canuck is French-Canadian for French-Canadian, and it has apparently fallen out of favor. Since this discovery, whenever I'm uncertain of the correct French word, I avoid the temptation of giving the English word a French spin. Mlle. Vachon picks up on that kind of thing in a flash. Margaux also told me that when I'm asked to recite in class, I would sound better if I shoved the words way down the back of my throat and then hacked them up as if I were about to spit. It actually works quite well, and now, with all her help, I seem to be holding my own.

The Mathieu house smells like absolute heaven. Margaux's mom has knocked herself out. She's not only prepared a tuna noodle and green bean casserole, but she's made a huge white cake with chocolate frosting, topped with 16 candles. We sit around and talk about everything and nothing for almost an hour, and when dinner is finally over, I can only grin and shake my head in wonder as they sing *Happy Birthday* to me. Afterward, Mr. Mathieu wants to be sure I know that the cake was made with his wife's new electric mixer, and he calls us all over to the sink where he demonstrates in a bowl of water. He turns it up to the highest speed, and we all get wet.

When everything is picked up and dried out, we take glasses of Tang into the living room to watch *The $64,000 Question*. Determined to get the strongest possible signal out of Portland, Mr. Mathieu spends almost the entire program blocking the screen while he fidgets with the dials. The rest of us sit around and talk about what we would do if we had that astonishing amount of money. Mrs. Mathieu says she would get one of those new Mangle automatic ironers so she'd have free time to think about what else she might buy. Margaux wants a house with a dozen clothes closets and a Corvette in the driveway. I say I'd settle for a tiny apartment of my own that doesn't use kerosene for heat, as I'm tired of hanging sweaters out the window at night to get rid of the fumes.

~

The fall slides by, as well as my homework. I'm so far behind, I think I'll never catch up. Algebra continues to be a complete mystery; biology is not much better. I've finished *A Tale of Two Cities* for the second time, but I have no idea what Miss Klarity expects us to write about it. I'm doing fine in civics, but that's because Mr. Seale doesn't give homework, and he talks about things that are actually happening instead of what went on a thousand years ago. In French, it turns out Margaux's birthday gift is of no use at all. When Nat's song came up in class, Mlle. Vachon harrumphed. She said Mr. Cole is not a Frenchman — as if we didn't know that, already — and that *Je Vous Aime Beaucoup* is entirely incorrect. She claims he should have sung *Je T'aime Beaucoup*, instead. The woman is impossible.

Other than homework, life is getting better. My father still has his job, and when he's off, I spend most of the time at Margaux's. He had to work on Thanksgiving, but Mom and I celebrated with the Mathieus.

Now, it's only four days until Christmas, three months since I turned Sweet 16. We don't have an indoor tree, but I put a candle in the front window, and lit it every night for nearly a week until Mom calculated the odds of burning the place down and made me put it away. The Mathieus have a glorious big tree that Margaux's father decorated with gobs of tinsel and a hundred blue lights. Her mother says it's gaudy and nontraditional, but we think it's terrific and spend hours in front of it, lying on the carpet, playing Christmas carols. But, not tonight. Tonight is lesson night.

It's a cold walk through the cut, but the night is clear and there is no wind. It has begun to snow, and the big flakes make perfect stars on the dark sleeves of my coat. I stop under the streetlight at the corner of Head of Falls Road and hold out my arms to examine the perfect creations in the split second before they disappear.

When I reach the clearing before the mill, I look out across the river and watch the swirling snow as it makes a gauzy curtain in the lights of the paper mill. To me, it's a beautiful sight, and I find it oddly comforting to see the big white letters of the newly painted sign on the mill wall. Mr. M calls it "the 38 million dollar sign," which is what Scott Paper Company paid to buy up Hollingsworth & Whitney back in October. Everybody agrees it was a good deal, all around. Except for bringing in a few bigwigs from the home office in Pennsylvania, little has changed. The union jobs have all been saved and the pulp logs are still piled up to the sky. The best part is that there are plans to make toilet paper, and as Margaux points out, everybody in the world needs toilet paper, especially La-Di-Das, who, she claims, need a lot.

Mr. M hears me stomp on the stoop and comes to hustle me inside. It's toasty warm, and there is the delicious smell of chestnuts turning dark brown on the top of the heater. A tiny tree on the table by the sofa is strung with popcorn, and Adagio, curled in a ball on the piano bench, is wearing a red and green ribbon. I believe she nods when I greet her.

Mr. M is never in a rush to begin the lessons, and tonight I sit next to the cat while he brings cookies to munch on as we chat about the day. He wants to know what I think about all sorts of things. Although he didn't come to this country by way of Ellis Island, he thinks it's a shame it's being closed. He's proud that Senator Smith, who comes from just up the river in Skowhegan, has helped bring down the hateful Joe McCarthy, and he's mystified by the news that a meteorite has conked a woman on the head in Alabama. I suggest it would be great fun to call down one of those things on Mrs. Bizier, and he holds his sides in laughter.

Finally, I shoo Adagio off the bench and we begin the lesson. Mr. M tells me how surprised and proud he is at how far I've come. In four months, I've gone through four of Mrs. Moussallem's old lesson books, each one taking me closer to the intermediate level.

Tonight, I begin by playing scales. He calls for them in random fashion, and I jump right on each one – major, minor, ascending, descending, it doesn't matter. I've practiced them so many times I hardly stop to think. We move on to a frisky sonata and then finish up with a dumbed-down version of Brahms' *Hungarian Dance No. 5*. The piece is still new to me, and he stops me now and then to remind me not to slouch, or to adjust my fingers. I tend to go too fast on the sections I find easy and then slow way down through the rough parts, and he shakes his head as he tries to keep me steady by chopping his hand in the air above the score.

He doesn't have any sticky stars, but when I finish he pretends to attach one at the top of the page just the same, and then he makes me blush when he stands up to applaud before he shuffles over to the sofa, reaches down and retrieves something from underneath. He returns with a long, flat package, wrapped in holiday paper. "For you," he says, holding it out. "Merry Christmas."

I am mystified, even after I've unwrapped it. In front of me are two long pieces of heavy cardboard, maybe eight inches wide, hinged together with tape at one end. I delicately set it on the floor and flop it open. It's plain as day, but I still don't believe what I'm looking at. It's a complete and perfect replica of a piano keyboard!

I squeal, but then can't help but give Mr. M a puzzled look. "To be perfectly honest," he says, "I'm not at all sure about this, myself. I confess I've never heard of anybody ever using one, but of course I've never known a student who didn't have a piano, either. He tells me he gave the matter a lot of thought and decided that even a silent keyboard is better than none at all. "At least," he says, "tapping your fingers on the keys will help you keep tempo, and having the keys drawn the correct size ought to help with your fingering."

I get down on my knees to examine the mysterious and magnificent thing more closely. It is drawn on white paper that has been carefully glued onto the stiff cardboard. The lines between the keys are perfect, and every black key is evenly filled in. The entire surface is clear and hard, shellacked, he says, with several coats. It must have taken him days. "Thank you," I say, trying not to cry. "Thank you so very much."

He beams, puts his hands on my shoulders and holds me at arms' length. I'm thrilled, and he knows it, but my heart sinks when I remember I have nothing to give him. When I apologize, he brushes me off, telling me that *I* am his gift, straight from heaven. "Come to think of it," he says, "if you don't mind, from now on I think I'd like to call you Angel."

"Of course you may," I say, rushing to put my arms around his neck and bury my head in his worn wool sweater. Then, as I stand there feeling warm, safe, and wonderful, I begin to wonder how it can be that a 16-year-old girl named Angela has never before been called an angel.

1955

New revolutions brew on every corner. Rhythm and blues has become rock 'n' roll, and teenagers launch a music revolt that won't end for another fifteen years. Half the nation's homes have television sets, and parents, already shocked by the lyrics of the new songs, are horrified at the sight of their gyrating performers. Hollywood joins the fray by releasing Rebel Without a Cause *and* Blackboard Jungle *in the same year, and the new recklessness is underscored in the fall, when teen idol James Dean dies in a fiery crash.*

Propelled by a courageous few and the immense power of television, a long overdue movement to assure civil rights for African-Americans is thrust center stage. In January, Marian Anderson, denied the stage of Constitution Hall sixteen years before, becomes the first black singer at the Metropolitan Opera. In April, Elston Howard breaks the color barrier of the New York Yankees, and in May the Supreme Court orders the desegregation of the nation's schools. There's much to debate over that summer and fall, and in early December it all boils over. A spunky Alabama woman named Rosa Parks is arrested for refusing to take a back seat on a bus, and the preacher Martin Luther King, Jr., leads a boycott that stings the consciences and the wallets of those who resist his cry for fairness.

All the while, money makes money. The hourly wage jumps from 75¢ to $1, and the average annual salary rises to $3,800. Americans buy eight million new cars, and General Motors admits to earning more than a billion dollars in profit. Growing consumerism brings with it the beginning of revolutionary shifts in business and industry. The new interstate highway system spawns shopping malls at the foot of its ramps, and Main Streets struggle to hold on.

Small industries are beginning to fold up or fold in as owners take their operations south in quest of fewer unions and cheaper labor.

Seven

I t's been four months since Mr. M gave me the cardboard keyboard, and I'm still not sure how it can possibly be of any use in the matter of making music. The night I brought it home, I opened it on the sill beneath the double windows in my room, and with a pillow on the footstool, I sat down, squared up to middle C and put my fingers over the fake keys. *Tap, tap, tap.* That's all. *Tap, tap, tapity tap.* It felt stupid, and I was ashamed. Mr. M spent hours making it, and to be fair to him, I've tried poking away on that dumb cardboard every day since, always giving up in disgust before I head down to Head of Falls in search of real music.

Now, it's Sunday morning, the first day of April vacation. My father went out early, with a paper sack under his arm, aiming to celebrate five days of sobriety; Mom is working at Jabbur's, and Gabe is off somewhere, dribbling a basketball. Margaux hasn't yet banged on the kitchen door. It's a good time to give the cardboard one last chance. On the real piano, I've been struggling to play a learner's version of *Habanera*, from the opera *Carmen*, and I lean the sheet music against the window and examine it closely. My mind goes deep into the song, and when I hit the first note, a B-flat, I nearly fall off the footstool. B-flat comes straight into my head, clear as a bell. *This can't be.* Maybe the note is coming from a bird, but there's no bird I know of that sings in B-flat, and besides, the windows are closed. Mystified, I start to play again: a quarter A tied to a staccato D, followed by a full A. I hear every single note, or maybe I don't. It might be *Habanera* after all, since it has magic in it. I try a different song, less lively, and the notes come to me just as if I were playing Mr. M's piano.

I play on for more than an hour, deep in this strange new world, hearing every single note, when suddenly I'm startled by the loud slam of the kitchen door. Mom is home. That very instant, the sound of music stops. *Tap, tap, tap.* Nothing more.

No one is ever going to believe a cardboard keyboard can make real music, so I keep the secret to myself all through vacation, until Saturday night, when I'm at the Mathieus', playing records. I get all caught up listening to the Four Aces sing *Love Is A Many Splendored Thing*, and in that weak moment, I blab to Margaux about the Miracle on Front Street. It's a big mistake.

She turns to me in horror. "You've completely lost your mind," she says. "And you know what happens to people who hear voices, don't you? They lock 'em up!" Her head bobs with certainty. "What do you think they'll do to somebody who says she hears music in a piece of cardboard?"

She covers her face with her hands, and I backtrack quickly before she suggests getting her father to drive me to the Augusta insane asylum. "Just kidding," I say meekly. "Made it all up."

You'd think I'd learned my lesson, but the next day at Mr. M's, I decide I have to tell him, too, and when I sit down at the Beckwith, I blurt it straight out. "Do you know," I say somewhat apologetically, "that sometimes when I play on the cardboard keyboard, I actually can hear the notes in my head?"

I cringe, waiting for him to laugh out loud. Instead, he grins from ear to ear. "Goodness me, Angel," he says, "I've suspected this all along." *Here it comes. He thinks I'm nuts, too.* "Well, of course you hear the notes," he goes on matter-of-factly, "and don't for a minute think there's anything strange about it. It simply means you have an ear."

I'm not sure what he means, but I giggle and tug on my lobes, which I'd really like to have pierced, but Margaux says it would make me look cheap. "In fact," I snicker, "I have two."

"No, no," he says, "You have an ear for *music*. Like those other two ears you were born with it. You don't get it by studying, it can't be bought, and it can't be stuck on later." He's proud as can be. "Plain as day," he says. "You have a special gift from God."

I stare at him, dumbfounded.

"Okay," says he, "let's prove it." Out of the blue, he begins to hum the opening of *Unchained Melody*. I know it well; Les Baxter made it famous. Margaux has the record. "Now," he says after he's hummed a few bars, "you play it."

"Without the music?"

"Without the music."

I pause for a second, and then slowly tap the notes on the Beckwith with my right hand: *c, d, c, d, e, c, c, g, b, d, e, c* ...

"You see?" he says, beaming. "You hear the music and you can play it. On the cardboard keyboard, you play the music and you can hear it. It's exactly the same thing, just in opposite directions. God's gift. No doubt about it."

~

Monday, with vacation over, I wake to the shrieks of a hundred crows leaving their overnight roosts by the river and flying up into town. The sky is clear, and the sweet smell of spring mud is nicely covering the stink of sulfur from the paper mill. All is well. My father has a job, and I have an ear. I wonder why I could not have started my life at age 16, and skipped the rest. There's only one thing wrong: school is about to start, and I know I'm about to face a very different kind of music.

I'm in no rush to get to school, and every so often Margaux breaks into an awkward skip and moves on ahead, waving back, urging me to hurry. "Today we'll get report cards for the last term," she says, as if I needed reminding. "You think I'll have to sign for you again?" Margaux has inked Mom's name on the *parent* line of my report card for the last three terms. Mom doesn't keep track of such things, and I don't tell her, because she'd get upset and light a forest fire of candles at St. Joseph.

We pass Sittu's Bakery and reach the top of Union Street before I get Margaux to stop talking about report cards by pointing her beyond the Texaco garage, toward the fire station. Margaux's obsessed with the fire department. If they didn't already have the Dalmatian named Spanner, she'd probably be their mascot.

Men in black rubber boots are out front, washing the new American-LaFrance pumper, which seems a most fitting name for a Waterville fire truck. Margaux marches right over, swings her bad leg onto the running board, and begins to climb into the seat. One of the men tries to give her a hand, but he backs off when she kicks at him with her good leg.

She's no more than settled behind the wheel when she asks if it's possible to adjust the tone of the alarm horn on the roof. I know where she's coming from. We were on King Court last night when the 9 o'clock curfew blew, and Mr. M covered his ears. He said the sound is grating because the horn is set somewhere between a flat E-flat and a D-sharp, and most definitely should be changed to something more tolerable.

None of the men seem to know if there's a thing can be done about it, so Margaux moves on. When it comes to fires, she's a lot like Fergie, a fanatic for every detail. She has all the call box numbers memorized, and she drags me to most every fire in town. In February, we shivered for hours in Coburn Park, watching as the old academy building burned to a shell. Last month, she got us to the corner of Main and Temple ahead of the trucks, and the firemen looked at us as if we'd started it. Just two weeks ago, three people died in a fire on King Court, not far from Mr. M's. I'm tempted to ask why there are call boxes all over the La-Di-Da neighborhoods, but none at Head of Falls, but I'm afraid to know the answer.

The men have finished washing the truck, and they're standing around, flirting with Margaux. It's time to go, and I get her attention by pointing to my wrist where a watch would be if I owned one, and coax her down.

We're already late by the time we cross the busy intersection in front of the Elmwood Hotel, and I yell impatiently at Margaux when she stops outside the First National store to check the payphone slot for change. As we head up Center Street, my stomach starts to clench. I'm in for it, I just know.

The bell has already rung, and I race for homeroom where, sure enough, Mrs. Aldrich has begun to hand out report cards. When she gives me mine, she speaks loud enough for the entire class to hear and tells me she wants to see me at the break. I can't bear to look at my report straight on, so I hold it off to the side and peek out of the corner of my eye. It looks a little like a musical scale, without the G. There's a C in French, a D in biology, an E for excellence in conduct, an F in algebra, an A in civics and the gift of a B in English.

"I'm so disappointed," Mrs. Aldrich says the second I walk up to her desk, "but you had your chance, and I'm afraid you didn't make good use of it." She looks genuinely sorry, and I feel terrible. "We'll begin by replacing algebra with home economics," she tells me, "then we'll see how it goes." Telling her about my obsession with a cardboard keyboard would only get me in a bigger mess, so I simply apologize and surrender.

It takes just one home economics class to cure me of my bad study habits. I'm forced to sit in a circle with a bunch of girls, yacking on about stupid boys while we put together a dumb quilt from scraps of cloth that must have come from botched attempts at more useful projects. I have to line up bananas at Cottle's after school, but the minute I get home I fold my magic keyboard, slide it under the bed, and work until midnight, polishing homework assignments and boning up on every subject. I even take a few minutes to patch my dungarees, so I can check off the requirement for Home Ec. In the morning, Margaux writes *Yara Jamal* in bold script on the back of my card and I turn it in to Mrs. Aldrich, taking the opportunity to assure her I'm fast getting all caught up and expect to be back unraveling algebra in no time. Her doubtful smile is not encouraging.

After an exhausting and boring week of doing what I *have* to do instead of what I *want* to do, I look forward to staying home Friday night and playing a few tunes into my head from the magic keyboard. Instead, Margaux insists we go to the dance at the Y. I tell her I have nothing to wear, but she knows better. She was with me when Mom gave me a poodle skirt she'd acquired from a customer whose daughter had gotten too fat, and she went with me on a shopping expedition to Sterns department store, where I got myself a fine new sweater on sale for two bucks. On the way home, we completed the ensemble with a colorful, like-new scarf pulled from the bottom of a bin at the Salvation Army. My excuse isn't going to wash with Margaux, and I give in.

~

The sun is setting by the time we arrive at the Y, and the crowd on the lawn out front is beginning to drift inside. It's been the warmest spring day yet, and even with the windows in the tiny gym wide open, there's barely air to breathe. It doesn't help that we're made to dance in our socks to protect the precious wooden floor, and piles of smelly shoes are fermenting in the corners.

Margaux and I find a place on a bench along the wall just as the DJ begins with Tennessee Ernie Ford belting out *Sixteen Tons* with the amps cranked up to the max. The dance floor fills up quickly. Except for one or two couples that have been physically attached since birth, the rest are mostly cheerleaders and football players. In the very center is Priscilla Bizier, the tall blond daughter of the wretched Mrs. Bizier, swirling around with the captain of the football team, Moose LeGrand. She must be wearing one of those new torpedo bras like Jane Russell has in *The Outlaw*, as her boobs jut straight out in a desperate attempt to escape. Margaux's eyes are following mine. "How does she even breathe?" I whisper, real catty like.

"She doesn't," Margaux hisses back. "Accounts for the brain damage."

I know we're not being fair. Priscilla is a snob and all that, but they say she's truly one fine piano player, and I admire her for that. Of course, it doesn't hurt that her mother's a teacher.

After two or three songs and no dance invitations, Margaux and I ponder the notion of dancing with each other, but then decide it's best not to risk it. Someone is bound to say we're queer. Instead, we head for the Coke machine just as Fergie appears, out of nowhere. "Hey," says he. "What's up?"

"Nothing," Margaux is snippy.

He ignores her, turns to me and calmly asks me if I'd like to dance. It's not like I have a long list of boys to choose from, and besides, at the moment Fess Parker is singing *Davy Crockett*, which is fast enough to keep Fergie from feeling the need to cling. Even though I consider myself a good dancer, it's hard to keep up with him. The poor boy starts and stops and jumps this way and that without any real plan, and I'm exhausted when it's over. Next up is *Melody of Love*, and I run for the girls' room.

When I get back, Gabe is talking to Margaux and Fergie. He gives me a hug and tells me he's heard all about my school demotion. I tell him I've got to work harder, that's all. Gabe says I need help, both with my piano addiction and with the decision-makers at school. He says he'll help on the school end of things, but I can't imagine how.

All the while, Fergie has been listening with his mouth wide open, and he immediately jumps in and says he'll help with algebra, even though I'm not taking it anymore. "It's all about x's and y's," he says. "Nothin' more to it than that." I'm about to decline his offer when everybody starts screeching, and we turn to watch Gabe's friend Spike at center court, jitterbugging like a madman and twirling this chick I've never seen before.

"Who's that?" I ask.

"Don't know," Gabe confesses, "and I'm not sure he knows, either."

Margaux shrugs her head. "Maybe he just wants to score."

"Well then," Fergie quips, not getting it. "Maybe he should play basketball."

Everybody laughs, and Gabe holds out his hand and invites me to dance. The heat in the place has already turned my curls frizzy, but I would never turn him down. He's as smooth as anybody, and we go off to the side and drift in a small circle while the Four Lads give us *Moments to Remember*. He'll be out of school in a few weeks. After that, I'm so afraid he'll disappear.

When we wander back to the bench, Gabe says he's going out to get some air, and Fergie goes with him, having suddenly decided he needs to read a chapter or two in his calculus book before he goes to bed. The rest of us aren't far behind. It is already ten o'clock, and the instant Pat Boone winds up *Ain't That a Shame*, the lights blink several times and everybody heads for the corners to sort out the shoes.

Outside on the steps, Gabe says he's going to stay at home tonight, and he'll walk with us. I'm surprised. Maybe he's not feeling well.

We haven't even reached the sidewalk when we hear Fergie, howling like a banshee as he comes racing back up Temple Street, arms waving. We meet under the streetlight in front of the Congo church and wait while he catches his breath. "The Lockwood's going out on strike at midnight," he finally gasps. "The mill's closed already."

A small crowd has gathered, and nobody says a word as we look at one another, slowly taking in the news. There's been talk of a Lockwood strike for weeks, but most people seemed to think it was just a bluff. Now, it's really happened. Moose LeGrand, laughing and backslapping only minutes before, begins to quietly sob. He has no father; his mother works at the mill. Several others begin to walk away, heads down, murmuring. Gabe reaches out and takes my hand. He doesn't say a word, but I know what he's thinking. Nothing good will come from having my father out of work, and it doesn't have much to do with the money.

Eight

Yesterday, within earshot of half the class, Mrs. Aldrich told me I was going to have to swap biology for something called general science, which as far as I can tell, amounts to not much more than learning how to translate temperatures back and forth between Fahrenheit and Celsius. This dumbing down of my courses is getting embarrassing, and it's not that I have college plans, because I don't. Most girls don't go to college anyway, and besides, I don't have the money. It's just that there's something special about being counted among the stars. Margaux said I should be looking on the bright side, because for someone who hasn't done a lick of homework all year, I should be grateful I've only been yanked out of two courses.

She's right, I suppose. At least I've managed to hold onto civics. I'd simply die if I didn't have Mr. Seale. Thanks to him, the kids in our class were better prepared for the news of the Lockwood strike than most people. We already knew cotton workers are the poorest paid workers in the state, that the local union gave back eight cents an hour three years ago, and that now the company wants them to cut ten cents more. He told us the owners aren't really as evil as people think, and they were just trying to keep the place up and running. He also warned us that when the local union joined the CIO in its threat to strike, the Waterville workers were just hitching a ride, playing by rules they didn't make and couldn't change. As if that wasn't scary enough, he says the cotton strike might be just the tip of an iceberg, and that the cost of labor might soon get the other mills in trouble, too. Even so, most of us still believed the whole mess would somehow disappear. Everybody thought for sure that Governor Ed Muskie, a Waterville man, could certainly fix it, but as we learned from Fergie after the dance, we were all wrong. The Lockwood managers shut down the looms at 11 that night, leaving the factory lights on just long enough for the workers to find their way out the door.

~

On Tuesday, three days into the strike, not a word is said about it in Mr. Seale's class. I'm not surprised. Word about his defense of the mill owners got around, and a whole bunch of angry parents demanded he stop talking about the subject. That was stupid. What do they think civics classes are for, anyway? Today, Margaux tried to slide him into a conversation about the strike with a question about the role of leadership in times like these, but Mr. Seale went directly to a conversation about Winston Churchill and his recent ousting as the British prime minister.

After school, as we collect in homeroom to await the final bell, Mrs. Aldrich ups and broadcasts another all-points bulletin, calling for me to see her before I leave. *Now what? Am I going to have to swap civics for a class in hula hoop?*

"I've got good news," she says the instant I tiptoe to the desk. "The decision has been reversed. Beginning tomorrow, you may resume your original classes." Her announcement is so abrupt and so formal that I think she's memorized it. I let the good news sink in while she goes on to say she hopes it's not all been too much of an inconvenience. It's been two days since my downfall; certainly not time enough for her to know I've found redemption. Maybe she's got herself a mole. Probably it's Margaux, but I won't ask. Instead, I simply paste a grin on my face and shrug my shoulders.

"It's all because of Mr. Fallon," she volunteers, "and apparently, your brother." The mention of Gabe is covered in ice, and so I waste no time in thanking her and head for the door. In fact, I'm in such a rush to get out of there before she changes her mind that I run square into somebody standing in the hallway, and spill my books on the floor. I bend down to get them, see a familiar pair of sneakers, and look up. It's Gabe, grinning ear to ear.

"What's new?" says he.

"You know what's new," I say, throwing both arms around his sweaty neck. "How'd you manage it?"

"It all has to do with a cherry bomb," he says, nonchalantly. I don't get it, but I do know all about the bomb. It went off yesterday morning, between second and third periods. The explosion shattered a urinal in the boys' room, breaking the pipes and flooding the floors. Everybody had to stand outside for an hour while they mopped things up. "Turns out," Gabe says, "I was leaving the toilets when the thing went off. Mrs. Rich, the art teacher, saw me and turned me in."

I'm still trying to make a connection to my good fortune. "What was it?" I ask. "A prisoner exchange? Me for the kid who lit the fuse?"

Gabe pretends he's hurt. "I'm not a rat," he says. "I just told Mr. Fallon that it wasn't me, and that he might want to talk to the only person in the boys' room when I left, a short, fat kid, with blond hair and glasses." I pause, then tell Gabe I don't know a single student who fits that description.

He laughs. "Me neither."

Gabe says Mr. Fallon was most grateful for the lead and they talked for quite a while, about all sorts of things. "He told me how glad he is that I'm about to graduate," he says, "and I reminded him he wasn't quite finished with the Jamals. He said he knew you and, if we didn't have the same last name, he'd never guess you were my sister."

I'm still waiting for the punch line, and at last Gabe finally explains that he told Mr. Fallon about what Mrs. Aldrich had done to me and asked if he could fix it. "He said he'd try, but made no promises." I can tell, Gabe is proud as a peacock.

"Now," he says, brotherly like, "you've simply got to find a cure for your piano addiction, and get down to business." I just nod. I don't dare tell him the piano is the most important thing in my entire world.

Margaux is waiting at the end of the hall, and I tell her the news while Gabe stands there, all puffed up. I wonder if she still thinks he's a turd, but won't ask, since she probably does.

At that moment, I hear a yelp and turn to see Fergie pop out of the principal's office and head toward us. He spends a lot of time in the principal's office. Margaux says he's brown nosing, but I know he likes to listen to the ham radio Principal Goode keeps on his desk. Fergie's out of breath. "There's a riot!" he gasps. "Up by the Wyandotte, where the Lockwood has a railroad siding. The scabs are unloading boxcars and the picketers have caught them. We've got to go, right now."

Gabe looks at me and scowls when he tells me my father is surely right there, among the picketers, and that he doesn't want to be within a mile. These last few days, Gabe has kept his distance, not only because my father has become a tyrant again, but also because his behavior is embarrassing. I understand, and I give my brother a squeeze before we head off in opposite directions.

Margaux leads the way down toward the river, bobbing up and down on her bad leg like a jackrabbit. The day is muggy, and the heavy air spreads the stink of the river all through the valley. On top of that, I can taste the sulfur in my mouth. When we exit the cut under the tracks, we see the blinking red light of a cop car far off to the right, parked in the middle of Head of Falls Road. A dozen men are milling around the siding, shouting and waving signs, most of them printed with the same words: WILL NOT WORK FOR STARVATION WAGES. Another half-dozen men are working by the open door of a boxcar, unloading crates onto dollies and piling them on a nearby truck. The picketers keep their distance, but the thin divide doesn't protect the scabs from a torrent of insults and clenched fists. Bernie Nelson is standing with several other cops in the middle of the road, keeping the two groups apart and trying to lighten the mood by chatting with men on both sides. Margaux turns to Fergie. "Not exactly what I'd call a riot," she says, disgustedly.

Fergie has just started to admit he got a bit too carried away when we see a man move across the imaginary line, jump onto the running board of the half-loaded truck and scream as he pounds on the window. The driver slinks onto the passenger side, and Bernie reaches in the cab and yanks the ranting man down off the truck. It's my father.

Margaux sees him, too. "He's shit-faced," she says in her usual delicate way. Since the first day of the strike, my father's either been picketing or drinking, usually both at the same time. Late last night, I was studying at the kitchen table when he came home, all full of beer and steam. Mom and I sat with our mouths shut while he carried on about the unfairness of life, cursing the scabs, and saying the most awful things about the same bosses who had taken him off the dole only six months before.

The police seem to have things back under control near the boxcar, but I can still see my father, red-faced and screaming, running back and forth along the picket line, looking for a chance to give someone a good whack. Bernie is strolling around the edges, waggling his baton, trying to keep the picketers behind the line. We're set to move in closer when he spots us and trots our way.

"I'll never understand how you three kids always seem to know where the action is," he says, "but, I'm tellin' you, this is *not* a place where you should be."

Fergie has a notepad, like a reporter, and asks how many men are on each side, and then wants to know how Bernie thinks the whole thing will end up. Bernie utterly ignores him, and turns to me. "Seeing as how you are already here, and seeing as how you're about to leave, I wonder if you would be kind enough to take your father with you?"

Margaux doesn't give me a chance to answer. "In a pig's ass," she says. "He's not a sheep, you know. He's a wild bull." Her deft combination of barnyard metaphors causes Bernie to pop his eyes.

I give Margaux a nasty look and answer for myself. "Just can't do it," I tell him. "He'd never agree."

Bernie shrugs. "Well," he says, "if he doesn't calm down, I'll have to take care of it myself."

"Go ahead, arrest him," Margaux says, as if she was granting a wish.

"I could if I wanted to," Bernie says, "but if I arrest a picketer, there'll be hell to pay from the union and everybody else. It's not worth the trouble."

I tell him I'm sorry I can't help, but that we'll obey his orders and leave. Fergie and Margaux seem to have defiance on their minds, but we retrace our steps, just the same.

We're almost at the underpass when we hear the startling quick whoop of a siren. It's Bernie, and we step off the road to let his car go through the narrow tunnel. He grins and waves as he goes by, and I glance into the backseat. My father doesn't see us. He's too busy screaming at Bernie, and looking somewhat silly as he waves his cuffed hands in the air.

We follow the car under the tracks, and I watch to see which way it's headed. I'm hoping it will turn left, down Front Street, toward the police station, but instead it turns the other way, toward my house. I watch as Bernie pulls up to the curb, gets out, and goes to the back door to haul my father out. They have a very animated conversation while Bernie removes the handcuffs and points my father to the front door. Instantly, I turn to my friends and tell them I've decided to go back down to Mr. M's. There's nothing to explain. They know why.

When I get back to the siding, the scab truck is gone and I can see the rear ends of the picketers, headed toward Temple Street, on their way down to the Lockwood gates, beyond the bridge. There's no rush, and I walk slowly down onto King Court. The sky has cleared and, in a seeming sign of peace, the setting sun casts a warm yellow glow on Mr. M's tiny house. His car is there, headed out as usual. That's good. I wasn't sure I'd find him home.

I've long since stopped knocking at the door, and walk straight in. Adagio jumps off the piano bench to greet me, purring as she weaves between my feet. Mr. M is on the kitchen side, making supper. "Homemade bread and molasses," he says, coming to the table and offering a plate. "Fit for an angel."

"Or, maybe a prisoner," I say, laughing before I sop a chunk of warm bread in a pool of thick blackstrap. I don't really care if I have a lesson or not, and he doesn't say a word about it. Instead, we linger at the table and talk.

As always, the first thing he wants to know is how I'm doing at school. I used to be somewhat vague on that delicate subject, but after my recent downfall I stopped keeping secrets. He's the only one I dare share my true thoughts with, and he can't help if he doesn't know the truth.

I tell him about Gabe's miraculous rescue, and his face lights up. "From now on," he says, breaking off another piece of bread and handing it to me, "you must work very hard. The piano can wait. I don't want any blame for bad grades." He then asks if I'm getting any help, and I list my small army of tutors. I tell him Fergie's been a great help with algebra and biology, even through the few days I was unenrolled; that Margaux has stepped up her French drills; and that I'm getting all the help I need in civics, right here on King Court. He nods throughout.

The discussion then turns to the strike. Nobody around here is talking about much else. He says he's worried about the strikers and their families, and when I tell him I believe it will all end soon, he disagrees. "Cotton workers in this neck of the woods are in trouble," he says. "All those people are going to have to find work in the other mills." There are still about 5,000 jobs around here, he says, and with all the comings and goings, there should be room for everybody who wants to work.

I don't say anything about my father, who's proven he's a lot better with the goings than the comings, but thoughts of him remind me I've forgotten to share the main event of the day, and I quickly tell him everything, from Fergie's riot alarm to my father's police escort home. I don't hold back. Mr. M already knows my father went back to his wild ways when the strike began. At the mention of his name, Mr. M's face grows serious and he leans over the table and stares me straight in the face. "Promise me something, Angel," he says. "If your father comes home in a bad way, make sure you get out of there. Go to the Mathieus', or come down here, or go somewhere else where it's safe. Promise me?" I nod. He nods. "I must tell you," he says, gazing absently out the window, "I'm not sure what I'd do if that man ever harmed you."

Nine

Mom wants to sit near the front at Gabe's graduation, as close to the stage as possible. A customer at Jabbur's has let her borrow a Brownie Hawkeye camera, and she's bent on getting a close-up of my brother the second he crosses the stage. She says she wants it for my father, who's decided to stick with the shrinking picket line at the Lockwood rather than attend graduation. His excuse is pathetic, but I keep my thoughts to myself. Now isn't the time to fret about my father, anyway. I've got my hands full dealing with my own feelings about Gabe's graduation. Ever since eighth grade, his friends have been dropping out of school like crazy, lured by the money, taking any jobs they could find from here to Connecticut. He's had a few bumps along the way, but he stuck it out, and I'm proud of him. On the other hand, I'm so afraid he's about to disappear from my life, entirely.

Mom fussed and moaned all afternoon about getting good seats, and since it was easier on the nerves to wait in the gym rather than at home, we walk up to school early. Margaux comes with us, all dolled up like she's headed for a wedding, and she slides into the front row first to let Mom have a place on the aisle for a clear shot. We're barely settled when skinny Fergie comes skipping down the aisle, all flushed with excitement, gushing greetings. Margaux quickly nudges me out of the seat next to Mom and takes it for herself so she won't have to sit next to him. It's fine with me, and he seems quite pleased with the arrangement as he settles in and immediately begins to scour the printed program for typographical errors. I resist the temptation to remove his smudged and streaked glasses to clean them for him, and while he chatters on, pointing out misspelled names and misplaced commas, I gaze around the gym, which has been miraculously transformed. The brown wrestling mats are all stacked up against the walls, and purple and white balloons have been strung from one basketball hoop to the other. The doors at the front by the stage have been propped open, letting in a bit of fresh air along with just a tinge of the locker rooms downstairs. Two long tables are in front of the closed curtain, and the folding chairs behind it are filling up with every imaginable local dignitary, from Mayor Dubord to Spike's father, William Moufette, Sr., Esq., chairman of the school board.

When things get underway, the seniors file in to the strains of a Sousa march, played by the school band. There's an obvious shortage of good bass players, since there's barely an oompah in the whole piece. Girls in white robes on the left, boys in purple on the right, they file into seats on opposite sides of the aisle. A double benediction takes care of both the Catholics and Protestants among us, followed by greetings from principal Goode and the mayor.

The featured speaker is Mr. Moufette, who resembles a slinking weasel as he struts to the podium, peers down his pointed nose, and proceeds to bore us to death for a half hour or more, telling the itchy graduates over and over that the entire world is in their hands. After his third warning I scan the faces of the graduates I know, and begin to have real concerns about the future.

At last comes the part we're here for. As assistant principal, Mr. Fallon is in charge of keeping the diplomas straight, and he checks each one carefully before passing it off to Principal Goode who hands them out, one by one, while Mr. Seale calls off the full names.

With her finger perched on the shutter trigger, Mom moves out of her seat and into the middle of the aisle while Mr. Seale is still calling off the A's. I pull her back and make her wait until Gabe has reached the bottom of the stage stairs, and then I let her go. Mr. Fallon reads off *Gabriel Elias Jamal*, and then surprises everyone when he stops the proceedings, walks around the end of the table up close to the podium, and gives Gabe a giant bear hug. The place erupts in gales of laughter. Mom, not getting the point, smiles proudly as she snaps a picture.

At the end, the band plays the new graduates out the door to the Waterville High Song, a counterfeit copy of another Sousa march, *Stars and Stripes Forever*. Outside, families and friends gather in small bunches on the lawn, laughing and taking pictures. Mom finishes an entire roll of film before she remembers she hasn't gotten one of Gabe and me together. With some fumbling, she figures out how to reload, and we start over.

The special evening has only begun. The Jabburs have invited us to the restaurant for a dinner in Gabe's honor, and we are each allowed to bring a guest. Of course, I ask Margaux. Not until this afternoon did I discover that Gabe invited Spike Moufette. Of course, I didn't tell Margaux. She would have insisted on going home to change into something low cut and outrageous, and would undoubtedly have made a dramatic entrance to the party, wearing far too much perfume.

It's after closing time, and we arrive to find we have the entire place to ourselves. The wood-paneled walls of the restaurant are covered with old photographs and maps of Lebanon, and the menus in a box by the door are written in both English and Arabic. Fewer than ten tables fill the entire place, each one covered with a green, checkered oilcloth and topped with a tiny vase of plastic flowers. Tonight, two of the tables have been placed in the middle of the room with chairs for six. Mom explained beforehand that my father said he would make it if he could, but I know she didn't believe him. We don't even bother explaining his absence to the Jabburs. It's just too embarrassing.

Mr. and Mrs. Jabbur flutter around in white aprons, pouring glasses of water before presenting an appetizer of flatbread chips with garlic dipping sauce. Margaux turns up her nose and refuses to try any of it. Instead, she ups and asks if they have any peanuts, which Mr. Jabbur agreeably brings to the table with all the ceremony of a waiter at the Ritz.

We've just begun to eat when there's the loud roar of an engine, then a second of silence before the startling explosion of backfire. Obviously, it's Spike. He's through the door in seconds, arms spread like the lord of the manor, requiring each of us stand up in turn to shake his hand. I can tell Margaux is pleasantly stunned. When he gets to her, she droops her hand like the queen. She's about to say something profound, when she chokes on a peanut, coughs it back up, and sends it flying over Spike's head. Everybody pretends not to notice.

Gabe and Spike sit at the end of the table, and they immediately begin a conversation that the rest of us don't understand. There's only so much that can be said about automobiles, but these two never seem to get to the bottom of it. While they jabber on about torque and horsepower, I watch Spike out of the corner of my eye and try to understand why I'm even mildly attracted to him. There's a great deal about him not to like, but now I'm curiously searching for reasons why his negatives might be overrated.

It's a most delicious meal, all planned with love and attention. Mrs. Jabbur has made baked kibbeh with lamb and a huge tureen of tabbouleh, entirely prepared, she proudly points out, with fresh ingredients – tomatoes, parsley, mint, lemon and green onions. It's difficult, but not at all impossible to find room for dessert: flaky squares of baklava, dripping with honey.

We sit and talk long after the dishes are cleared. Mom comes right out and asks Gabe what he intends to do with his life now that he is a degree-holder. I don't think she's ever really flat out asked him the question before, and it's probably the warmth of the moment that allows him to answer her frankly. "I'd really like to get into the auto repair business," he says, "and if there was ever a time to do it, it's now." He admits he doesn't have the training, but says he's determined to find a way to get it. In the meantime, he says he's going to look for any kind of a job that puts him close to cars.

Margaux, Spike and I won't graduate for another year, but Margaux says she already knows what she wants to do, and proudly announces she will be a nurse. I figure her polio experience put her off in that direction, and I can't help but think that if she had a little more patience, she might be very good at it. "Why be a nurse," I ask, "when you could be a doctor?" She gives me a queer look and shrugs.

Spike, no surprise, proclaims he wants to be a lawyer, like his father. He says he's thinking of going to Yale or, if he can't get in there, maybe to Dartmouth. Margaux, who has hung on his every word all night, can't help herself. "Well, aren't you the La-Di-Da?" she says before making a face that plainly says she'd like to take it back.

Although I've never said it to anybody, I find myself declaring I won't be at all surprised if my future has something to do with music. "For a start," I say, "I might work for Al Corey, selling records and giving piano lessons to kids."

Mom wipes a drip of honey off her chin and looks up at the clock on the wall near the kitchen. "My gosh," she says, "ten o'clock already, and I have to be back here at five. We'd better go." There are hugs all around, with special thanks heaped upon the Jabburs. "I can honestly say," Mom tells the pair, "I've never been to such a wonderful party in all my entire life." She means it. The same is true for me.

Spike offers us a ride home, but it's only a short way, and Mom and I decide to walk. I can tell Margaux would rather go with Spike in his shiny black Crestline, but she shakes her head and makes believe she doesn't care. Gabe climbs in with Spike and says they're headed off to the Ford garage on Charles Street to look through the windows into the lighted showroom and see the newest models. The Fairlane has replaced the Crestline model, and Spike said at supper he'd like to have the new one. My brother is more interested in the latest T-Bird, which, he likes pointing out, has so much horsepower that they actually offer seat belts to go with it.

It takes only a few minutes to walk up Hathaway Street and cut through Allen Road to get to Front Street near Joseph's Market. As we near the house, my wonderful meal suddenly rises, foul tasting, into my throat. My father is standing there, under the light on the porch, his arms crossed.

"Where have you been?" he barks, the instant we reach the steps.

"It was Gabe's graduation night," Mom says, voice trembling.

"I know that, ya damn fool," he comes right back, "but graduation was over hours ago."

She reminds him of the invitation to dinner at Jabbur's, but doesn't say a word about his forgetting. "Here," she says, holding out a tiny package wrapped in a paper napkin. "I brought you some baklava." At that, he reaches out and wildly slaps her hand, sending her offering flying into the ditch.

Margaux slips quickly past and runs up the driveway. I'm frozen in fear, and then I remember Mr. M's warning about what to do if my father gets out of hand. I run to catch Margaux and ask if I can stay overnight, and she pushes me ahead of her into the house.

Margaux has a big double bed, and we crawl in together. I'm still shaking. "I've simply got to do something about it," I whisper in the dark. "One of these days somebody's going to get hurt real bad, and I'll hate myself if I've done nothing and let it happen."

"Bernie Nelson would help if he could," Margaux whispers back. "Trouble is, your father has to break a law before the cops do anything."

Her mention of the law puts me to thinking. "The law is already being broken," I say, "whether my father is the one to break it, or not."

Margaux flips on the light by the bed. "I get it," she says, sitting straight up. "Tomorrow we'll march ourselves down to Archie's and do a little law enforcement of our own." I make her promise to let me do all the talking.

~

The North Street pool has been open for two weeks, and we have to stay on as lifeguards until the five o'clock closing. If my father keeps his usual picketing schedule, he'll be down at the Lockwood, and we can go to Archie's without having him know a thing about it.

The day seems to last forever, but when the last padlock goes on the gates, we're off in a flash. Within 20 minutes, we cross lower Front Street and arrive at Archie's. A cock-eyed sign on the door says they're open, and we walk straight in. It's dark inside, but it's easy enough to see the place is empty. The day crowd has gone home and the all-nighters aren't yet in.

A man with huge arms that bulge out of a dirty white tee shirt is standing behind the long bar, washing glasses in the sink. Archie, I presume. He turns toward us the instant he hears us. "What are you doing here?" he growls. "You can't stay. Have to be 21. Law says so."

Quickly forgetting her pledge of silence, Margaux jumps right back. "I'm 21," she lies. "This girl here is my guest."

"Don't matter," the man barks. "No minors on the premises. Period. Now, get out."

I take a deep breath, gather every ounce of courage I can find, and sidle up to the bar. Calmly, I trace slow circles over the glass jar of pickled eggs with my finger. "Actually," I say, lifting the same finger to point at the man, "the law is what we're here to talk about."

"What law?"

"The law that says you can't serve alcohol to someone who is drunk."

"What makes you think we do that?" the man says. "And, who are you to be asking, anyway?"

I stand and lean over the egg jar, look him straight in the face. "My name's Angela Jamal. My father's name is Ashur, and he's drunk most of the time from the beer you push at him when he comes in here every night."

The man's eyes dart back and forth between Margaux and me. He seems momentarily confused, not quite as angry. "Look here," he says, almost nicely, "I'm not a babysitter. I've got a living to make, just like everybody else. I know your father, and he drinks a lot, but he never makes any trouble for me and I'm not about to make trouble for him."

Now, the man's admitted making my father drunk, and it makes me mad. "No, *you* look, Archie," I answer back. "Stop serving him when he's drunk, or I'll turn you in to Patrolman Nelson and then you'll wish you had."

At that, the man flops open the bar gate and bolts through the opening, shouting. "You two get out of my sight right now, or I'll be the one to call Bernie Nelson."

We're almost at the door when Margaux spins around on her good leg. "One more thing," she snaps. "If you so much as breathe a word to her father about our little visit, this place is gonna disappear." She makes a slow gesture of pretending to scratch a match on a box and throw it on the floor. "You got it?" she hisses. "Poof! Goodbye Archie's." At that, we both run out the door.

"What d'ya think?" Margaux says when we're safely on the sidewalk. I allow as how a threat to burn the place down wasn't part of our script, and even so, I'm not at all sure he's about to stop serving beer to my father.

We're not far from Mr. M's, and I suggest we have a visit. Margaux says her hair is a mess from all the chlorine at the pool, and she has to go home and wash it out so it'll be ready for another bleaching in the morning. I head off to Mr. M's by myself.

As always, he's delighted to see me. I sit on the piano bench and he goes to his Morris chair, hauling Adagio up into his lap before I begin my long report. His face slowly changes with his mood as I detail all that has happened over the past two days. His eyes twinkle when I relate the details of Gabe's graduation and last night's party at Jabbur's. He scowls when I tell him about getting home and finding my father in a rage, and his face takes on a look of horror when I take him through tonight's confrontation at Archie's Bar.

"You shouldn't have done that," he says when I'm finished. "Archie's is not a place for young ladies, and Archie doesn't like anybody telling him what to do. When you run a place like that, you build a crust, and you and Margaux are no match for it."

I'm pretty sure I'm in for more scolding when the front door suddenly swings wide open and a man is standing there, all stooped over, maybe even older than Mr. M. His shoulders are shaking, and his face has no color. He looks sadly at Mr. M and heaves a great sigh. "She's gone," he says. *Oh dear, the poor man has lost his wife.*

Mr. M goes and puts both arms around the man's neck. "I'm so sorry, Salem," Mr. M says. They hug each other for a long moment before Mr. M turns back to me. "This is my friend Salem Habib," he says. "He worked at the Lockwood all those years while I worked at the Wyandotte. We retired at the same time." I take the man's trembling hand, and Mr. M nods at me. "And this here is Angela Jamal, my dear young friend who's taking lessons. I call her Angel. We all need to have an angel. She's mine."

Mr. Habib nods and smiles just a wee bit, then turns back to Mr. M. "They did everything they could to try to save her," he says. "But they weren't able to do it." Now, I feel really horrible.

Mr. M tries to lift the mood. "Think of it this way," he says. "She gave us 80 good years, and there are lots of people who are a whole lot better for having her around."

I'm beginning to think we might not be talking about a wife after all, and then Mr. Habib cinches it. "They say she's closed for good and, by the end of the month, the place will be liquidated and they'll be moving everything out, looms and all.

I let out a long whoosh of air. He's talking about the Lockwood.

Ten

Except for having to clean up after the occasional kid who takes in too much water and throws up all over everybody within a half-mile, a lifeguard assigned to the shallow end of a swimming pool has plenty of time to think. This summer I've used the time to take stock of where things stand in my life, and I must say, things are looking up.

I'm still nuts about the piano, but I've managed to squeeze in the far less interesting things I'm expected to do, like homework. My grades went up in the last term, and I no longer feel doomed to a lifetime cursed by dress patterns and recipes. The cardboard keyboard allows me to practice almost any time I want, and Mr. M says the hard work is paying off. Not to mention, the salary for lifeguards jumped up to $20 a week this year, and I'm able to help Mom with the rent and have enough left over for a few sale records and used clothes. And right there at the top of the list of good things is dear Margaux who, unlike weathermen and parents, is most reliable. While I can never tell which path she might take in any given situation, I can count on her being right there with me at the finish. I don't know what I'd do without her.

Of course, life is never completely perfect. The come-to-Jesus meeting Margaux and I had with Archie didn't bring any miraculous conversions, and the evil man is still pouring beer down my father's throat as long as he's able to pay. My father no longer even pretends to be out looking for work, and his drunken rages are getting more horrible by the day. Thankfully, it's summer and the long days allow flexibility in the matter of arranging comings and goings from the house. These days, most of them are goings.

This morning, Margaux and I sit on opposite arms of the wooden lifeguard chair, and my fond thoughts about her foolishly prompt me to reach out and pat her shoulder. She jumps about a foot in the air and looks at me as if I've got sunstroke, which wouldn't be at all surprising since we're in the middle of a heat wave as bad as Maine ever gets. It's been above 90 degrees all week, and now that Doctor Salk has solved the polio problem, most every mother in town is packing her inoculated brats off to the pool every morning to let Margaux and I do their babysitting. Right now, I think I could actually walk on their little heads, like logs in the river, and go from one side of the pool to the other without getting wet.

I shade my eyes against the sun and take inventory. It's not easy; the waterlogged little buggers don't stay still. *Where's the little one, Charlie somebody, whose mother laced him into a blue plastic donut and dropped him off without a howdy-do? Check. Where's that chubby girl, Sheila Mercier, who has a hissy fit when anybody gets in front of her dog paddle? Check. And, how about that tubby, freckle-faced troublemaker, Freddie Pelletier? There he is, the little jerk. Check.*

With the census as complete as I can make it, I'm about to sit back and take another slug on my Orange Crush when there's a great commotion, right square in the middle of the pool. Kids are plowing out and away in every direction, like spokes on a wheel, screaming and knocking each other over as they frantically head for dry land. Alone in the middle of the newly created oasis is, no surprise, Freddie Pelletier. Margaux has already spotted him, and she's wallowing like a tugboat in his direction "He's got a plastic turd," she yells back. Joe's Smoke Shop up on Main Street keeps them behind the counter, and they've been selling like hot cakes all summer.

The little jerk has met his match. Margaux hooks into the back of his trunks and suspends him mid-air with one hand while she scoops up the fake turd with the other. Once back on shore, she drops him abruptly onto the hot asphalt before setting the shiny object on my towel so everybody can see it's fake. Then, with the rapt attention of every gawking kid, she yanks Freddie onto his feet and herds him twice through the fresh water showers before shoving him out the main gate. Gradually, the little brats wallow back into the pool, boys bravely out in front, girls more cautious.

All the while, the head lifeguard, Stan Chilton, has been leaning on the chain link fence behind us, grinning. When Margaux returns, he walks over to us and she wilts like a picked flower in the sun. Uncle Stan does that to her every time. He's a gorgeous hunk with hair on his chest and muscles like Johnny Weissmuller. Behind his back, we call him the Pool Prince.

"Well done," he says to the shamelessly blushing Margaux. "I guess the little shit never heard about your reputation for using brute force when necessary."

It's an inside joke. Last summer, as part of our lifeguard tests, we had to make water rescues. The pretended victim was Uncle Stan. You might think he'd calmly allow himself to be saved, but oh no, he had already explained that drowning victims tend to fight off their saviors, and nothing will do but what he has to thrash around and battle every one of us. When it comes Margaux' turn, I'm worried. Never mind her infirmities, even at 100 percent she's not half his size, and it's plain he's not doing her any favors. The two are in about seven feet of water when he screams for help. Margaux bears down, bum leg churning twice as fast as the other one. She circles him while he flails his arms, then treads water at a safe distance until he insists he's going down for the third and final time. At that, she disappears out of sight before she suddenly pops up in front of him, rears back, and clocks him square in the face.

The man is plainly dazed, and Margaux seizes the moment to grab him by the hair and side-wind him to the asphalt beach. I'm pretty sure she's gotten herself demoted to the towel room, but the Pool Prince holds his bleeding nose and laughingly announces she has passed.

Now, as he congratulates her for dispatching Freddie, Margaux gives him a drooly look that it would make you sick. Either he doesn't get it or he doesn't care. It's probably the latter, as he'll be a senior at Colby in the fall, and he's way beyond high school girls.

If there are troublemakers left in the pool, they've moved on to a different section, and in the momentary peace, I glance up to the deep end and see good old Fergie coming our way, zigzagging along the water's edge to keep his feet from burning on the blacktop. "We're working," Margaux snaps, the instant he reaches down to grab my towel, "and we can't be distracted."

"Well then," he says, "you just look straight ahead and tend to your own business." She glowers, and he goes on. "Come to think of it, you two should probably be separated. I don't think lifeguards are allowed to bunch up." He looks over at Uncle Stan, who is nursing a root beer.

Margaux won't let go. "You don't know squat," she says. "When there's a crowd in the shallows, we need to work together. You know what I mean, four eyes?"

Fergie doesn't catch the word emphasis, and looks hurt as he reaches up to straighten his streaked glasses. "She means four eyes are better than two," I translate, trying to keep the peace.

Margaux is still ogling the prince, and I'm afraid she's going to drool down her front. "This *boy* here is bothering us," she finally says, pointing at Fergie.

"Tell you what," Uncle Stan says to Margaux, "you just follow me down the pool a ways so he can't bother you any more." She scoots after him like a puppy chasing a tennis ball.

When she's gone, Fergie takes Margaux's spot on the arm of the lifeguard chair. "Well, just you look at that," he says, pointing up along the hot-top beach.

"At what?"

"The shimmer."

"The what?"

"The shimmer. The black tar is absorbing the sun's energy, making the air above it hotter and less dense than the rest, causing the light to change direction and speed. That's shimmering."

I give him a dumfounded stare. "Look Fergie," I say, "I've just managed algebra. Calculus is next, not thermal physics."

He seems pleased to move on to a more general discussion of classes. He already knows about my own miraculous recovery. In fact, he gets credit for helping in both algebra and biology, where I earned most respectable B's. Together with A's in French and civics, I got myself on the honor roll for the first time since fourth grade. This fall, I'm going to let Mom sign my report card.

Fergie wanders off, calculating the number of holes in one section of chain link fence, and Margaux returns in time for closing. It takes forever to get the kids out of the pool and through the showers, where they are rinsed of chlorine, diluted urine, and God knows what else. After the last towel is collected, we amble across the way to the North Street Dairy Cone and cough up 25¢ each for double chocolate soft-serves to lick on the long walk home.

It's Thursday. Two more days of work, then all of Sunday to do as we please. I'm going to have a lesson with Mr. M in the morning, and then we plan to take our bikes up Mayflower Hill for a picnic near the college water tower. It's peaceful up there, and any troubles seem to disappear when we look out over the valley, sometimes all the way to the Camden Hills on the coast.

When we reach the bottom of Union Street, I pop the tip of the cone into my mouth, and begin to think of possible excuses for not going home. Mom will be there, fluttering around, worrying about things that won't happen and not worrying about things that will. My father is almost certain to be home, and in a great rush for something to eat so he can get back to Archie's. I don't expect to see Gabe, as he and my father are now never home at the same time.

I'm about to invite myself to the Mathieus' for the fourth time this week, when I look up the street and see a figure standing on our front porch. It's Gabe. His hands are stuffed in his pockets, and his face looks troubled.

Margaux gives him a quick nod and scoots on ahead. "Fancy seeing you this time of day," I say, feeling scared but trying to act normal. He comes slowly down the steps, onto the sidewalk, and puts an arm over my shoulder. "I've got to talk to you," he says, steering me up the gravel sidewalk, away from the house.

I can't imagine what he's about to say, but I don't have to wait very long. "I joined the Army today," he says, popping the announcement as casually as if he were reporting the score of one of his games.

My stomach clenches. I don't know what to say. Deep down, I knew he would be going somewhere, but not the Army. He bends and looks directly into my face. "I tried, Angela," he says, "I honestly did, but there's nothing for me to do around here. With the Lockwood closed, there's lots of people looking for work, and some have families. Even if I wanted a mill job, it wouldn't be right to get in ahead of them." He says he really wanted to work on cars, and that he went to see Mr. Desmond at the Ford garage on Charles Street. "He's such a nice man," Gabe says, "and he'd like to help me, but he needs mechanics. He said if I went into the

Army maybe they would train me and he'd give me a job when I got out."

"So," I say, angrily, "you just be-bopped off and signed up for the Army?" He nods. I ask who else knows, and he tells me Spike went with him to the recruiting office, and that he's just now told Mom and my father. "What did she say?" I ask.

He grins. "You know Mom. She reminded me that President Eisenhower is a military man, and that he's bound to drag us into another war, where I'll most certainly be killed and returned in a box." We can't help but laugh, and then I ask about our father. "I thought he might go off on me," he says, "and when he got up from the table and headed my way, I was set to run. Instead, he just shakes my hand and says he's real proud." There is a pause as Gabe's eyes mist over, and he stares blankly down the street. "I don't remember him ever saying anything like that to me, before."

"And, what about me?" I blurt it out.

"You're the only reason I feel bad about any of this," he says earnestly, "and I'm really sorry, but you already know I'm not much use to you, anyway. I'll stay in touch, I promise." He probably won't, but it helps to hear him say it.

I'm just beginning to get the shocking news settled in my head when he tells me he'll be leaving at ten in the morning on the train to Boston and then on to Fort Dix, somewhere in New Jersey. "Tomorrow?" I ask, wondering if I've heard him right. He nods his head.

Margaux is stunned when I tell her, but she recovers quickly and commences to recite all the reasons why things will be fine after Gabe's gone. "The big turd was never around, anyway," she says, again betraying her general view of men. "We'll make out just fine without him."

I tell her I plan to see Private Gabriel Jamal off at the station in the morning, and she agrees to cover for me at the pool. "Uncle Stan's very patriotic," she says, knowingly. "After all, he's in ROTC at Colby." I don't bother to explain that every Colby boy who can walk is taking ROTC, and promise to get back to work as soon as I can.

Gabe is already at the station when I arrive. The Flying Yankee is parked on the tracks nearest the old cobblestone platform. Only a few passengers are waiting to board, and he's standing off by himself near the first car. He looks so small. He's wearing a tee shirt and dungarees, and he's carrying the worn, little canvas bag he's used a thousand times to lug his gym gear. He sees me, and rushes to give me a hug. We embrace for a long time without saying a word.

When the conductor calls to board, Gabe reaches into his pocket, draws out two large coins and presses one into my hand. "Silver dollars," he says. "One for you and one for me." I turn the coin over and over in my hand. I've never seen one before. "Peace dollars," he says, real serious. "Peace for you, peace for me. Home and away." He swings one foot onto the car step. "If you need me," he raises his voice above the squeal of the releasing brakes, "just squeeze Miss Liberty real hard and she'll yell loud enough for me to hear."

I look through the windows as he finds a seat on the platform side and puts his face close to the glass. He's managed a grin, but as the train pulls away, I catch a look of doubt. There's nobody else around, and I run alongside the car, beneath his window, clutching my precious coin and waving, all the way to the end of the platform before I stop and sadly watch the silver bullet disappear into a cloud of summer dust.

Eleven

It's Sunday. The bars are closed, and my father will no doubt remain passed out in bed until well after noon. Mom is off to her second Mass at St. Joseph, and I'm in my room, playing away on my silent keyboard, when the music in my head abruptly stops, replaced by the rude thrumming of a car engine. It's so loud the windows rattle. I know in an instant it's Spike Moufette, but for the life of me I can't imagine why he's come when he knows perfectly well my brother's gone.

Downstairs, I peek through the curtains and watch as he makes a full circle around his precious Ford, using a rag to wipe an occasional speck of dirt, and I realize the reason he always parked on the street when he came for Gabe was to avoid our muddy driveway. I give him a careful once-over as he stops to apply some spit to a stubborn speck on the continental kit. He's all duded up like a greaser. His dark hair is slicked straight back, and he has a pack of weeds tucked into a rolled-up sleeve of his white T-shirt. He's wearing dungarees that have never seen a lick of work, and the wallet in his back pocket is chained to his belt. I must admit, he looks pretty nifty, and I think to myself it's a good thing Margaux isn't here, or she'd be making a perfect fool of herself.

Spike looks up and sees me, and he tosses the rag in the trunk. "How ya doin', kid?" he asks, swaggering to the bottom of the steps.

I block the door. "Kids are goats," I say, arms folded. "Gabe's not here. You know it."

"Not here to see Gabe," he says. "I'm here to see you." *Well, blow me over.* "Gabe made me promise I'd keep tabs on you," he goes on, "and that's exactly what I'm doin'."

I start to assure him I'm managing just fine taking care of myself and don't need any help from him, but I've been too snippy, already. "Well, that was very nice of my brother," I reply sweetly, "but it isn't necessary. Not necessary at all."

At that, he looks up and gives me a lop-sided, ice-melting grin. "All the same," he says in a sing-songy voice, "a promise is a promise." He holds out his hand and looks me straight in the eyes. I melt a tiny bit more. "What say you and I go to the street dance Friday night?"

Is it even possible that Spike Moufette, the Adonis of Waterville High, has just asked me, Angela Jamal, on a date? Has Colby College moved back down on College Avenue? Is the world coming to an end? It seems I wait an hour to reply, but it's really only seconds. "Sure," I say, surprising myself and stopping right there, before I change my mind.

"Good. Pick you up at seven," he says as he turns and prances back to his car, cranks the radio to 100 decibels and throws gravel in the air as he roars down the driveway to the sound of Dean Martin singing *The Naughty Lady of Shady Lane.*

The whole thing is over before I've given his invitation a lick of thought. Never mind that Margaux will have an apoplectic fit when she learns I'm going out with Spike, but she and I already agreed we'd go to the dance together. In fact, we've talked about little else for days. It's the last dance of the summer, and besides having a DJ for the popular tunes, Al Corey and his band will make

91

a special appearance. Up to this moment, I couldn't wait for the day to come.

There's no waiting now, either. Dean wails *oh, what a girl* as Spike turns the corner at Temple Street, and Margaux bounces out her front door and heads for mine. I feel a huge confession coming on.

"Who the heck was that?" Margaux asks, bobbing past me into the kitchen.

"Spike."

"Spike Moufette?"

"Who else?"

"What'd he want?"

"He asked me to go to the street dance."

My penance comes in an instant. Her face turns an odd color, and she somehow manages to project jealousy, anger, and disappointment, all at the same time. I rush to my own defense. "He's only doing it because Gabe asked him to look after me," I explain. "Otherwise, he wouldn't be giving me the time of day." The last sentence is no more than out of my mouth when it comes to me that I'm probably telling the truth, and I get all snippy again. "I might just tell him to go take a leap."

Quite by mistake, my threat produces the perfect response. "Oh, no," she says, her color slowly returning normal. "This is all very interesting. You must definitely go. It's fine with me. I'll go, too, and keep an eye."

First Spike, now Margaux. Four too many eyes, if you ask me. Before I can think of what to say, her enthusiasm gushes out. "Now, let me give you some pointers on dating," she says, as if she knows anything about dating. "First of all, if you go some place to eat, make sure he pays. He's got the money, and that's the way it's supposed to work, anyway." I nod. She moves on to point two. "You can't dance just with him. People will think it's more than a simple date and get the wrong idea, if you know what I mean." I know what she means. "Finally," she says, wagging a stiff finger under my nose, "don't you ever, ever, under any circumstances, get into the backseat of his car." She pauses for me to digest this last rule, then adds gravely: "These days, there are more babies made in the backseats of cars than in all the bedrooms of America." I get the point, but she obviously isn't sure that I do. "You realize, don't you," she says, her finger still wagging under my nose, "that there's hardly any distance between a simple kiss and going all the way?"

I didn't know that, but neither do I feel the need for more sex education. She's forgotten that last year she discovered a worn copy of *The Kinsey Report on the Sexual Behavior of the Human Female* hidden under the spare wheel in the trunk of her father's car, and we spent hours in her bedroom, digesting the details of every chapter. When we were finished, we both agreed that, even though some of the women in Mr. Kinsey's study were obviously lying, the two of us were nonetheless well behind the curve in the matter of sexual knowledge. Even so, we also agreed we were about as brushed up on the subject as two virgins could ever possibly be.

Margaux's dating instructions have taken her mind off Spike, so I'm happy to pretend I'm interested in what she has to say until I see Mom walking up the driveway, and I put a finger to my lips. My mother has never said one single word to me about sex, and if she doesn't know enough about it to talk with me, I'm not about to teach her. Besides, now is not the right time. She's still wearing her black veil from church.

"Angela has a date with Spike Moufette," Margaux blurts out the instant Mom walks up. I watch my mother's face carefully, and I can tell her brain is searching for some reason why this is not good news.

She does not disappoint. "Oh, dear me," she says. "That boy drives way too fast. You'll have a crash and get hurt, or worse. I just know you will."

Margaux stifles a giggle, and I offer a quick solution. "Well then," I say, "maybe I'll just have to ride in the backseat." Mom nods agreeably, and Margaux pokes her finger in my ribs. It seems a perfect time to collect our bikes and ride to Mr. M's for my lesson, and we excuse ourselves and zip down the familiar way to King Court.

We are no more than settled at Mr. M's kitchen table when Margaux reissues her bulletin of the day. "Angela has a date Friday night," she proclaims. Next, I expect she'll rent a hot air balloon and announce it to the entire city. "It's with Spike Moufette," she says, adding unnecessarily, "of *all* people."

Mr. M is holding Adagio in his lap, and he continues to pat her calmly. "Isn't he the boy who's got that big, black Ford Crestline?" Margaux nods eagerly. "Those are nice cars," he says, "but I've heard the backseats are very uncomfortable." I'm not sure if he's making a simple observation or if he's in cahoots with Margaux. Before I can say a word, he drops the subject right there, leaving me to wonder what he really thinks about his angel and Spike Moufette.

Mr. M shuffles off to the sideboard and returns with a plate of Oreo cookies. I'm hoping Margaux will stuff her face and stop talking, but no such luck. She shoves the cookies to one side, reaches into her pocket, and produces a folded piece of paper that she promptly opens and spreads out in front of him. "See here," she says, pointing. "Don't you think Angela Jamal ought to be a part of this?" I have no idea what she's talking about, and I move in to look.

Piano Recital

Come Hear Waterville's
Finest Students Perform

Friday, September 16, 1955
High School Gymnasium,
Gilman Street
7 p.m.

Open to the Public

Nadine Bizier, WHS Music Director

Mr. M breaks into a broad grin. "Well, I should say. We can certainly find a piece to play, and we'll have three weeks to polish it up. Plenty of time." He then turns to me. "First thing, Angel, is to get you signed up. Go see Mrs. Bizier next week, the day school opens." I'm not at all anxious to pay that wretched woman another visit, but I can't disappoint Mr. M, or Margaux, for that matter, and I agree.

Margaux grabs her first Oreo in celebration, and I wait for her to pop it in her mouth before I point to Mr. M's mayonnaise jar on the table, already half full of coins. "You'll be getting that new TV any day now," I say. He tells me it won't be new, as new ones cost about $300, but he's seen a perfectly good used TV at Drapeau's on College Avenue for half the price, and he's got his eye on it.

~

I've begun to think Friday will never come. All week, Margaux and I have debated what I will wear. I don't have a ton of options, and we end up just where I thought we would. There's nothing wrong with the red pleated skirt I got at the Army store. It's made of that new polyester and wouldn't wrinkle if you ran it over with a truck. It must have been too small for the girl who had it first, as the only thing that needed fixing was a pulled-out button at the waist. It goes nicely with my only black sweater, which, Margaux claims, gets more appealing the older I get. To top things off, Mr. Mathieu has drilled a tiny hole in my precious silver dollar, right through the top of the B in LADY LIBERTY, and I can wear it on a chain around my neck, ready to squeeze if anything goes wrong.

Spike comes at seven on the dot, and holds the door while I climb in the front seat. The car is gorgeous on the inside, and I can tell he likes having me ooh and ahh as I run my fingers over the leather seats. When he shuts my door and walks around to the other side, I sneak a peek into the back and gasp when I see an old plaid blanket, folded neatly on the seat. It's too late to run, and so as he settles in behind the wheel, I take inventory of the owner of this moving bedroom. He's gone from being a greaser to a Teddy boy. His hair is glued down, cropped in a duck's ass, and he's wearing a blue blazer with tan chinos that finish up well above his socks. The chalk stick for covering blemishes on his white buck shoes is resting in the open ashtray.

I've already begun to wonder what I've gotten myself into, and it doesn't help that my mother was right. The boy drives way too fast, and my head snaps back and forth at every stop sign. Temple Street is blocked off for the dance, and we take the long way around and park on Charles Street, in front of the Ford garage. We have to stand there while he drools for a full five minutes at the new T-Bird in the show window. He makes a big point of telling me he's going to talk his father into buying it for him in exchange for his summer's work at the law office. I can read the sticker. It says $3,300. I made about $200 in ten weeks at the pool, and most of it's gone, already.

Tons of people are milling around on Main Street, and lots more in the grass park near City Hall. A bandstand has been set up on the lawn near the street, alongside the big white bulletin board that lists the names of all the war veterans, whether they made it home or not. I spot Margaux, sitting on a bench nearby. She all but drools as she gets up to greet Spike before she sits down again and, as an afterthought, says hi to me, as well. "Where's Fergie?" I ask.

"Einstein's gone to the men's room in the Opera House," she says, pointing to the marquee over the theater entrance at City Hall. "Must have had too much soda. If we're smart, we'll move before he gets back." I tell her to behave herself, and Spike and I sit and share the bench.

The music is every bit as terrific as I had expected, and I marvel at the mix. The old people dance gracefully as Al Corey plays Big Band music, but his slow-paced renditions of Tommy Dorsey and Glenn Miller send most of the kids to the sidelines. Everybody, young and old, dances when the DJ plays soft syrup like Patti Page or Pat Boone, but when he puts on the new rock 'n' roll, everything changes. At the first notes of Chuck Berry and *Maybellene*, the old folks move to the sidewalk and stare disapprovingly as the kids swarm the street and begin to gyrate. I point out this curiosity to Spike, but he doesn't get it and his eyes glaze over. He changes the subject by asking me to dance.

We're in the middle of the street when the DJ announces *Earth Angel*. Everybody is watching, and I know it's because Spike has the reputation of being the Fred Astaire of Waterville. It doesn't take long to discover his reputation is greatly exaggerated. He has all the moves, for sure, and he twists and bobs, arms and legs flailing in all directions, like no one else. The problem is he rarely matches the beat, and he's impossible to follow. Worse, he can't stop twirling me around in half loops and figure eights, and it's all I can do to keep my silver dollar from jumping up and breaking my jaw. The music slows at the end, but Spike doesn't, and I'm exhausted and a little dizzy by the time the Penguins sing the finish: *I'm just a fool. A fool in love with you.*

We dance a few more songs, and, because of sore shoulders and Margaux's instructions, I suggest we each dance with someone else. I've already spotted the tall blond he brought to the Y, but I still don't know her name. "Why not dance with *her?*" I ask, pointing.

"That's Gloria Bousam," he replies. "I can't possibly dance with her. We broke up over the winter, and now we can't even speak to each other." I've never heard about that rule, but I'm fine with it. The girl has everything her name implies, and I can't offer much in the way of competition, at least below the neck.

Margaux is still on the park bench, and she's sprawled out over the seat so Fergie has no place to sit. He's standing behind her, tapping his feet, grinning at everybody. I suggest to Spike that we ask them to dance, and he pauses a bit too long before he gives in.

Margaux giggles and acts the fool when Spike asks her, and her words come out like she's playing a 45 on a 78. "She's glad to," I interpret. Fergie doesn't wait to be asked, and when we take to the street I watch over his shoulder as Margaux gets the spin from Spike. It's hard enough to dance to *See You Later, Alligator*, but when it comes to rhythm, Margaux is his perfect match as she doesn't have any, either. I shake my head as she nods to the crowd whenever Spike takes off on solo flight.

Fergie's face is shining with sweat, and his movements are a little too stiff, but his timing is flawless, and his feet hit the pavement on the beat. I'm more comfortable than I've been all night, even though he whispers algebraic equations while we waltz to The McGuire Sisters singing *Sincerely*.

The rest of the night we alternate between dancing and sitting, and by ten o'clock I'm ready to leave. Spike wants to know if I'd like to walk up Main Street to Park's Diner for a treat before we head home, and I make the mistake of asking if he means to include Margaux and Fergie. He looks at me like I'm nuts.

The converted railroad caboose is crowded. The booths are full, and we take adjacent stools at the bar. Spike fishes for a nickel to play the jukebox, but I tell him to save his money. There's a console at every booth and each one is playing something different. Spike gets French fries with gravy and I settle for a chocolate doughnut. We both want Cokes, and he suggests we share one with two straws. I tell him I want my own.

I find there isn't much to talk about when we're alone, but an endless stream of his friends wander by, give me the once over, and then carry on with stupid talk and inside jokes. At last, he gives the man behind the counter a dollar bill and, while he waits for change, he turns to me. "Settle up," he says, "and we'll get out of this madhouse." I fish out the last quarter in my purse and hate myself for breaking Margaux's first rule.

In order to get out the front door we have to shuffle sideways down the narrow aisle, and we're near the door when I rub into Mrs. Bizier's leggy daughter, Priscilla, coming in. She greets me like a long-lost friend, but I'm not silly. It's because I'm with Adonis. "Well, fancy meeting you here," she says, somehow implying I'm out of place.

"Fancy meeting you, too," I say, giving it back. "Did you have a good time at the dance?"

"I thought it was fine," she says, flipping up a hand with at least six bracelets, "although the Al Corey band did go on a bit long, if you ask me." Having betrayed her narrow taste for music, she promptly puts me down again. "I understand you are trying to learn how to play the piano," she sniffs, "and that you're taking lessons from that Mr. whatever."

"Mr. Moussallem," I say, "and he's an excellent teacher. I've come a long way in a very short time."

"Oh yes of course, Mr. Moussallem. The weaver. Well, I'm sure he's just fine for a beginner." I'd like to smack her and, while she's on the floor soaking up the cooking fat, tell her I can play as well as she can. Unfortunately, the place is so crowded that there's no room for her to be spread out on the floor. Unaware that she's narrowly escaped my rage, she plows on. "Tell me," she says. "Have you found a piano to use for practice?"

I want to scream at both her and her mother. Instead, I look the skunk straight in the eye. "In fact, I have," I tell her. "It's a *Corrugated Steinway*, Model 88. Very rare. You've probably never heard of it."

We're blocking the door to the diner, and Spike is already outside, waving at me. I'm about to go join him when Priscilla pipes up again. "You would be most welcome to come and hear me play," she says. "We're having a recital coming right up, on September 16."

"Oh yes," I say, icicles forming on my tongue, "I'll most certainly be there, as I intend to participate myself."

She looks at me like I've got six heads. "Indeed, you're most definitely *not* participating," she says. "That recital is only for my mother's students, and you're not one of them."

1956

Americans buy 20,000 television sets a day, and the nation is spellbound by quiz shows and situation comedies that depict family life as it should be instead of as it really is. The quarter-hour evening newscasts can only skim the headlines, yet the country is more brushed up on current events than ever before.

The last French troops leave Vietnam. The Italian liner Andrea Doria *sinks off Nantucket. Egyptian President Gamel Abdel Nasser grabs the Suez Canal, then lets it go when Israeli, British and French troops help change his mind. Brave Hungarian students launch a revolt against Soviet rule and are crushed by 200,000 troops encircling Budapest.*

Racial integration plods along, moved more often by the forces of state courts than by displays of goodwill. There is a bus boycott in Tallahassee, Martin Luther King's home is bombed in Montgomery, singer Nat King Cole is attacked on a stage in Birmingham, and in South Africa, Nelson Mandela is charged with treason.

In Maine, commerce and industry still thrive in the cities. The spring brings 50,000 cords of wood down the Kennebec to the mill in Winslow, ready to make paper. The National Interstate and Defense Highways Act has engineers planning the largest public works project in U.S. history, and while most of the 41,000 miles will be laid out point to point, in Waterville the route will bend and add a mile or so to avoid the new campus of Colby College. The new highways are cheered by a nation in love with automobiles, but Americans are killing themselves in record numbers. Ike goes on television to plead with people to slow down, but at the same time, new cars from Michigan are bigger and faster, and even sprouting wings.

Twelve

Everybody says the January weather has been milder than usual, but the readings certainly weren't made down here where I live, in Siberia. Mom turns the heating stove on at about four in the afternoon so it'll be toasty when my father stumbles in for supper at five, but the minute he heads back to Archie's Bar, she turns it off again. The rest of the time, we sit around and watch our breath, or go somewhere else to get warm.

Being cold is not Mom's fault. Kerosene is expensive, and this leaky house gurgles it up as fast as you pour it into the tank behind the stove. The curtains fly straight out into the room when it's the least bit windy, and if you set a cup of tea on the windowsill, it'll freeze before your second sip. We used to keep the oil barrel at the side of the house filled, but the fuel man wants cash on delivery, and it's not possible to pay. Instead, on the way to school I drop a five-gallon can off at Goodhue's Texaco and fill it on the way home with whatever change I have in my pocket.

It would be nice if my father contributed something, but it's been nearly a year since the Lockwood closed and he's not spent a minute looking for work. Instead, he's a giant siphon, draining money from Mom's purse, sucking up great quantities of beer, and hogging the heat for the few hours he's at home. He says he's waiting for the Lockwood to reopen, but even Mom, who believes most everything she hears, knows that's complete nonsense. Nobody's going to be silly enough to re-open a mill in this neck of the woods, and besides, half of the old place has already become the Hathaway shirt factory. In any case, being a slacker is the least of my father's sins, and I sometimes wish he'd simply up and disappear.

Worrying about my father makes me miss Gabe terribly, but when I wish he were home, I know I'm being selfish. He writes to Mom – more often than I thought he would – and never forgets to include a poorly coded message to me, asking how things are going when I know he really wants to know about my father. I write back and tell him everything is fine, even though it isn't. He can't do a thing about it, and I settle for knowing he's happy. I'm pretty sure he is, because he sent a snapshot of himself from Fort Bragg, and pictures don't lie. He's wearing the new stripe of a private first class, and he's standing with one foot on the running board of a monster truck. The Army has repaired his teeth, and the results are right there in the broad grin on his face. Mom keeps his picture in her purse, and I sometimes sneak it out to have a look. It's foolish, I know, but I touch it with my silver dollar before I put it back.

Things go better for me when I plan my comings and goings from the house, and the endless game of hide-and-seek with my father works pretty well during the week. The weekends require more thought. Today, as on most Saturdays, I will escape to the Mathieus'. Tomorrow, I'll have a glorious long afternoon with Mr. M and the piano.

After a morning of mopping floors at Cottle's, I pick up my weekly check and rush to cash it before the bank closes at noon. The $19 is all but spent. I'll give Mom $12 and hold back $5 for kerosene. The remaining $2 is mine, and no matter what, half is going for the Elvis Presley 45 with *Don't Be Cruel* on one side and *Hound Dog* on the other. The record went to the top of the charts early this month, and I won't be surprised if it stays up there forever.

The can of fuel is awkward and heavy. I change hands every ten steps or so as I make my way down the cobblestones on Union Street, and then stop at Sittu's for a minute, to rest. It's cold, but the exercise warms me up, and I'm panting when I come through the door. Mom isn't home. That's good. She's probably off to St. Joseph, attending some meeting, whether she belongs to the particular group, or not. If there's not a meeting, she'll be kneeling in the front pew, asking Jesus for a hand.

I turn right around and go to Margaux's. Her father welcomes me in, and he points to a bologna sandwich Mrs. Mathieu has left for me on the table. "Aha," he says, eyes twinkling, "our lost boarder has returned." There was a time when such a remark would have embarrassed me, but not now. He and I have a running joke about my frequent visits, ever since he first suggested it would make things a whole lot easier on Mrs. Mathieu if I told her when I wasn't coming for supper instead of when I was.

Margaux and her mother come to join us at the table, and Mr. Mathieu directs the conversation. He always loves to tell stories, and today he's full of news about last month's move of his beloved shirt factory down to the old Lockwood. He tells us that after 103 years on Appleton Street, the Hathaway is now making more shirts than ever before. "In business," he says in the fashion of a teacher, "advertising is the key to success, and showing our shirts on a man wearing an eye patch is working miracles." He claims the entire country is buying Hathaway shirts faster than anybody could ever imagine, but I find it hard to believe a man with only one eye can be responsible for selling that many shirts.

After lunch, Margaux and I retreat to the living room. The TV is unplugged because Mrs. Mathieu is convinced the thing emits invisible lethal rays, and she only plugs it in for the shows we're allowed to watch. Right now, TV doesn't matter. We've got other things to do. Last fall, after Priscilla Bizier snippily explained the piano recital wasn't open to ordinary human beings, we decided we'd try out for the school play, coming up in March. The parts will be announced on Monday, and while *Guys and Dolls* has plenty of starring roles, Margaux says the leads will go to the usual La-Di-Da favorites. Instead, we've set our sights on singing and dancing as Hot Box Girls, and I'm pretty sure we'll be picked. We both have good voices, and when it comes to dancing, Margaux never gives a second thought to her polio leg.

As soon as Mr. M learned about the tryouts, he went straight off to Al Corey's and surprised me with a book of sheet music for the entire production. Together, he and I have learned almost every piece. As Margaux and I settle down to rehearse, I suggest I run home and get my cardboard keyboard. She looks at me like I'm nuts. "Nobody can hear that damn thing but you," she says, "and I'm not even sure about you." So much for that idea. Instead, we go at it a cappella, practicing the numbers most of the afternoon.

Supper is served on TV trays. Elvis Presley will be on the Dorsey Brothers Stage Show at 8 o'clock, and we're not going to miss a minute. Everybody in the world knows about Elvis, but up to now, not many have actually seen him sing. Tonight is his first time on national television, and I'll bet every last person in the US of A will be tuned in.

Mrs. Mathieu has made a fluffy meatloaf, special for the occasion, and for dessert there are cups of tapioca pudding, topped with cherries. Two minutes before eight, Mr. Mathieu lets me adjust the dial on his new electric antenna rotor, and when I put the arrow on the exact spot he has marked for Channel 5 in Bangor, it's astonishing to watch the snow slowly melt off the screen as the bow tie on the roof turns north.

Despite Mrs. Mathieu's warnings of evil rays, Margaux and I sink onto the carpet, inches from the screen, and stare up intently. When Elvis is introduced, he appears to be dressed in black and white, although it's hard to be sure. His shirt is surely black, and the tie is white. He has on a tweed jacket and dressy pants with a shiny stripe. His long hair is slicked back, but not so much that it doesn't bounce. He's simply over-the-top gorgeous.

His first number is *Shake, Rattle and Roll,* and somewhere in the middle, he leans over to one side and strums his guitar barely inches from the floor. When he straightens up, every part of his body is keeping the beat. Mrs. Mathieu is standing behind us, finishing her tapioca, and when Elvis thrusts out his hips for the first time, she chokes on a maraschino and rockets it over our heads onto the floor. Mr. Mathieu isn't even watching the TV. Instead, he's staring at Margaux and me, shaking his head. "I don't believe it," he says. "And, they're going to have him back next week?"

Elvis sings two more songs – *Flip, Flop & Fly* and *I Got a Woman* – and when he begins to twist, the live audience pauses in dead silence for a second or two before applauding in a stunned sort of way. At the very end, when the dear boy says *Thank you. Thank you very much, ladies and gentlemen*, Margaux and I shriek uncontrollably. It takes a whole commercial to recover.

It's only nine o'clock, still plenty of time before I risk running into my father when I get home, and it doesn't take much to convince me to stay on and watch *The Jackie Gleason Show* with its skit, *The Honeymooners*. It's good, but it can't compare to Elvis.

~

The next morning it's freezing in my bedroom, and I open one eye and look out to see big, lazy snowflakes drift down a dishwater gray sky. It's Sunday. There's no need to hurry, so I decide to stay under the warm covers a bit longer. Unfortunately, I stay too long.

It's ten o'clock by the time I head downstairs. Mom has gone to Mass, and I'd hoped my father was still in bed. It was too much to ask. When I walk into the kitchen, he's sitting there, elbows on the table, two shaky hands holding a cup of coffee. It's been months since we were even in the same room, and I'm shocked by what I see. He hasn't shaved for days, and the thick black hair on his head is curled over the frayed collar of the same filthy sweatshirt he's worn all winter. He looks up with bloodshot eyes, rimmed in red. "Good morning," I say timidly, while creeping slowly toward the door.

One hand shoots up in front of me, and his mouth makes a sneer. "Not so fast, young lady." The tone startles me, and my heart pounds. "It's time we had a little talk about that frog you're dating," he says, straight out. He's talking about Spike.

"If you mean Bill Moufette," I say carefully, "I'm not really going out with him, but I do see him once in awhile." I should stop right there, but I don't. "And, I don't think it's nice to call French people frogs."

Red veins pulse on his swollen nose. "I'll call him any gawd damn thing I like," he snarls, "and he most certainly is a frog. Worse than that, his father's the crooked lawyer who worked for the Lockwood in the strike. They're traitors, the whole bunch, and Roman traitors at that. I want you to stop seeing him and go find yourself a good Maronite boy."

I know this is not going to be a two-way discussion, but the idea of having my father pick my friends for me is more than I can stand. I look him square in the face, and then surprise myself. "You've never bothered to tell me what to do before," I say as natural as a breath, "and you're not going to start telling me now."

In a split second he leaps out of his chair, grabs me by the arm, and slings me to the floor, all the while yelling terrible things. I howl in pain, and try to get to my feet, but my arm hurts so much I can only roll off to one side as he reaches down to grab me again. "You little bitch," he screams, "your mother spoils you, but I'm gonna teach you a lesson you won't soon forget."

I manage to get to my knees and am set to plead with him when a shadow falls across the floor in front of me. I look up. It's my mother. She's standing in the doorway, a veil over her face and the snow shovel in her hand. "You leave her alone, or I'll kill you, I swear I will." Never in my life have I heard her talk this way, and I'm stunned. So is my father, and he turns and heads for her, but she calmly backs down the steps, waving the shovel in front of her as she goes. I use the moment to grab my coat and slip past him and follow Mom into the driveway.

"He won't dare come after us," Mom says in a voice loud enough for him to hear. "The neighbors would find out what kind of a man he really is." I figure we're in for it now, but she's right. He turns and storms back into the house, slamming the door behind him.

We walk all the way to St. Joseph before either of us says a word. When she turns to go up the granite steps, I grab her arm. "Will you be all right?" I ask.

"Don't you worry," she says, her jaw still firmly set. "You go for your lesson. I'll be in church for an hour or so, and by the time I get home, he'll have simmered down. He always does. Most of the time he feels terrible about what he's done. And in case he doesn't, I'll apologize all over the place, just to make peace." She gives me a tiny grin. "I'll even promise to make *you* behave."

I throw my arms around her neck and hold on for a very long time. When I finally let her go, I choke back tears as I watch her frail body disappear into the church. There's something truly wonderful about discovering she'll stick up for me, but there's something terribly sad about knowing she won't stick up for herself.

I head on to Temple Street, and I'm at the corner before I realize I've left my sheet music behind. No matter. I'm surely not going back home, and besides, Mr. M has a piano bench full of songs. We'll find something new.

I stand in the road outside the house for a minute to collect my thoughts. Mr. M can't know there's been any trouble. He'd feel terrible, and I'm not sure what he might do. The snow has stopped, but I see the plow truck has left a pile at the foot of the driveway, covering the headlights of the old Buick. I make a mental note to shovel it out before I leave.

Inside, I'm greeted by the wonderful smell of kibbeh, and realize I haven't had breakfast. Mr. M is in the kitchen end, setting two places at the tiny table. He looks up with a grin. "Best day of the entire week," he proclaims. "Special for the Lord, and special for you and me, too."

Adagio is curled in a ball near the heating stove. Except for a tiny twitching at the very end of her tail, she doesn't move. "Is she okay?" I ask, pointing.

"Just old," he says, "like me." Then he shrugs it off by humming a few bars of *Don't Get Around Much Anymore*. We both laugh, but now I'm worried about both Mr. M *and* the cat. The dear man is cold most of the time, even in the summer, and right now the house must be at least 80 degrees. I shed my coat and toss it in the chair by the door. The instant I sit at the table, he points at my right arm and gasps. "What's that?" I look down. There are four ugly red welts where my father grabbed me. He shakes his head sorrowfully. "He did that, didn't he?"

I'm caught. "Yes, but it will be fine, don't worry."

"No, it's not fine," he says, "not fine at all. Tell me what happened." He doesn't say a word while I tell the story, but I hear him mutter "no" under his breath, over and over. When I'm done, he holds his head in his hands and stares at the floor for a very long time before he looks up and leans in close. "Angel, I'm going to tell you something," he says in an even voice, "I promise you, he'll never, never hurt you again." The edge in his voice gives me a chill, and I want to change the subject, but he's not finished. "If that arm's not better in the morning, you go see the school nurse, first thing."

"Oh, I couldn't possibly do that," I say. "One look and she'd know what happened, and then there'd be questions I don't want to answer."

"Well then, you come down here after school and I'll run you up to the hospital for a check. I need to get my car out of the snow bank, anyway. There's a meeting of the Knights at 7 tomorrow night." I assure him I won't require a trip to the hospital, but that we'll get his car unstuck just the same. He seems to be satisfied, and he takes a spatula and gives me a big diamond of kibbeh. I wait for him to serve himself and then dive in, devouring most of it before he's taken a bite. All the while, he tells me how he missed too many Knights meetings this winter and wants to be sure they don't think he's dead. I don't like the way he puts it, but at least we've gotten the conversation away from my father.

After lunch I go to the piano bench and rummage around. I'm surprised when I find the score for the song on my cracked Tony Bennett record, *Rags to Riches*. It's one of my favorites, and Tony is the best. I beg him to let me give it a try, but he's doubtful. He says the piece might be over my head, but we work on it anyway, and we take turns playing the melody and the chords. Two hours later, he admits he was wrong. I can play it, two hands, smooth and strong, with feeling and without a mistake.

It's getting late, and we still have to shovel. As he struggles with his coat and boots, he fusses about my arm and we argue about who's going to do the shoveling. When we get outside, I grab the shovel and won't let go. He occupies himself with the broom, cleaning off his precious Buick. When I stop to rest, I playfully toss a bit of snow onto the windshield he has just cleared, and that starts a delightful snowball fight that sends us into gales of laughter that don't stop until he's exhausted and holds up his hands in surrender. He leans to kiss my forehead when I finally head off for home.

A westerly wind has swept away the noise of the woolen mill, and the world seems peaceful. *Rags to Riches* is stuck in my head, and I quietly sing as I skip along Head of Falls Road toward the cut. Along the way, I begin to think about the marvel of having gone from utter misery to total happiness in the span of a single day, and I stop dead in my tracks to dream how wonderful it would be if my life could follow that same upward path for weeks, or months, or even years.

Thirteen

I know it was a mistake to leave my silver dollar on the kitchen table when I came home last night, but I was tired and wasn't thinking. This morning the necklace is right where I put it, but its clasp is open and the coin is gone. I wish I dared to march into my father's bedroom and demand it back, but my aching arm tells me I'd better let it go.

Of course, the minute we set off for school I report the theft to Margaux. She knows what that coin means to me, and she immediately begins to scheme a way to get it back. First, she suggests we pull the firebox on the corner and then sneak back into the house when my father comes stumbling out to see what's going on. I tell her that won't work. My father wouldn't hear the horn if it was mounted in his bedroom. She then says we should tell officer Bernie Nelson to get a search warrant for my father's pants, and the very idea makes us both giggle. She finally slows down when I tell her I'll write Gabe and ask him to send another one.

With that, Margaux clams up and doesn't say another word the rest of the way to school. She's rarely at a loss for words, and I would ordinarily think she's sick, but in this case I know what's bothering her. Grades come out today, and she needs a good mark in biology if she's going to have a shot at nursing school. Our junior year is barely half gone, but classmates are already beginning to plan the rest of their lives. I really haven't a clue about where I'm headed, even though I've claimed an interest in music, but at least I'm not worried about second-term grades. I already know I got an A in every class. Mrs. Aldrich whispered the good news to me after school on Friday, just before she gave me a great big hug. When I re-issued the report to Margaux, I could tell she was jealous, not so much about the good grades, but it annoys her that I get on so well with Mrs. Aldrich. I've tried explaining there's a big difference between being a brownnoser, which I am not, and being a teacher's pet, which I most definitely am. Margaux doesn't buy it, even when I point out Mrs. Aldrich is proud of having had a hand in saving me from perpetual home economics, and that the poor soul doesn't get many chances to gloat over her students. She doesn't teach any real classes, and her job mainly consists of managing our homeroom, policing the cafeteria and the parking lot, and coaching the girls' basketball team. On top of that, she has to supervise after-school detention, and as everybody knows, there aren't any prizes in that box of Crackerjacks.

The hallway in front of the principal's office is clogged with students, pushing and shoving in order to get a glimpse of a notice tacked on the bulletin board. Mrs. Rich has posted the cast for *Guys and Dolls*, and Margaux starts to drag me into the mob when I notice Fergie is behind us, leaning against the opposite wall, shoving his glasses back up on his nose and beckoning us over.

"Congratulations, Hot Box Girls," he announces, all smiles. He apparently came to school early and has memorized the list.

Margaux asks who got the lead parts, and Fergie runs them off. Doug Doyon, the little peacock who has had a major role in every play since sixth grade, will be Nathan Detroit; and Priscilla Bizier will play the moll, Adelaide. Margaux gives a knowing shrug, claiming the ink was dry on those assignments long before tryouts.

Fergie continues with the all-French cast. The football captain Moose LeGrand is playing Nicely-Nicely. No surprise there. They put an athlete in every play in order to entice the jocks to fill the seats. Spike is the gambler, Sky Masterson, and Spike's old girlfriend Gloria Bousam is Sarah Brown. I've read the script, and it tickles me to think that when the lights come on, Gloria will be chasing Spike again. In real life he says he's done with her, but my gut tells me she's not finished with him.

Right now, Spike is clowning around for the cheerleaders, who are strung out along the main corridor, bouncing their boobs and practicing with their pompoms for tomorrow's basketball game. He sees me and he waves awkwardly, but I pretend not to notice. I don't care about him as much as I did at first, when dating him seemed like such a big deal. His money took me in, and I got a kick out of the envious stares from the La-Di-Das. But since then, I've learned there's not a whole lot more to him than what you see. I'm bored with hearing him talk about himself, and I'm not at all happy he keeps asking to go parking up by the Colby pond. I suppose he hopes I'll be overcome by carbon monoxide or something, and that he can have his way with me, but I'm not stupid. Margaux's rule about not getting into backseats still makes perfect sense to me.

Fergie hasn't said if he has a role in the play, and I'm about to ask when he announces he's going to be the stage director. I'm glad for him. He's not much of an actor, but he's the only one in the entire school who knows how to run the lights.

The mob by the bulletin board has thinned out, and Margaux and I move in to confirm our spots. It's nice to see a couple more Lebanese girls listed in the chorus. Leyla Ayoub, the weaver's daughter, is there along with Sheila Maroon, a quiet girl who had to be teased to try out. Tacked below the listing is a note that says the first cast meeting will be at 4 o'clock this afternoon. Lucky for me, I worked Saturday at Cottle's and have the afternoon off.

The day passes quickly, mostly because I'm up to speed in every class. Pre-calculus is the only real challenge, but Fergie doesn't mind giving me after-school lessons. English with Miss Klarity is a breeze. Margaux's father is helping me with French, and now that we're done with conjugating verbs and on to reading *The Hunchback of Notre Dame*, I'm doing just fine. I'm not as fond of U.S. history as I was civics, but taking history is the law. Besides, it's a cinch to steer Mr. Fallon away from the boring past and into the more interesting things. We covered the history of slavery in the fall, so now we're into a discussion of modern-day integration. Mr. Fallon tells us people in Alabama have been giving rides to the black folks who boycott the buses, and the police are arresting the drivers, left and right. Just last week, the preacher Martin Luther King was jailed for driving 30 miles an hour in a 25-mph zone, just as if people couldn't see right through that kind of nonsense. Waterville has only one black family, so of course it's hard to understand what these poor people are having to put up with, but it's interesting to think about what might happen if the Lebanese people around here got together and held a sit-in at the local country club.

By 4 o'clock, the cast has filled the front rows of wooden seats that rise above the basketball court, and Mrs. Rich is standing in front, clipboard in hand. We're accustomed to seeing the art teacher in outrageous get-ups, but as play director she's gone way over the top. She's applied some kind of black grease to enlarge her eyebrows, and her cherry lipstick is traced in the shape of a bow, rising far above the line of her lip. She begins by telling us Spike Moufette has been called away by his father and won't be here. She doesn't elaborate, but Fergie fills in with another whisper. Sky Masterson is upset because his father needs help moving the last boxes of important papers out of the big shot offices at the Lockwood, and the job won't be done before the rehearsal is over. I laugh to myself. It's a sure bet Spike is pretty upset about that.

Not only is he missing a chance to flirt with the girls, but he's also probably doing the most work he's ever done in his life.

Mrs. Rich introduces her helpers. Gabe's old friend, Mr. Fallon, doesn't know diddly about theater, but as assistant principal he's become very good at making order out of chaos. Mrs. Aldrich draws her assignment simply because she's the assistant director of just about everything that goes on around here.

The old upright piano I'm not allowed to play has been pushed up close to the sloping seats, and when Mrs. Rich recognizes "our wonderful pianist," Mrs. Bizier does a grand flourish up and down the keyboard before she stands and jangles her bracelets in acknowledgment of what seems rather tame applause.

Mrs. Rich then tells us she has a terrific surprise. We will practice at the high school, she says, but the dress rehearsal and final production will be at the Opera House downtown. Better than that, she says when we move to the theater, the Fred Petra Band will be joining Mrs. Bizier on the accompaniment. With that, the cast members go nuts, stomping their feet and pounding on the backs of the seats. Fred Petra is the best horn player around, and his new band is already famous. For me, there's the added comfort of knowing that, no matter how poorly we sing, at least the background music will be terrific.

At the very end of the meeting, we're told that while the school will rent costumes for the lead players, the rest of us must provide our own. Yikes! The chorus girls will require a number of costume changes, and I'll do well to be able to scrape up a single one. Margaux, who's back in high spirits after learning she earned a B in biology, reads my concern and promptly waves it off. Hot Box girls aren't supposed to have much taste, anyway, she says, and besides, her mother can outfit us just fine. "Big hats, sweaters, circle skirts, and pigtails for *A Bushel and a Peck*," she says before adding she'll be happy to straighten my hair for the pigtails.

None of this is reassuring. For one thing, Lebanese girls don't wear pigtails. Even if they wanted to, it's not possible. The only time Margaux tried ironing my hair, she got one side straighter than the other, and for weeks I had to turn sideways when I talked to somebody, just so they wouldn't be confused.

It's a bit after five by the time Mrs. Rich finishes with her business, and she suggests we practice a song or two before we leave. Since Sky Masterson is absent, she starts with *Take Back Your Mink*, requiring only the chorus and the needy Miss Adelaide, played by the equally needy Miss Bizier. It doesn't go well at all. The piano-playing Bizier drowns out the singing Bizier, and Mrs. Rich tries to avoid a mother-daughter catfight by pumping her palms up and down in an effort to get the elder to lay off the keys. Even then, it doesn't get much better, and we give it up at six with a promise to practice a whole lot before the next rehearsal.

An inch or so of late afternoon snow has covered the icy sidewalks, and it takes a half hour of slipping and sliding to get down to Front Street. We're late. Mrs. Mathieu will be holding supper, and as we rush up the steps, out of the corner of my eye I catch a blinking red light coming from the street in front of my house. Margaux sees it, too. "Cop car," she says. "Maybe Bernie's bringing your father home." I peer to look as we round the corner, and sure enough, Officer Nelson is starting up our front stairs. I glance around, but I don't see my father anywhere.

Bernie tips his hat, but there's none of the usual banter. Instead, he's all business and his face is so grim he scares me. "Your mother home?" he asks. I tell him I'm sure she is, and Margaux and I step past him and go through the door. Mom hears us, and she walks out of the kitchen, wiping her hands on a towel. Her mouth drops when she sees Bernie, inches behind us.

"Evenin', Yara," Bernie says, his eyes cast down at his uniform cap that he's slowly turning in his hand, like a steering wheel. Mom and I swap glances, waiting. The quiet is awful. Finally, Bernie sucks in his breath, lets out a long sigh, and tells us there's been an accident.

"Ashur?" Mom asks, right off.

I know the answer even before Bernie nods his head.

"Is he hurt bad?" Mom asks. "Oh, dear God. You must take us up to the hospital. Please, Bernie, you must. We don't have a car."

The officer gazes at the floor for long seconds, and when he looks up again, his lips are trembling. "Oh, Yara," he says. "There wasn't a thing anybody could do. I'm so sorry, but I'm afraid ... I'm afraid he's dead."

Fourteen

Somehow, I knew my father was gone the minute Bernie Nelson headed up the steps without him, and as we waited for the officer to squirrel up the courage to tell us why he'd come, I felt like I was reading a book I'd read before, where the scenes unfold predictably and the ending is always the same. After Bernie finally says what he came to say, no one moves or makes a sound until Mom slumps to her knees on the cold floor and begins a keening prayer. The wailing causes Margaux to stiffen, and she grabs me by the arm. I yelp, then shiver.

"Sorry," Margaux says, pulling back her hand even as she moves close to stare into my face. She's trying to read me, but I'm frozen like a statue, as if I've somehow left my own body and am looking down upon myself from somewhere else. My mind swirls with oddly mixed emotions. I feel sorrow for Mom, who loved my father in a way I'll never understand; and bitterness, because her love was not returned. I'm ashamed by the surge of relief I feel for having at last escaped the fear of him and of coming home. And worst of all, there are awful pangs of guilt for so often having wished him dead.

Now that he's managed to deliver his sorry message, Bernie's confidence is restored. He's bent over Mom, gently patting her shoulders while he tells her he understands the shock of it all, and that he's sent for Father Ataya, who will be here any minute. Hearing that, Mom gets back on to her feet and, still in a stupor, begins to wander about the front room, straightening doilies and using the dishcloth to dust the furniture. "Oh, dear," she mutters more than once. "Father Ataya? Coming here?" Bernie shakes his head and assures her no special preparations are required.

It's as if I'm listening to someone else talk when I ask Bernie exactly what happened to my father. He speaks slowly as he explains that a woman came to the police station shortly after six to report a man lying on the sidewalk a short ways down below, on Front Street. "I ran there," he says, "and I knew right off it was Ashur, but there was nothing I could do." Again, he says he's sorry. "We've had no accident reports, but we think he was hit by a vehicle traveling north. Marks in the snow show his body went on an angle up the street and onto the sidewalk, on the left."

"Hit and run?" I hear myself ask calmly.

"Looks like it," Bernie replies. "We'll know more tomorrow. The case has been assigned to our detective, Norman Gates, and I'll be working with him. We'll get to the bottom of this, I'm sure. Gates is a bulldog. The vehicle that hit your father has to be damaged on the left front. We'll get word out to the auto repair places; they'll be on the lookout."

"Exactly where did it happen?" Margaux has joined the interrogation, and Bernie tells us it was almost directly across the street from Archie's. "Figures," Margaux says.

"Maybe so," Bernie concedes, at the same time holding up a finger, "but I've just come from there, and Archie claims Ashur wasn't in the bar at all today."

Margaux shrugs her shoulders. "Well then, Archie's lying."

Bernie goes on to say the three customers who were still at the bar all agreed with Archie, whereupon Margaux promptly declares the whole lot of them turds. "It's possible," Bernie comes back, "that he might have been out doing errands, or maybe looking for work down at the new Hathaway?"

Mom speaks up for the first time. "No," she says, clearing her throat. "That's not possible." Bernie seems pleased to have made a connection with Mom, and he looks at her cautiously. "I'm afraid there has to be an autopsy," he says. "It's the law. It will be done in the morning at Thayer Hospital. After that, we'll know more."

Fortunately, Mom doesn't have time to think about autopsies as, just then, Father Ataya comes up the front steps. The priest's cheeks, pink from the cold, stand out sharply in a sea of darkness. He's wearing a heavy black Mackinaw, a black fur hat, and a black wool scarf, wrapped twice around his neck. His thick, horned-rimmed glasses fog quickly in the warmer air, and he takes them off and wipes them with a handkerchief, magically produced from the folds of his black cassock. He's blinded for the moment, and I watch him search the room for shapes. He stops at me and reaches out. "Oh, dear Yara," he says.

"Angela," I say. "Mom's right here." I take his hand and point it.

"Oh, yes," he says, putting his glasses back on his face. "Let's go into the kitchen and have a talk." Mom leads the way and puts a kettle on the stove.

Bernie starts for the front door, mumbling something about having to get back to work, and Margaux follows right behind him. "Oh, please don't go," I say to her, sounding pathetic. She turns to explain she has business to take care of and she'll be right back. Through the window, I watch her on the front porch, waving her arms at Bernie and yacking away. I can't imagine what she's talking about, but Mom calls me from the kitchen and I go to her.

Father Ataya is sitting with Mom, calmly sipping tea while offering words of comfort and, at the same time, working in answers to questions that haven't yet been asked. Perhaps there's no need for a wake, he suggests. He's certainly right about that.

121

Who would come except my father's friends, looking for a free nip? Then he says we can have a funeral on Thursday morning, three days from now. "Assuming, of course," he says, "the body has been released and there's time for Gabe to get home."

Mom gasps. She's forgotten about Gabe, but I haven't. I've been thinking about the need to call him, but I'm not sure how to do it. It can't be as simple as calling up Fort Bragg and asking to speak with Private Jamal. Fortunately, Margaux is back, and she says we can use their phone and that her dad will help get us through.

A big question is still unanswered, and I turn to Father Ataya. "We don't have any money, you know. I can't imagine how we'll pay for things."

"Oh, never you mind," he says, kindly. "Your father's a veteran. There are benefits. The VFW will help, too. Then, there are the Knights. Don't fret about a thing." At that, he stands abruptly, promises to come back tomorrow, and casts a blessing over the three of us. Margaux provides the "amen," and we see him to the door before heading over to the Mathieus' where sympathy assignments have plainly already been handed out. Margaux's mother takes Mom into her arms and murmurs words of sorrow. Her dad does the same with me, and we stand there for a minute or two, listening to kind and thoughtful words about my father that, were he still alive, would have brought bolts of punishing lightning.

The telephone has already been placed on the kitchen table, its long black cord stretching from the tiny phone desk in the hallway. Mr. Mathieu dials the local operator, and for the next half hour the dear woman stays on the line, guiding us all the way to North Carolina. When she finally gets the operator at Fort Bragg and explains the situation, she's told they will get hold of the Red Cross and Gabe will call us shortly. It doesn't take any time at all. Within fifteen minutes the phone rings, and I pick it up. It's a miracle. It's my brother.

"Something terrible has happened," he says. "Is it Mom?"

"Mom's fine," I tell him. "It's our father. He's dead." There's a very long pause, and I wonder if the connection has been lost. "The Red Cross came," he finally says. "I knew someone had died, and I'm ashamed to say I was mostly afraid it was Mom, or you." I warn him he's just begun to deal with the mixed up feelings, and then we talk about him getting home. He says he's sure the Army will fly him to Boston, and he'll hitchhike from there. I can't think of anything more to say than "I love you," and pass the phone to Mom.

~

It's a real shame no one has ever come up with something better to say than "I'm sorry" when someone dies. Sorry for who? The dead person? The ones left behind? Or, maybe for themselves, at not being able to come up with something better to say.

Our long parade of sorrys begins in the morning. Mom is earnestly into mourning, and she's off to Mass, wearing the long black dress she borrowed last night from Mrs. Mathieu. I'd like to go to school, but Mom says it would be disrespectful, so instead I take the cardboard keyboard out of my cold bedroom, set it up on the kitchen table, and begin to run through the music of *Guys and Dolls*. I'm playing *Adelaide's Lament* for the second or third time when the music in my head is overrun by a knock at the door. It's Fergie. He's walked a mile out of his way to school, just to see me.

"Sorry," he says the instant I open the door. He then stares at me intently, as if I might have been somehow transformed into another person overnight. Once he's satisfied that I'm me, he reaches to give me a hug, a most awkward tangle of arms during which we dislodge his glasses and send them skittering off the side of the steps. He drops to his knees and gropes in the snow, chattering all the while. "I heard the news last night," he says. "It was too late to come, but I worried about you all night long."

I don't tell him that I didn't lose a wink of sleep. "Don't you worry," I say, "I'm fine." With that, he's quickly run out of things to say, and there's an awkward moment or two before Margaux appears. "This is perfect," I announce. "You two can walk to school together." Margaux gives me a dirty look and, as they head off, I can't help but grin when I overhear Fergie begin to explain to her the chemistry of embalming.

Mom returns from church just as the Jabburs arrive with a parcel of food from the restaurant. They stop inside the kitchen door and both say, over and over, how very sorry they are. Mr. Jabbur assures Mom she won't need to come to work until next week, and that she'll be paid just the same. When they learn Gabe is coming, they invite us for dinner at the restaurant the night before the funeral.

After awkward moments of grunts and nodding heads, the Jabburs turn and leave just as a car pulls into the driveway. I'm confused until the passenger door opens and I see Mr. M get out slowly and begin to pick his way across the icy driveway. His friend, Saleem Habib, the man I met the night the Lockwood closed, has brought him.

Mom sets out a bowl of hummus and flatbread from the Jabbur gifts, and we all sit at the table. The scene brings on yet another strange feeling when I realize I've never seen Mr. M outside of his house on King Court. In my wildest dreams, I never expected to see him here, in mine.

Mom goes to make tea, and Mr. M reaches for my hand. He doesn't say a word, but I read his eyes. He's never said it flat out, but he hated my father and I know he worried endlessly about me. After a few awkward moments, he finds a way to tell me what he's thinking. "Don't you worry, Angel," he says, patting my hand. "The stars will shine the brightest on the darkest nights." The silent Mr. Habib nods agreeably, and I'm still pondering that heavy thought when Mom returns, a trembling cup of tea in each hand. "That's a fine daughter you have," Mr. M says to her, "and quite a marvelous piano player, indeed."

Mom seems proud. "She plays that keyboard you gave her all the time," she says, "but of course I've never once heard it." Everybody laughs, including Mom, while Mr. M goes on about my playing, making me blush. When the two men stand up to leave, Mr. M tells me he's been feeling a bit under the weather and is not likely to be at the funeral. I understand what he's not saying and nod agreeably. I promise I'll come see him when it's over.

The two have barely left when Father Ataya and Bernie Nelson pull in from different directions. The Jamal house has never seen this much traffic, and I'm beginning to feel like an usher at the Haines Theatre. Father Ataya tosses his heavy coat on the sofa and points my mother into the kitchen. He says he wants her to help pick hymns for the funeral Mass. I'm tempted to join them, as I have an idea or two, but I'm pretty sure Mom won't think *Ode to Joy* is proper, even though Ludwig would probably say it's perfect. Instead, I stay with Bernie in the front room.

"I don't really need to see your mom," he says. "You can tell her the autopsy has been done. It proves that your father was hit by a car, or maybe a small truck. The backs of his legs are bruised, but the coroner says that's not what caused his death. He thinks he died when his head hit the curb." I wince at the thought as he goes on to say there's a big gash on my father's forehead and that it might be a good idea to leave the casket closed. That's all fine with me. It's hard enough to remember him as he was, never mind what he might look like now. "One more thing," he says. "They found chips of black paint on the rivets of a back pocket of his dungarees. That might help us identify the vehicle."

None of this is the least bit interesting to me. What does it matter? All I know for sure is that my father was wandering drunk in the middle of the road, and there's no one to blame but him. It's not like someone was actually out to kill him.

Bernie starts for the door, and then turns back with a tiny grin. "Oh my gosh," he says, "I most forgot." He wrestles to pull something out of his pocket and holds it out in his hand. I can't believe what I see. It's my silver dollar!

He can tell I'm confused, and he quickly explains that Margaux told him the story of the missing coin last night, as he was leaving the house. "I went back to the bar," he says, "and asked Archie if I could have a look into his till. He said he had nothing to hide, and when I found the silver dollar he claimed that someone else had passed it. I knew right away he was lying because the hole was just where Margaux said it would be, right in the 'b' of 'liberty.'" Bernie holds his shoulders back and smiles. "He knew I had him, dead to right, and he fessed up right then and there. Admitted your father had been in the bar all afternoon and left soon after six."

I turn the beautiful coin over and over in my hand, all the while showering Bernie with thanks. He's relishing it, and says he isn't finished. "Just so you'll know," he says. "Archie's Bar is closed. The mayor pulled the license this morning. It doesn't always happen that way, but he'd been warned more than once about serving drunk customers. It's on the record. Besides, the man lied to me about your father's whereabouts the first time around. He could be charged with hindering an investigation, but I guess they decided to close the bar, instead."

I'm astonished. Margaux told Archie she'd burn his place down if he kept serving my father, and while she didn't exactly torch the place, the result is the same. Maybe Mr. M is right, after all. The stars are already getting brighter.

As far as I'm concerned, the day could end right here, but a loud roar tells me the parade's not over. There's no mistaking the sound. Spike has come to say he's sorry. I wondered if he would.

Mom and Father Ataya are still discussing hymns, so I pull on my jacket and meet him on the steps.

"Hi," he says, somewhat sheepishly. "I'm really very sorry."

"You are indeed," I agree, scanning him up and down.

"Gabe coming home?" he asks, abruptly ending the condolences.

"Yup," I say. "Not sure when."

"Maybe you and I can get together when this is over," he says.

"Maybe."

That's it. He gets in his car and peels backwards into the street. Despite freezing temperatures, his windows are wide open and the last thing I hear is Little Richard: *Wop bop a loo bop a lop ba ba*. I'd say *Tutti Frutti* describes the situation perfectly.

~

It's Wednesday afternoon before Gabe arrives, and Mom and I are in the kitchen when he bursts through the door. For a moment, he seems unsure about what he might find, but when Mom lets out a shriek of delight, he sweeps her off her feet and they both hug and laugh as he twirls her around the table. I watch in sheer joy, and then my mind flashes back and I remember my brother racing around that same table to escape my raging father. I hold onto that bad memory until Gabe lets go of Mom and heads for me. We clutch so hard I'm afraid our necks will break, and then I hold him out at arm's length. His once-long hair has shrunken to a boxy crew cut, and polished brown boots have replaced the smelly sneakers. He doesn't have a whisker, and the green Army jacket makes him look like Ike himself. I'm tempted to go and find Margaux so we could trot him up and down Main Street.

We spend the evening at Jabbur's, just the three of us. No one watching would ever guess we're having a family funeral the next day. We talk about almost everything, but my father's name does not come up. Gabe tells tales of his Army training, and his eyes sparkle when he says he expects to be assigned to the motor pool, where he'll be learning all about big engines. He stops only long enough to grab another meat pie, making me marvel at the capacity of his stomach and wonder if anybody's fed him since he left.

Mom doesn't have a whole lot to say, but she hangs on Gabe's every word, and for the moment, seems to have set aside her grieving. My brother makes us cross-eyed with detailed descriptions of what he calls the "deuce-and-a-half" truck. Then he turns to me and asks how I'm doing at school. When I tell him I'm knocking off A's faster than Ted Williams hits home runs, he smiles broadly, and then, out of the blue, says I should be thinking about going to college. I can't help but laugh, and then explain to him that a girl who's lugging kerosene to keep warm and eating tuna casserole to stay fed isn't likely to find enough money for college. Mom nods sadly. Gabe does, too, but then goes on to tell us he can't begin to spend all the money he's earning, and that he's going to start sending more of it home to help out.

We talk well into the night, and when I finally go to bed, a bitter cold wind howls me off to a deep and satisfying sleep. In the morning, the sky seems fittingly gray as we trudge our way to St. Joseph. There are lots of things I'd rather be doing than going to a funeral, but it doesn't bother me as much as I thought it would. Only two things trouble me. I'm so afraid Mom might melt down and cause a scene, and I worry about what Father Ataya might have come up with to say about my father. Some sort of eulogy is required, but I can't imagine how the dear man is going to manage in this case.

There are plenty of empty pews. I spot some of Mom's friends, and recognize three or four of my father's drinking buddies, no doubt praying for the resurrection of Archie's Bar. Fergie is here, as I expected, and I know that as a Congregationalist, he's going to have lots of questions when this Mass is over. Spike is seated on the aisle, and gives Gabe a wave as we pass by. Margaux, sitting with her parents, wags a gloved hand and manages a smile.

Otherwise, there's only the Jabburs and a few others, including the lady who always sits in front to cue the visitors in the matter of standing, sitting, and kneeling.

It's a full Mass with all the bells and whistles, and I find comfort in the mysterious but familiar Arabic chanting and the biting smell of frankincense. When Father Ataya draws us into the communion of saints and prays for the safe passage of my father on his way to paradise, it strikes me that he might be a little too confident about exactly where my father is headed. The least I can do is pray for a safer passage than the one he had crossing Front Street.

My worries about Mom turn out to have been needless. She sits like a black statue throughout, and takes communion without a sniffle. When the time comes for Father Ataya to talk about my father, I draw my neck into my shoulders and nervously twist my fingers. "Ashur Jamal was a well-known member of our community," he begins. *That, he certainly was.* "He was a patriot, and served our country well." *Yes. Soup. At Fort Dix.* "He was the husband of a most faithful member of our church, and the father of two of our wonderful children." *Can't argue one bit with that.* "He will be missed." *Well, at least by his cronies at Archie's.* "We must pray for his redemption," he winds up. *We certainly must.* With that, he's escaped without a single lie and the Mass is over before I know it.

Gabe had warned us he'd have to leave as soon as the funeral was over, but still, I wasn't ready. It's a good thing there's no time to fuss. He'd brought his duffle bag to church and, after we shake hands at the door, he goes to the foot of the church steps, sticks out his thumb, and is picked up by the first car coming down Front Street, headed for the bridge. As he climbs in, I hold up my silver dollar up for him to see, and he waves back with the clenched fist that holds its mate.

Mom's friends are going back to the house with her, and I'm not worried about leaving her long enough to pay a visit to Mr. M.

129

It's true that he hasn't been feeling well, and I worry about him as I make the cold walk down Temple Street. When I turn onto King Court, I glance ahead and am relieved to see smoke rising from his metal chimney and warm light coming from the two front windows. Still, there's something strange about what I'm looking at, and it takes a few seconds to figure out that it's the car. Always before, the black Buick has been parked headed out, toward the street. In fact, that's the way it was left on Monday, when we shoveled. This afternoon, it's heading straight in. I'm about to go inside and ask Mr. M about his odd parking, but something makes me want to take a closer look.

When I walk to the front of the car, my knees go weak, and I'm overtaken by terrible thoughts. The left front headlight is smashed, and there's a good-sized dent on that same side of the hood, near the fender. Mr. M was on Front Street Monday night around six o'clock, and Bernie said the vehicle that hit my father was probably black. Most frightening of all, Mr. M hated my father for the way he treated me, and I remember his exact words when he told me to stay away from my father when he was drunk. *"I'm not sure what I'd do if that man ever harmed you."* Is it possible Mr. M could have killed him for my sake? My heart says never, but my head says maybe.

Fifteen

I t's been a month since my father died, and in these new days of
adjusting to a peaceful home, Margaux and I spend hours
hanging out in the front room, doing anything we please. Elvis has
a top-ten tune on the charts for the very first time, and my old 45
has given *Heartbreak Hotel* at least a million spins. Every time that
handsome hunk drops to a sexy low pitch, we try to make our
voices as deep as his, and when we can't, we burst into great gales
of laughter.

> *Well, the bell hop's tears keep flowin',*
> *And the desk clerk's dressed in black.*
> *Well, they been so long on Lonely Street*
> *They ain't ever gonna look back.*

When the song first came out I thought for sure the house on
Lonely Street was mine, but it certainly isn't now. These days,
Margaux often hangs around for supper, and we joke about how
the Mathieus' grocery bill must have plummeted. Fergie, who had
never before been inside my house, now stops by regularly, always
unannounced. Margaux cringes every time he comes up the steps,
but she's growing fond of his usefulness, especially in providing an

audience for our concerts and in solving the mysteries of pre-calculus.

Mom doesn't yet realize, but the month has been good for her, as well. While she'll never be entirely cured of fussing, she doesn't carry on half as much as she used to, and it's nice to see her sometimes smile. Yesterday, I was able to convince her that her tips would improve if she wasn't moping around Jabbur's in mourning clothes, and even though she had vowed to wear the black dress for a whole year and a day, she took it back to Mrs. Mathieu this morning and then rummaged around in her own spare closet for the things she considered "suitably dull."

Of course, life is never without worries. The investigation of my father's death hasn't progressed an inch, and while finding out who ran him over doesn't matter much to me, I do care about Mr. M, and I'm so afraid the poking around is going to lead to him.

After the funeral, when I saw his damaged Buick, I simply had to confront him or I would have gone positively mad with worry. The instant I walked through his door, I came right out with it. "The Buick," I said. "You always park it facing out, but now it's headed in?"

"Oh, that," he replied with a simple shrug. "Had a little accident." He went on to remind me I had helped him shovel out the night before my father died so he could drive up to the Knight's meeting. "It was snowing, and the roads were slick," he said. "After the meeting, I stopped at Joseph's Market to get some flat bread, and I was doing just fine until I headed home." The story rolled out as calmly as if he was talking about the weather. "I went by way of the cut under the tracks, and when I got to Head of Falls Road I didn't make the corner. The front wheels turned, but the old Buick didn't, and I slid into a snow bank. That might have turned out all right, except there was a telephone pole in the middle of it." The thought made him chuckle, but he saw my look of alarm and quickly said he wasn't hurt and was able to back up and get right back onto the road. "When I got home, I pulled her straight into the driveway. People around here know how much I love that car. I didn't want anybody to know what I'd done to her."

Without any sense of my fears, he had explained it all, and I believed he was telling the truth. He'd hidden the damaged car from the neighbors, not the cops, and he got Mr. Habib to drive him to my house the next day for the same reason. The accident might also explain why he didn't come to the funeral, although I couldn't imagine him wanting to join prayers for the safe passage of my father, in any case.

Being convinced of Mr. M's innocence is one thing; having to prove it to someone else would be quite another. Today, when I visit him, I begin to think about Bernie Nelson telling us of the alert that had been issued to local body shops, and I try to be nonchalant when I ask about his plans for car repairs. He tells me Mr. Habib took him up on the Oakland Road on the way home from my house that morning and, from his description of the damage, his friend Arnold Weeks thought he could fix it up, good as new, for about thirty bucks.

"So, when will you be doing that?" I ask calmly, trying not to raise his suspicions. He explains he needed a month to get the money up, and that the work couldn't be scheduled until today. I make a sour grimace, then try to turn it into a smile.

~

The mandatory week of mourning turns out not to have set me back at school. Margaux and Fergie kept me stocked with homework, and when I wasn't playing the cardboard keyboard or greeting sorry visitors, I kept up with the reading. My friends were very eager to help out, as it gave them an opportunity to make certain I knew how very sorry they were about my father. Some were actually truly sorry, but I could tell that some weren't. Even so, it was enjoyable while it lasted.

I missed three *Guys and Dolls* rehearsals, but even that didn't do any harm. The troupe made very little progress while I was gone, and right now I'm no more behind than all the rest. Throughout this afternoon's long rehearsal, poor Mrs. Rich is a fountain of frustration, yelling and scolding, even sobbing a flood at the end of a particularly bad run through *Sit Down, You're Rockin' the Boat*.

I can't blame her for being worried. The performance is only three weeks from today, and nothing has gone well. The actors forget their lines, the singers mumble over words they haven't memorized, and Mrs. Bizier continues to insist on playing fortissimo when I know perfectly well the score calls for something a whole lot softer. And then there's Spike, overtaken by his role as Sky Masterson, who's apparently seen the movie version as he's parading around imitating Marlon Brando, cocking his head with his eyes half shut and holding a stick of chalk like he's smoking a butt.

The rehearsal is over in time for me to race down to Cottle's for two hours of arranging bananas, and when I leave work I dig for enough change to buy two cans of tomato soup. Mr. M's car is probably in the shop with the paint drying, and he hasn't been able to get out. He'll need something to eat.

The cold wind off the river has turned lower Temple Street into a sheet of black ice, and I use the soup cans for ballast until I get onto the sure, gravel footing of King Court. As I round the corner, in the dim light over the door of Mr. M's house I see a car parked in the driveway, but it's not the Buick. There's a light on the roof. It's a police car. My heart sinks.

I open the door without knocking. Mr. M is in his chair, and he gives me a meek wave. Bernie Nelson is standing behind him and another officer is in front. It can only be Sergeant Gates, the one Bernie said was in charge of the investigation.

"Sit down, Angel," Mr. M says, nodding toward the piano bench. "You know Bernie. This here's Sergeant Gates." He points to the other man, whose glare makes me feel a little foolish as I stand in the doorway with a can of soup in each hand, and I head off toward the tiny kitchen.

"Not so fast," the sergeant barks. "We're having a private conversation here. Police business. You're going to have to leave."

Mr. M straightens himself in his chair, and seems ready to object when Bernie holds up his hand. "It's fine," he says to the sergeant. "She's family."

Gates doesn't have a clue about who I am, and he shrugs. "Well then, you may stay, but you're not to say a single word, do you understand?" I nod. I wouldn't want to talk to the awful man, anyway. He's younger than Bernie, somewhere in his twenties, and he's standing there like a fat peacock. His potbelly nearly hides his holster belt, and his sour face looks like it's never, ever been wrinkled by a smile.

"Now then," the wretched man says, turning back to Mr. M, "let's go over this one more time." Mr. M looks weary. I don't know how long they've been here, but it's plain they've tired him out. I wish they'd just leave him alone, but the sergeant seems not to care. "You were driving your car on Front Street at about 6:30 on the night of January 30, is that right?"

"Yes, I told you that."

"And, you had an accident, did you not?"

"I told you about that, too."

"Now then," the sergeant says, sniffing his nose, "you didn't really care much for Ashur Jamal did you, Mr. Moussallem?"

"Not especially."

"In fact you hated him, didn't you?"

"I didn't like him."

"And, suppose you tell me why you didn't like him?"

Mr. M gives me a cautious glance before he answers. "Because of the way he treated his family. He was a nasty drunk, didn't have a job, and didn't contribute a thing. He took food money and wasted it on beer. He had a vile temper." He pauses for only a second and lowers his voice. "Sometimes, he beat them."

None of what he's saying surprises me. The dear man has never said these kinds of things to me, but I've always known the way he felt about my father. The sergeant leans in inches from Mr. M's face. "You hated that man enough to kill him, didn't you?"

"No," Mr. M says firmly, "I did not."

Gates won't let up, and stands with his hands on his hips. "Well, now," he says, "I'm told you've kind of adopted Mr. Jamal's daughter, a girl named Angela, and that you're teaching her to play the piano." Mr. M turns slowly to look at me, and in that second a light goes on somewhere in the sergeant's head and he whirls toward me. "You!" he says, his eyes bugging out. "You're Angela Jamal, aren't you?" I shrug my shoulders. "I knew it. You shouldn't be here. I told you that." He turns to glare at Bernie.

Bernie, who outranks him in age if not in rank, jumps in to protect us. "Too late now," he says, holding up the palms of his hands like stop signs. "Let's just wind this up, right now."

I can tell that the fat sergeant is smarting at being tricked, and again he leans rudely into Mr. M's face. "Well then," he says, digging for space to slip his thumbs under his belt, "it would seem to me that we've got everything we need. "You'd do anything to protect this young lady," he says, gesturing at me, "and right there is the motive. You were on Front Street when Mr. Jamal was killed, and your automobile certainly hit something that night, as you fully admitted and as we could plainly see when we went up to the body shop this afternoon. On top of that, the black from your car seems to match the paint found on Mr. Jamal's trousers. If you ask me, when you put that all together, it adds up to murder." I want to jump off the piano bench and slap his face, but I sit tight, holding my breath.

Mr. M slowly bends forward, puts his head in his hands. The sad sight causes me to ignore the sergeant's order of silence. "This whole thing is ridiculous," I speak up from the bench. "This poor man hasn't killed a soul, and I think you know it perfectly well." I glare to Bernie for support, and then turn back to Gates. "Just how do you account for the fact that in order to go to St. Joseph and continue on to the market, he would have to have turned *right* at the top of Temple Street, and for him to be anywhere near Archie's Bar when my father left, he would've had to turn *left*?"

I can tell the sergeant hasn't given the question a thought, but he stares daggers at me, then fakes a cough before waving his hand dismissively. "Who's to say he didn't turn left? If he set out to kill your father, then of course he turned left, not right, like he said."

"Maybe so," I jump back, "but even if he did turn left, whoever hit him was traveling north, in the opposite direction." The daggers keep coming, and I press on. "Besides, how would Mr. M have any way of knowing what time my father was leaving the bar that night?"

The sergeant bristles. "Oh, so you call him Mr. M, do you? I don't suppose a young lady who's so fond of a man that she's given him a nickname would be the least bit prejudice when it comes to defending him, now would she?" His smirk begs for a good slap, but I keep my hands in my lap as he rambles on with a warning. "You best leave the investigation of a murder to the professionals, young lady, and stick to the piano." I think he's finished, but for some reason he feels obliged to answer my last questions. "Just so you won't think you've got all the answers, let me tell you that Mr. Moussallem could easily have driven to the end of Front Street and turned around and headed north. As far as knowing when your father left the bar, everybody in this end of town knows he left every day about six to head home for supper." There's no point in me going on. It would just make the man angrier, and that won't help.

As the two officers start for the door, the sergeant turns and waves a fat finger under Mr. M's nose. "We'll be back," he snips.

"In the meantime, don't go anywhere, and, if I were you, I'd find myself a good lawyer."

After they leave, it's some time before either of us utters a word. I go to the kitchen to warm the soup and pour some milk in a saucer for Adagio, who looks even more forlorn than the last time I saw her. Mr. M stays slouched in his chair, staring absently out the window, his glasses reflecting the lights from the woolen mill across the way. He clearly needs some cheering up.

I set two bowls of steaming soup and a few crackers on the kitchen table, and motion him to come. As he shuffles slowly toward me, I ask if he thinks he needs a lawyer. "Maybe I do," he says, sadly. I remind him Spike's dad is an attorney. "Yes, well," he says, "but I guess I'll talk with Lester Shapiro. He's a good man. Often helps people in this part of town. Doesn't charge much, sometimes nothing. He'll know how to handle this mess." He glances up at me. His eyes are sad and there is no color in his face. I've never seen him look so old. "I didn't do it, you know," he says.

"I know. I've known that from the beginning," I answer, trying not to leave any doubt. "Let's have our soup, and then I'll play you a tune." He nods agreeably. I sense he already knows what I'm going to play.

I learned the first section of Beethoven's *Für Elise* early on in my lessons, soon after I was able to play by sight. Mr. M said the piece was perfect for learning the pedals, and for putting emotion into what you play. Any student can learn the notes, he told me, but the trick is in the pace and the touch. "When you get this one just right," he told me once, "you can hear the angels sing."

His reference to the angels is a private thing between us. When he first gave me the piece, he explained that no one really knows who Elise was, or even her place in Beethoven's life. He must have been in a great rush when he wrote it, because he just scribbled the name on the top. Mr. M says maybe it has been misread all these years, and for all we know, Ludwig could have written it "Für Angela," instead.

We finish our soup, and then I play it for him. He sits quietly, eyes closed, directing me with tiny movements of his hands, cueing me for the expression of the sound and for the tempo. The color slowly returns to his face. He's hearing the angels, and he's happy again, but I'm so afraid it will not last.

Sixteen

After the final dress rehearsal, Mrs. Rich assembles the cast and tells us she honestly doesn't think we'll ever get one bit better. She says it in such a way that we're left wondering whether it's a compliment or a sign of despair, and my teacher-savior, Mrs. Aldrich, steps in to try to clear things up. "Just you wait," she tells us, "when Fred Petra and his band join us tomorrow night, you'll think for sure that you're on Broadway." Her cheerful observation pleases everyone but Mrs. Bizier, who's annoyed at the prospect of being upstaged by Fred Petra, and she slams the lid over the keys before stalking out of the pit in a huff. Mrs. Aldrich follows inches behind her, apologizing all the way.

Despite Mrs. Rich's constant fretting, the final rehearsal goes very well, especially considering we are in the Opera House for the very first time. Fergie and his stage crew manage the sets without much confusion, and everybody except Spike remembers their lines. Spike might have been flawless too, but when he sings *I've Never Been in Love Before* to Sarah Brown, he completely loses his concentration. Gloria Bousam's missionary uniform is so tight it's a miracle she can button it up. Somewhere in the second verse, Spike's mind shifts and he forgets the words. Gloria has to sing them for him.

~

It's going to take some planning to fill the time before tonight's performance, and I begin right after breakfast when I run down to King Court to check on Mr. M. Three weeks have passed since the awful meeting with Sergeant Gates, and nothing's happened. Mr. M told me last week he has been to see Lester Shapiro, and the man has agreed to defend him if it comes to that, but there's not been another word from the police. Mr. M tells me I shouldn't worry, but I can tell he's not taking his own advice. His wonderful smile comes hard, and his mind often wanders. This morning, he's forgotten what piece we've been working on, and I have to remind him. When I finish, I turn to watch him gaze dreamily out the window. To lift his spirits, I point out that his mayonnaise jar is fast filling up, and that he'll soon be able to get his TV, but it doesn't help. He tells me he's more likely to have to spend it all to settle up with Lester.

I'm back at the Mathieus' by ten. Margaux's mom has called the four Hot Box Girls for a final fitting of the costumes. One by one we stand on a kitchen chair for adjustments. For the roles as chorus numbers, we're wearing long dresses with pleated skirts, each of a different color, chosen on our own. Mine is pink, chosen from the rack at the Army store. With black tights and black sweaters slung over our shoulders, we look like we belong together, even though we're all different sizes. Margaux needs extra adjustments around her sloping shoulders. Leyla Ayoub is tiny, and her outfit requires tucking. My dress must have belonged to a beanpole, as the skirt has to be let out to the very limit of the seams. Sheila Maroon is already perfect, and she has nothing to do but hold the pins.

The Farmerette costumes are simple: cut-off dungarees and plaid shirts. We've discovered the straw hats won't stay on our heads with all the dancing, so we add chinstraps. That part is easy.

141

The biggest challenge is the outfits for *Take Back Your Mink*. Mrs. Rich gave Mrs. Mathieu a picture taken from an advertising poster for the movie, but she completely ignored it. "Much, much too sexy," she huffed. Instead, she's gone and put shoulder straps onto what look like one-piece red silk bathing suits that come almost to our knees and, instead of mesh stockings, she insists we all wear tights. It takes almost an hour to get these outfits ready, and much of it is spent talking about cleavage. Margaux and Sheila want a lot. Mrs. Mathieu doesn't want any. Leyla and I don't much care. Everybody gets just a little.

When the costumes are set, there's still most of the whole afternoon to wait, and Margaux and I head off to my end of the house to fill the time with gabbing and playing records. Mom is in the kitchen getting ready to go to her second job, which she likes even more than waitressing at Jabbur's. Soon after my father died, Father Ataya offered her weekend work tidying up the sanctuary before every Mass, and if there was ever a job made in heaven, this is it. She's at church most of the time, anyway, and now she can pray and be paid at the same time. These days, when St. Joseph worshippers flop to the kneelers, you can bet they stand back up without a trace of dust.

The instant we settle by ourselves in the front room, Margaux asks for news about Mr. M, and I put a finger to my lips to make her whisper. I've never told Mom that Mr. M is a suspect, and it would set her back in her recovery if she found out my father was still haunting us, even from the grave. Margaux, of course, knows the whole story. I told her about Sergeant Gates' grilling the minute I got home from Mr. M's that night, and it sent her into an awful rage, prompting her to declare the sergeant a turd, and a lot worse than that.

Mom comes to say goodbye, and as she stuffs cleaning rags into a sack, reminds us she'll be in the front row in time for tonight's performance. She's barely out the door when Margaux steers the conversation back to Mr. M. I tell her I'm terribly worried. "This is what we're going to do," she says as if she's about to clear the whole thing up. "We're going to find Bernie Nelson and ask him just what in hell is going on. It's not fair to keep Mr. M hanging this way. If they haven't got enough to arrest him, then they need to march themselves down to King Court and tell him so."

Of course, it's not as simple as it sounds, but Margaux is in a twist and she's not about to listen. I try to warn her by setting the needle on the 45 so we can hear *The Great Pretender* and then tell her no cop, not even loose-lipped Bernie, is going to tell a couple of kids about an ongoing murder investigation. Margaux ignores both The Platters and me. "Tomorrow," she declares, "we'll track him down and remind him it's *your* father we're talking about, and *you* have every right to know."

Turns out, we don't have to wait for tomorrow. At five-thirty we put on our chorus dresses, bag up the rest, and head off for the Opera House. As we trudge along Main Street, giggling at the catcalls from passing cars, we spot Bernie up ahead, chalking tires in front of Sterns department store. I warn Margaux we only have time to say hello, but her ears are turned off.

"By golly," Bernie says when we draw up close. "If the two of you don't look like movie stars. Tonight's the big night. Everybody's going. I'm on patrol duty, but I plan to stand in the back and catch what I can."

"Nice to know our tax dollars will be hard at work," Margaux snips. "Speaking of which, suppose you tell us how those dollars are doing in the stupid investigation of Mr. Moussallem's supposed involvement in the death of this girl's father." She points at me as if I'm a full partner in the prying.

Fortunately, Bernie knows Margaux well, so he's not at all taken aback by her tone. Instead, he shakes his head and grins. "You two know better than ask those kinds of questions," he says,

Earl H. Smith

just as I thought he would. "But, I will tell you something," he goes on, just as Margaux thought he would. "I've got a hard time believing the old man did it, but you must admit the evidence is pretty strong. He was on Front Street that night, and he had an accident of a kind that fits our suspect." He turns to me. "To top things off, he truly hated your father."

Margaux huffs. "Skimpy stuff, if you ask me," she says. "Where's your witness? Where's that proof? You and the sergeant are just guessing, that's all, and it's not fair. Not fair at all."

Bernie twirls his chalk stick under the streetlight, and I can tell he's thinking of what to say. Finally, he gushes it out. "You know, don't you, that I'm not the one in charge here, and I really shouldn't be telling you this, but Sergeant Gates is a very ambitious young man. He's up for another stripe, and making an arrest in this case would help his cause. I've tried to slow him down," he goes on. "In fact, the only reason for the delay is that I've managed to convince him we ought to sit back and wait to see if another suspicious car turns up. So far, I'm afraid, there's been no such luck."

Bernie's all blabbed out, and the conversation could just as well end right here, but Margaux needs the last word. We're already pointed toward Castonguay Square when she spins back on her solid leg and points a finger. "I'll tell you one thing," she hisses, "if that dumb sergeant arrests Mr. M, the only decoration he's gonna have is scrambled egg all over his stupid face." I can hear Bernie chuckle as we round the corner.

~

The old brick Opera House is aglitter, and the white marquee, ringed with blinking white lights, gives me the chills.

144

TONIGHT 7:30
Waterville High Presents
Guys and Dolls
Tickets 50¢ Children 25¢

Old gas sconces, long ago re-fitted with electric bulbs, cast a warm glow on the red-carpeted staircase as we climb to the second floor theater. Inside, the house lights shimmer on the blue velvet curtain and reflect off the gilding on the curved face of the balcony. Margaux and I linger at the backstage door to take it all in. I've never been in any kind of fairyland, but I'm pretty sure I'm in one right now.

Although it's still an hour before the show, most of the cast has already arrived, and everybody is milling around behind the curtain, chattering like monkeys. Mrs. Rich is nervously fluttering here and there, clipboard in hand, giving orders to get costumed and go to the tiny backstage room where Mrs. Aldrich is applying makeup. Margaux and I already have our first costumes on, so we get in line behind Priscilla Bizier and watch while Gloria Bousam, the pious missionary, gets a final touch of powder to seal in all the blush, lines and shadows painted on her face. Up close, the result is shockingly stark, but Mrs. Aldrich assures us it will all look grand from a distance, under the lights.

When it's Priscilla's turn, the room is nearly filled with her taffeta gown. Mrs. Aldrich shrouds her in a huge apron before applying the foundation that includes a thick pink paste, designed to hide the pimples. Priscilla has had a recent outbreak, no doubt brought on by stage fright or her mother, or both. She's clearly going to need extra time, and while we wait we listen to the Fred Petra band go through its warmup. The glorious, clear sound of his cornet rises up above the rest, and then, just like those moments when my trances at the cardboard keyboard are rudely interrupted, the music stops. Margaux turns to give me a puzzled

145

look, and we hear loud groans from the cast and the sound of feet crossing the stage and headed for the orchestra pit. We surrender our places in the makeup line and rush to have a look.

The stage curtain is open a tiny crack, and Margaux drops to her knees, dives through the slit, and peers over the edge. I lean over her shoulder, and I'm shocked by what I see. Mrs. Bizier is seated with her back to the baby grand, crouched way over, holding her head in her hands and throwing up all over the place. Daughter Priscilla, her unfinished face half porcelain and half pimples, is already in the pit, taking care to keep a safe distance from her puking mother, wringing her dainty hands and cooing words of comfort. Mrs. Rich is down there, too, calling out for towels.

Margaux scrambles back onto her feet, pinching her nose. "Oh, my," she honks, "that woman is one sick puppy."

"Something she ate?" I ask.

"Spaghetti," Margaux says decidedly, "From the color, I'd say it was Franco-American."

We turn back toward the stage where Mr. Fallon, who up to now has been quite willing to leave the play directing to Mrs. Rich, has taken charge and is huddled up against the first drop curtain, talking with Mr. Petra, who is carefully wiping something off his horn. When they are finished mumbling, Mr. Fallon turns to the rest of us and claps his hands. "I'm sorry to have to say this," he announces in his most official assistant principal voice, "but we don't have a piano player, and Mr. Petra says we really can't go on without one. I'm afraid the performance has to be postponed, or maybe even canceled. There's nothing else we can do."

His proclamation is met with a sea of disappointed faces. The guys are groaning, the dolls are weeping, and Mrs. Rich is sobbing uncontrollably, sending broad streaks of mascara coursing down her cheeks. Someone pipes up and suggests Priscilla can sit in for her mother, but the idea is dismissed in an instant. Priscilla is Adelaide, and Adelaide is a lead with no understudy. Someone else asks if Mr. Petra has a piano player, but he explains that Gerry Wright, his regular keyboard man, wasn't needed for tonight's performance and has another gig at Colby, playing at a fraternity dance.

Everybody is standing around awkwardly, staring at each other in disbelief. Everybody, that is, except Margaux, whose nose is about an inch from mine and whose face is lit up like the theater marquee outside. Finally, she gives me a wicked wink and turns to the rest, raising both hands as if she was casting a blessing. "Angela plays the piano," she practically shouts. "She can do it." The only sound is a gurgling burp from the pit.

Everyone turns to look at Mrs. Rich, who seems unsure. "Well now," she stammers, "I…well, I just don't think…"

Margaux cuts her off. "I'm telling you, she can do it," she declares in that shut-up-and-listen voice of hers. "She's a wonderful pianist, and I've heard her play every piece in the show at least a dozen times. No one will ever know there's even been a substitute." There is another pathetic retch from down below, and bubbles rise in my own stomach. Mr. Petra, bless him, breaks the awkward silence by inviting me to follow him into the pit.

We arrive in time to see Mrs. Bizier being led away on wobbly legs by the gym teacher, Miss Paton, who's apparently volunteered to take the victim home. Fergie is down here with his stage crew, mopping up and running a fan at high speed to clear the air. He grins when he sees me and sticks both thumbs straight up.

Mr. Petra puts an arm around my shoulder. "I guess you've been put on the spot," he says gently, "but don't worry. I won't let you do it if you can't handle it." He reminds me that the piano part takes the lead in many of the songs, and suggests I find one of them and play it for him. I pick *I'll Know* from the first act, taking care to switch from B-flat for Sky Masterson to A for the scratchy soprano, Adelaide. Mr. Petra stops me before I'm even half finished. "That's enough," he says. *Yikes. Enough for what?* I suck in

147

my breath and follow him back on stage where he promptly waves at Mr. Fallon. "She's terrific," he says. "The show is on!" Everybody cheers.

It's already a minute or two after 7:30, and there's no time to even think about what's just happened. Cast members are already scrambling for their places by the time Mr. Petra and I drop back into the pit. I open the piano score to the first page, place it on the rest, and then stand up quickly to look out over the now dimly lit house. The place is filled, even the balconies, but I spot Mom there in the front row, looking altogether amazed.

Mr. Petra gives hasty final instructions to his band. The drummer is in the back, and the others – trumpet, bass trombone, euphonium, and tenor sax – are arrayed in front of him. "Follow me carefully," he says, looking at me. "I'll cue you with my horn." I reach up to brush back my hair, now tightly curled and damp with perspiration. My heart is thumping. I take a deep breath, and we're off.

We play the *Overture* before the curtain opens, and then move on to *Runyonland* and *Fugue for Tinhorns*, where I stay comfortably in the background for the wonderful brass. I've never played in an ensemble before, but Mr. Petra makes it easy, facing the stage and setting the tempo by bobbing the bell of his cornet and cueing with his eyes. My own eyes flit back and forth from the score, to Mr. Petra and, once or twice, over my shoulder and up onto the stage. I take an extra long look when the Hot Box Girls come out singing *A Bushel and a Peck*. Somehow, they've managed to fill the gap I've left, and are doing just fine with only three.

By the time we reach the end of Act I and Sky is crooning his heart out to Sarah, I am quite at home with the music, but I'm still not used to the swell of applause that comes after each number. The clapping, while not for me, is nice, but it tends to mess up the timing.

At intermission, the entire band comes over to the piano, mopping their faces with towels and grinning. "Well now," Mr. Petra says, "I think we've just discovered Waterville's best-kept musical secret." The others nod. "A student of Mrs. Bizier's, are you?"

"No, I am definitely not," I say with too much emphasis. "My teacher is Elias Moussallem, and he's wonderful." The mention of his name makes me think how badly he's going to feel when he finds out what has happened. If he'd known I was going to play the piano, he would have been here, no matter what.

His name doesn't register with Mr. Petra, I can tell. "I'm sure he's very good, indeed" he says, "and so are you."

The second act goes by quickly and without a hitch, and when it's over I'm wishing we could do it all over again. Moose LeGrand has the audience in stitches when Nicely-Nicely does *Sit Down, You're Rockin' the Boat*, and Doug Doyon, as the handsome baritone Nathan Detroit, steals the show with *Sue Me*. Give Priscilla full credit. Adelaide is terrific in every number, and it's impossible not to notice she's more relaxed than she's ever been at the rehearsals when her mother eyeballed her from the keyboard.

At the very end, the audience stands and claps wildly while we play the reprise over and over to let the cast return for curtain calls. The four leads come last. Spike, Gloria, Doug and Priscilla join hands, and when they take a bow, the place explodes. Spike is so deep into being Sky Masterson that he's all puffed up like a Kewpie doll and jumps out in front of the other three, taking not one but two extra bows. It's disgusting. I can see Margaux, standing in the back with the chorus, sticking her tongue out at him.

When the curtain finally closes, Mr. Fallon comes out between the flaps and signals for quiet. "Thank you, thank you," he says to the audience, like Elvis. "Before we go, we must recognize some behind-the-scenes people who have made this all possible." One by one, he thanks Mrs. Rich, Mrs. Aldrich, Fergie and his stage

149

crew, and then the Fred Petra band. Mr. Petra waves a hand from the pit, and then points at me. Mr. Fallon catches his cue. "You may not have realized it," he says to the audience, "but our wonderful pianist, Mrs. Bizier, was taken ill just before tonight's performance, and we were fortunate to find a replacement in our very midst." He motions for me to stand. "Please, let's thank Angela Jamal for saving the day." I am dismayed by the long, loud applause that rolls over me, and I stand there, not knowing what to do with my hands, wishing the moment would never end.

When the house lights come up, Mrs. Rich tells the cast to leave by the back door and hurry around to greet the audience on the front steps. I stay with the band, and we follow behind. The night is cool, but clear, and the fresh air is a welcome change from the stuffy theater. Right off, I spot Mom, under a light at the foot of the stairs, and she whoops me a greeting. "I just can't believe it," she says when I go to her. "I've *seen* you play a hundred times, but this is the first time I've ever *heard* you." I don't know what to say. I give her a big hug. Tears are running down her cheeks. "You're wonderful. Praise God."

Mom says she and Mrs. Jabbur are going back to the restaurant for a celebration cup of coffee, and as she turns to leave, there's a tap on my shoulder. It's Fergie, still all sweaty, grinning from ear to ear. He reaches behind his back and hands me a single, wilted, red rose. "Left it in the footlights by mistake," he says, making an apologetic grin. "Gave one to Margaux, too. It was more dead than yours." Just then, Margaux herself appears, carrying the proof.

"Let's go," she says, using a finger to flick the last of the hanging petals onto the sidewalk, "before *she* gets here." She tosses her head back. *She* is Priscilla, who's already too close for me to escape. I give her a doubtful greeting.

"Honestly," Priscilla starts right off, "I can't believe how far you've come on the piano, and all without a piano of your own. I think maybe one of these days you're going to catch up to me."

She has left such a wide opening with that snide remark that I am tempted to jump on her, rake off her makeup with my fingernails, and expose every one of her stinkin' pimples. Instead, I simply nod. Nobody, not even Priscilla, is going to wreck this night for me.

A second chance for a wrecking comes along only minutes later, as Margaux and I walk up Main Street, headed home. She has crossed the street to look in the Woolworth windows, and I hear the honk of a horn as Spike pulls up to the curb and reaches across the seat to wind down the passenger window. "Great job," he says. "And, what did you think of old Sky Masterson?" He's fishing for a compliment, but I'm not biting. "Want a lift?" he yells above Dean Martin singing *Memories Are Made of This*. "Maybe we can go by way of the Colby pond?"

Margaux is back, and she has sneaked up to his side of the car, running her hands along the fender and looking doubtfully into the forbidden back seat. He doesn't see her until she barks through the window as if he had invited her. "Why would we ever want to ride in a scratched up old Ford," she sniffs, "when we're walking on air?" He looks surprised.

"I guess he didn't know you were with me," I say as the Crestline disappears up Main Street.

"Who knows?" she laughs. "Maybe he wanted to get both of us in the backseat."

"And what was that about walking on air?"

"Well, aren't we?" she asks as she begins one of those awkward skips of hers, and at the same time, flapping her arms like a bird. "Aren't you just so proud of yourself that you could float?"

"Pride is something you have in someone else, not yourself," I tell her as she spins around and hops back to me.

"Well then," she demands, "exactly what were you thinking when all of those people got on their feet and cheered?"

I wait for her to settle in front of me. "I was thinking about Mr. M, for one thing, and how much he means to me." She nods, understanding. "And, there's something else," I say. "I also had this strange and wonderful feeling of knowing, for the very first time, exactly who I am."

Seventeen

Mom and I stayed up most of the night, hashing over every last detail of my surprise appearance as the piano. The way she sees it, the evening was nothing short of a heavenly miracle, ranking right up there with the transistor radio. By the time we went to bed she had herself convinced that Douglas Edwards was coming down from Bangor with his TV crew to interview me on the front steps. It's no use telling her Douglas Edwards is not in Bangor, because she insists that since Channel 5 comes from Bangor, that's where he must be.

This morning, it seems I've barely gone to sleep when there's a racket in the kitchen. Margaux has let herself in the back door and is yelling her lungs out for me to come. I stagger downstairs and she's standing there, all gussied up for church, holding a copy of the *Portland Sunday Telegram*. She says her dad walked up to Joe's Smoke Shop before breakfast to get it, and then proceeds to throw most of it on the floor, keeping only the Maine news section, which she spreads out on the table.

"Lookie here," she says, pointing to a photograph below the fold. "We're famous." It's a picture of last night's performance, from the second act, I can tell, where Sky sings *Luck Be a Lady*. "That's me," Margaux says, jabbing a finger on the upper right of the picture where I can barely make out the muddy faces of the chorus. In a short review under the photo, the writer begins by calling it "a fine high school performance," which sounds a little like Mrs. Rich's lukewarm assessment of the dress rehearsal, but then there are lots of nice things said about the actors, and at the very end, there's this: "The play was nearly called off because of the last minute illness of the school pianist, Nadine Bizier. However, Angela Jamal, a junior, filled in brilliantly and saved the day." I read it twice. My name has never been in the newspaper, unless there was a birth notice, which I doubt.

"How very nice," I say.

"My picture or your name?" Margaux wants to know.

"Your picture."

"Got anything to eat?" She's starved, and I'm barely awake. I bring chocolate doughnuts I got in the day-old section of Harris Bakery on Friday, and as we dunk them in milk to make them chewable, I absentmindedly scan the rest of the news. A tiny item near the bottom of the page catches my eye, and my mouth drops open.

**Waterville Man Arrested
In Hit and Run Fatality**

WATERVILLE – Elias Moussallem, 82, of King Court was arrested Friday morning on suspicion of vehicular homicide in a January 28 accident in which Ashur Jamal, 42, also of Waterville, was killed. Sgt. Norman Gates, who led the two-month investigation into the death, said further charges against Mr. Moussallem could be made. The accused has been released on his personal recognizance, and a probable cause hearing will be held on Wednesday to determine if the case will be bound over to the Grand Jury.

My hand is trembling when I stick the piece in front of Margaux. "Gates couldn't help himself, could he? He just had to do it, and Mr. M knew it when I saw him on Friday, but he never said a word."

I tell Margaux we've got to help him, and she tackles my thoughts, in order. "Gates is a rotten turd. Mr. M didn't want to upset you before the play. We'll figure something out, but we don't have very much time before Wednesday."

Mom joins us in the kitchen, and there's nothing to do but explain the whole thing to her. The story will be all the buzz at St. Joseph this morning, anyway, so I show her the clipping and explain. When I'm finished, she turns slowly to the sink, fills the percolator, and calmly sets it on the stove. "I thought Ashur's death was an accident," she says, turning back to me. "Are they saying he was killed on purpose?" I nod. "Well," she says, "if that's true it most certainly wasn't Mr. M, now was it?"

I feel a sudden surge of affection for this dear woman who fusses so much but somehow manages to take the rotten things in stride. "He would never harm a flea," I agree, and go on to tell her Mr. M has a lawyer. She says she knows Mr. Shapiro, who often has lunch at Jabbur's when he's working at the courthouse in City Hall. "He's a fine, sweet man," she says, "and a darn good lawyer, from what they say. You really must go and talk with him." Mom's not an especially good strategist, and the suggestion startles me.

"Only if we have something new to contribute," Margaux jumps in. "So far, we haven't got much." She makes a tiny smirk. "I'm afraid the point you made about Mr. M having to turn left instead of right at the top of Temple Street that night didn't impress anybody, but of course nobody's going to pay much attention to you, anyway. You'd defend Mr. M if he was Attila the Hun."

"Well, surprise, surprise," I come back, "suppose I tell you I *do* have a little extra evidence?" Margaux perks up, and I spell it out. "Mr. M's Buick was damaged on the fender, near the headlight. It seems to me that if somebody got struck there, they would have gone *under* the car instead of off to the side of the road, which they say my father did."

"Or, maybe *over* the car and onto the side of the road?" Margaux appears to be working for the prosecutor.

"Yes, but in either case there would have been cuts and bruises, and Bernie told us that, except for the backs of his legs and his head where it hit the curb, there weren't any."

Margaux returns to the defense. "Guess what?" she says. "I've been thinking about this, too, and I think I might be able to prove Mr. M couldn't *possibly* have done it." I ask her how, but she says that what I don't know won't hurt me. "If I'm right," she says, "we can clear Mr. M, but if I'm wrong it will set us back." I have no idea what she's talking about.

Mom gets up, pours herself a cup of coffee, and motions us to the door. I ask her where we're going, and she says we're going to the Mathieus' so I can use the phone to call Mr. Shapiro and arrange a meeting.

"On a Sunday?" I'm surprised.

"Not a problem," Margaux hunches her crooked shoulder. "He's Jewish."

Mrs. Mathieu offers us muffins the instant we come through the door, and Mr. Mathieu inquires about his Sunday newspaper. Margaux has left it on my kitchen floor, and she heads back while Mom explains why we need the phone. Mr. Mathieu goes to look up the number.

Margaux is back by the time Mr. Shapiro picks up, and all four stand in front of me, like birds on a line. "Hi," I say, much more meekly than I intended. "It's Angela Jamal."

"I feel as if I know you," he comes back in a kind voice. "I was at *Guys and Dolls* last night, and Mr. Moussallem has told me all about you. He'll be so proud when he finds out what you've done." I thank him and tell him I understand he's agreed to defend Mr. M, and that Margaux and I think we might be able to help. I explain there are things about Sergeant Gates' investigation that seem incomplete, and ask if we can possibly meet before the court appearance on Wednesday.

I hear a tiny chuckle. "So," he says, "Nancy Drew and Bess Marvin want a meeting? Fine with me. Let's say tomorrow after school, about 3:30?" We agree to meet in front of Archie's bar, and I give a thumbs-up to the birds and thank him again. "One more thing," he says before he hangs up. "If we're going to talk about evidence, Sergeant Gates ought to be there, too. I'll see to it." The thought makes me shiver.

We're finished barely in time for the Mathieus to head off to Mass at Sacred Heart, and I leave to walk down to Head of Falls. A hazy fog hangs like a shroud all along the cold river, and I find myself wondering if it's too much to ask for a bit of sunshine to arrive before Wednesday and lift the gloom that's overtaken us.

Mr. M doesn't get out of his chair when I come through the door. His eyes are dull, and his face is drawn. He knows I'm about to scold him for not telling him about the police charges, so he doesn't give me the chance. "Sorry," he says, first thing, "but I just couldn't bear to tell you before the play." He doesn't even yet know that I ended up playing the piano instead of being a Hot Box Girl, and I don't tell him. It would make him even sadder that he'd missed it. Instead, I tell him about the meeting tomorrow with Mr. Shapiro and assure him things will turn out fine, but I don't feel anywhere near as certain as I sound.

He and I spend the lazy Sunday afternoon together, a little piano playing here and there, and lots of talking. He tries to be cheerful, but his mood doesn't lift very much, and I reluctantly leave him with a big hug, promising to return with a full report of tomorrow's meeting.

~

In school on Monday, I spend the hours in a total fog. When Mlle. Vachon calls on me to recite in French, I can only say "huh?"

and I don't flinch when she scolds me for not paying attention. All I can think about is this afternoon's meeting, and about what's at stake if we can't turn the tables on the awful sergeant.

Margaux meets me within seconds after the last bell, and we run down Gilman Street, headed for home. The day has been warm, and in the narrow space between the sidewalk and the road tiny mounds of slush and snow are the last reminders of the long winter.

When we turn onto Front Street, I see that we're the last to arrive. The tall man I presume is Mr. Shapiro is standing in front of Archie's place, talking with Sergeant Gates. When we get near, Margaux points her thumb at the shuttered bar and gives me a satisfied nod. The "CLOSED" sign on the inside of the front door is hanging askew, and the windows are splattered with mud. Bernie Nelson is there as well, and he greets us with a friendly hug. Mr. Shapiro introduces himself and turns to Sergeant Gates, who's wearing a sour puss, and barely grunts when we say hello.

"Well now," Mr. Shapiro says. "We've called this meeting to see if we can shed some light on the charges made against Mr. Moussallem. Some of us believe they may be incorrect." He begins with what we already know – my father was intoxicated when he left the bar behind us; he was struck by a vehicle as he crossed the road; and his body was thrown up onto the curb on the left, where he died. He goes on to recite the allegations against Mr. M. "There's no argument," he says, "that Mr. Moussallem was driving on Front Street about the time Mr. Jamal died, or that the man had an accident that night. We just don't believe the two are in any way connected."

Gates bristles throughout Mr. Shapiro's opening remarks, and when the lawyer is finished, the sergeant produces a thick, brown folder. "I have the evidence. It's all here – means, motive, opportunity – what more does anybody want?"

Mr. Shapiro is abrupt. "What we want is the truth," he says before he turns to me and asks if I have anything to say. I swallow hard once or twice and ask the sergeant if his folder has a photograph of Mr. Moussallem's car before it was repaired. He fishes out a large black and white print and hands it to me. It's just as I remember.

"See here," I say, pointing to the bent bumper and the dented fender. "Don't you think if someone was struck this way they would have been knocked down and run over instead of being shoved off to the side of the road?"

"Makes sense to me," Mr. Shapiro is quick to answer. Even Bernie nods, and Margaux adds the explanation point. "Well, of course," she says, "any fool can see that."

"Not necessarily," the fool answers. "If you had investigated as many of these accidents as I have, you'd know that a struck body might go in any direction." It's like he's talking to a kindergarten class. "If you don't mind," he continues, "I have some important things to do."

Mr. Shapiro is annoyed. "What've you got to do that's more important than saving a man's life?" he asks, stepping into the sergeant's path.

Gates stops, rolls his eyes, and Margaux wheels around to face him. "Do you happen to have a picture of the accident scene?" she asks. He heaves a sigh and retrieves another picture, this one taken in the very spot where we're standing, showing the road with the trail in the snow made by my father's body, leading to the curb. She takes a long look before innocently inquiring if he found anything at all in the street that night.

"We found nothing," he sniffs. "It was snowing, and it was dark."

"No glass?" she asks, pointing to the shattered headlight in the first picture.

"Someone must have stopped and picked it up."

"Not likely," Mr. Shapiro says. "It would have been hard to see any glass in the snow, and even if anybody did, they would have seen the body first and gone to report it instead of stopping to pick up glass, don't you think, sergeant?" Gates doesn't reply.

"Do you think," Margaux says all innocent like, "that the headlight glass might still be where Mr. Moussallem said he hit the pole, down at the corner of Head of Falls Road? Maybe we ought to go down and have a look."

Mr. Shapiro brightens, then scowls at the sergeant. "You did check out Mr. Moussallem's alibi, didn't you?"

Gates isn't shaken one bit. "It was many days later when we discovered Mr. Moussallem's damaged Buick," he explains. "Much too late to verify his accident story."

"Not too late to check for glass though, was it?" Mr. Shapiro seems to have caught Margaux's lead. "Well then, what say we check it out, right now?" Before you know it, he and Bernie have started off down the road with the sergeant trailing behind them, sputtering all the while. Margaux and I bring up the rear.

"You've seen the glass, I presume?" I whisper to Margaux.

"Oh, no," she says. "Just a hunch."

There's a lull in the traffic along Front Street, and I fail to lower my voice. "A hunch!" The sound carries up ahead, and all three men turn to look. "A bunch," I shout to cover my mistake. "A bunch of dandelions." I point to the side of the street where there isn't a dandelion in sight. The men turn and continue up the street, and I grab Margaux by the arm. "What do you mean," I say, lowering my voice to a hiss. "We're hanging all of this on a hunch?"

Margaux doesn't say another word as we make our way up to the railroad cut and down Head of Falls Road. All the way, I'm horrified that Margaux has taken us far out on a limb, and we're about to crash. The snow pile in front of the lone pole at the corner has dwindled to less than a foot of dirty slush. Bernie kicks at it with his foot. Nothing. He kicks deeper. Still nothing. The sergeant stands there, arms folded, looking smug. My heart sinks.

Mr. Shapiro watches closely, then suddenly drops to his knees in the wet gravel and begins to scrape away the mush, all the way to the bottom. "Here we go," he says after a second or two. He stands and opens his palm to show a piece of glass as big as a clamshell. It's slightly curved and has lines through it. Headlight glass. Has to be.

I whop Margaux on the hump of her back and struggle not to cheer out loud. Mr. Shapiro and Bernie are smiling at each other. Gates still isn't buying. "Could have come from any car," he says dismissively. "Doesn't prove a thing."

Mr. Shapiro has run out of patience. "There's probably more glass down there," he says, pointing at the scattered slush, "and it won't take much to figure out whether there's a match with the other headlight on Mr. Moussallem's car." Gates starts to interrupt, but Mr. Shapiro holds up his hand. "I suggest you get down there and collect the evidence and do your job. When you're done, you'd better do the right thing, or else I'll be filing a few charges of my own."

The party breaks up, right then and there. Margaux goes on ahead with Bernie, gesturing and jabbering about something. I have no idea what she might be talking about, but that's nothing new and it doesn't matter, anyway. Mr. Shapiro and I leave Gates on his knees, grumbling while he picks up tiny pieces of glass from beneath the pole.

"Goodness me, Nancy Drew," Mr. Shapiro says when we're out of the sergeant's earshot, "you girls have done one fine bit of detective work. I'm pretty sure your friend Mr. M will be off the hook before this day is done." I look up toward the cut. It's dusk, and the setting sun has slid under the clouds, making the tower of St. Joseph shimmer in gold and red. He looks in the same direction, and we stop to gaze. "Truth is like the sun," he says, turning to me.

"You can shut it out for a time, but it doesn't ever go away." I'm completely astonished. It's an Elvis quote, and it's coming from a guy who must be all of 50 years old.

At home, Margaux and I gobble down a supper of leftovers, and quickly return over the same route, down to King Court. It's dark when we get there, but I can see Mr. M standing on the front steps under the light, his round cheeks pink again, grinning from ear to ear.

"You just missed him," he says when we get close. "Lester came to say the county attorney has filed a motion to have all charges against me dropped. He says it's an automatic. I guess that means I'm free." We all stand there, cheering into the night, like three perfect fools.

Inside, I take my usual seat on the bench, back to the piano, and Mr. M goes to his Morris chair, flops down, and heaves a contented sigh. His world is back in orbit, and I have the same warm feelings I had on Saturday night, when the Opera House crowd cheered for me.

The thought makes me remember that Mr. M doesn't know about my piano adventure. Mr. Shapiro knew, but he must have saved the news for me. I start to tell him, but Margaux interrupts and begins to limp around in front of him, waving her hands, excitedly animating the entire story. Not surprisingly, her version is greatly exaggerated and most embarrassing, and when she compares me to Arthur Rubinstein for the third time, Mr. M is laughing so hard she needs to stop and get him a glass of water.

"I'm so very proud," he says when Margaux finishes up with an imitation of the applauding audience. "And just to think, it all began with a cardboard keyboard."

"And a genius teacher with a Sears & Roebuck Beckwith," I reply, turning to face the old piano.

"Play it," Margaux says. "Play *Furry Legs*." She means *Für Elise*, but she never remembers the name.

"Yes, of course," Mr. M agrees, "play it and Beethoven will join the party." Even Adagio manages to twitch her tail to the music, and when I'm finished, Mr. M takes a long look at me, then Margaux, then closes his eyes. A single tear runs down each cheek. "Hush for a minute," he says, holding up his hands. "I think we can hear the angels sing."

Eighteen

Just when I'm beginning to think summer might give me a little free time to sort out the latest sharp turns in my life, things begin to happen that suggest the world is not going to slow down just to let Angela Jamal catch up. The next surprise comes on a fine Saturday morning in June, when Bernie Nelson pops through the kitchen door and announces he's come to make a "courtesy call." His choice of words is fair warning. Bernie's so-called "courtesy calls" began when he used to come drop my drunken father on the doorstep, and he's kept at it like Hermes, the messenger of the gods, delivering one bit of bad news after another. Mom would never shoot the messenger, and she greets him like a newly arrived cousin from Lebanon.

"We found the car that hit Ashur," Bernie says the second he's through the door. "There'll be a piece about it in tomorrow's paper, but you won't learn the name. The driver was a juvenile. Name's protected, you understand."

I've gotten pretty good at sorting out the important things in life from those that aren't, and I'm happy enough that he hasn't brought news that the Two Cent Bridge has fallen into the river, or something like that. Still, he's piqued my interest. "So, what's the charge?"

"Leaving the scene."

"No manslaughter, no murder, huh?"

"Nope. No recklessness and no motive for murder. Turns out, the driver was frightened half to death, and really quite sorry. Made a full confession."

"Too bad they waited to be caught before they fessed up," I observe. "Might have helped Mr. M if they'd found Jesus at the get-go."

Bernie and Mom both know where I'm headed, and Mom jumps in to steer me off. "Oh, my," she says, pointing to Bernie's sleeve. "What's this?" She pats the three newly sewn-on gold stripes on the sleeve of his uniform, and he grins when he says he's been promoted to the rank of sergeant.

"Congratulations," I say, "and, pray tell, whatever became of the sloppy sleuth?"

"Gates? Well, he's back on the beat, walking the south end, brushing up on his French, I'd say." At that, we all have a good laugh, and when the new sergeant excuses himself, I follow him out the door and head down to King Court at a full trot to share the news.

When I repeat the tale for Mr. M, adding my own opinions as necessary, I'm surprised to discover that he's more concerned about the young driver than he is with having further proof of his own innocence. "It's so sad," he says. "Young people aren't prepared to drive, these days. Someone just gives them the keys and off they go. It's dangerous. People are getting killed, everywhere." He pauses to consider his somber declaration, and then, out of thin air, tells me he thinks it's high time I learned to drive.

My jaw drops like Charlie McCarthy's. *What would I do with a driver's license? We don't even have a car.* Mr. M knows what I'm thinking, and gets all serious when he tells me he doesn't feel as easy about driving as he used to, and if I got my license I could be his chauffeur in the Buick Special, maybe even run some errands for myself. Next thing you know, he ups and proclaims the first lesson will be tomorrow, Sunday, when there won't be many big trucks on Head of Falls Road.

Until you reach a certain age, Maine requires a parent's approval for driving and for getting married, the two things in life that can get you in the most trouble. When I ask Mom for permission to learn to drive, she's horrified and promptly finds her rosary and proceeds to tell me about the alarming rise in the number of automobile accidents, reciting the gruesome statistics as if they are strung into beads. She relents only when I promise I'll never drive out of town. Even then, her approval is lukewarm.

Telling Margaux about my plans is not required by law, and as it turns out, a huge mistake, which I compound by agreeing to take her along for the first lesson. She's all wiggles and giggles the next morning when we arrive at Mr. M's, and I can tell he has his own doubts about including her, but doesn't say a word. Instead, he reintroduces Mr. Habib, his kindly neighbor, who's been lined up as my official instructor. "This man hasn't had an accident since he wrecked his Model A in 1929," Mr. M says, proudly establishing the man's credentials. As if to clarify the record, Mr. Habib quickly explains that the long-ago mishap was the horse's fault, not his.

The Buick, facing out as usual, is just about filled to capacity when I slide behind the wheel. Mr. Habib is in the passenger seat, and Mr. M is in the back with Margaux, who has taken dibs on the seat right behind me, so that when I adjust the mirror I'm startled to see her grinning puss resting on the mohair, inches from my head. I tell her to sit back.

Mr. Habib has obviously given some thought to his instructor role, and begins by drawing an imaginary H on the dashboard and explaining the position of the gears – first, second, third, and reverse. He then points to my left foot and the pedal next to it and tells me it's the clutch and to push it in. "Now," says he, "turn the key all the way to the right." I jump when the engine roars to life, and Margaux, who has ignored my order and is still on her perch, giggles in my ear.

I soon discover there's a great deal to remember in the operation of an automobile, and not much time in which to do it. Mr. Habib points to the accelerator and tells me to give her a little gas and let the clutch out slowly. I pause for a second, wondering how he knows the car's a girl, and then I give her way too much gas and completely remove my foot from the clutch. She leaps out of the driveway and dies right there in the middle of the road. Margaux roars, and now it's Mr. M who tells her to sit back and be quiet.

The day is warm and sunny, and lots of folks are on the porches of the tenements. As we lurch up the road, starting and stalling like a frog being poked by a stick, a number of neighbors lean over the railings to whoop and cheer. Margaux shrieks in horror one second, laughs like a fool the next. I'd like to make her get out and walk.

Just when I think I'm getting the hang of things, we come to the end of Head of Falls Road, and Mr. Habib says for me to let off the gas and step on the brake.

The brake? Nobody's said a word about any brake.

I turn to give Mr. Habib a puzzled look, and we shoot straight through the intersection, not coming to a stop until we're up to the car windows in the puckerbrush.

"Holy shit!" Margaux yelps, eyes bugged out like she'd stuck a finger in a light socket.

Again, I turn to Mr. Habib, whose face suggests he's not only astonished by Margaux's language but also embarrassed at omitting any mention of the brakes. Thankfully, from the backseat, Mr. M assures me no harm is done.

They say the new Chryslers have something called power steering, but the 1941 Buick prefers to be moving when it's turned, and I'm in a spot where I definitely need to turn before I can move.

After much wrestling and conflicting advice, I'm finally able to get turned around and headed back. This time it's a smoother ride, and after three more trips up and down Head of Falls Road, I begin to feel like Stirling Moss at the Grand Prix.

Over the next few weeks, Mr. M takes me out for more lessons. Mr. Habib is no longer needed, and I'm careful to hide my driving plans from Margaux.

At the end of the last day of school, Mr. M drives me to City Hall for my test. He waits on the granite steps while the examiner, an old geezer who's more interested in the old Buick than he is in me, makes me drive up Front Street by the river, then up to the stop sign on Union Street, where I'm expected to keep the car from rolling back down the hill. I give her too much gas on the takeoff, and we vault over the cobblestones and onto College Avenue without giving up a backward inch.

As we go down Main Street, the man points to a space along the curb at Woolworth's and tells me to park. I ignore the honking horns, and slowly pull in and then back out again, barely nudging the bumpers of the cars in front and back. Once we return to City Hall, Mr. M comes to peer anxiously into the car window, and the examiner gives him thumbs up. I pass.

On the way home, Mr. M says that if I'm back before dark, I can take the Buick, and Margaux and I can go up to Rummel's for an ice cream celebration. I beg him to come along, but he claims he can't possibly leave poor Adagio at home by herself twice in one day. It's an excuse. He wants me to fly solo.

~

Several days of warm weather have popped the lilacs on the lawns of the grand homes on Silver Street, and Margaux insists on opening the windows "to take in the glorious smells." That's not true at all; what she really wants to do is hang halfway out the passenger window and wave at everyone in sight, including people she doesn't even know.

Rummel's is packed, but I'm able to creep into a newly vacated spot near the serving window. We agree to splurge on double chocolate cones, and I give Margaux my quarter and stay in the car while she goes to order. I watch as she limps to the end of a long line of kids, shouting and laughing in a way that only happens on the last day of school. I'm not sure why, but watching her makes me sad. The poor soul doesn't have a driver's license, and with her bad leg, her father isn't likely to let her get one. She might have known the joy of playing the piano, but polio got in the way. And, worst of all, she's nearly 18 and hasn't yet had a single date. I have wondered if the boys avoid her because she's kind of crippled, and the very thought of it makes me want to spit.

At this moment, Doris Day is singing *Que Sera, Sera* through the scratchy speaker above the serving window, and it comes to me that Doris has got it all wrong. Leaving your fate in someone else's hands is the easy way out. You don't have to shrug off a bad thing when you can perfectly well do something to fix it. Right then and there, I decide I'll find Margaux a date, no matter what it takes. There's really not much choice in the matter. She's not cut out to be a spinster, and God knows, with her foul mouth, she doesn't have a prayer of becoming a nun.

Margaux finally arrives at the serving window, and when I glance back toward the street I'm surprised to see Spike Moufette, on foot no less, strutting in my direction like Yankee Doodle Dandy. He sidles up with a big grin. "Well, lookie here," he says, real snotty like. "Nice wheels."

"Suppose it's better than no wheels at all," I say, "and where's your fancy chariot, anyway?" He doesn't answer, but instead asks if I'd like to go see *The Seven Year Itch* at the Haines Theatre tomorrow night. I'm about ready to tell him that I can't when I remember my freshly made resolve to get Margaux fixed up. On top of that, I've wanted desperately to see that movie. I don't say anything in reply, but instead nod my head toward my friend, who's just now hitching toward the car, carefully holding a cone aloft in each hand, dark rivulets of chocolate running down her forearms.

Surprisingly, Spike catches on. "She can go with Fergie, maybe?" His suggestion immediately tells me my dating plan for Margaux isn't going to work out exactly like a fairy tale. She has never much liked Spike, except from afar, and while she's warmed to Fergie, she won't be at all excited about being paired off with him.

She's almost to the car, and I'm quick to give Spike an answer before she can hear. "Sure," I say, "we'll go." Then I wait for her to hand my dripping cone through the window and go around and settle in the passenger seat before I tell her. It's a good thing Spike can't look through the roof and see her pretend to gag. "It's settled then," I say, praying that her first big slurp of melting chocolate will keep her mouth occupied.

The instant Spike is out of sight, Margaux starts taking me apart, piece by piece. Anyone would think she'd be grateful for my kindness, but instead she's furious, more about me going with Spike than about her going with innocent Fergie, who doesn't yet know a thing about it. She finally calms down when I explain we're only going to the movies after all, and promise that we'll all sit together, with her right next to me.

~

Even the theater seating arrangement doesn't work very well. Spike is still without his car, and he and Fergie are late picking us up for the Saturday matinee. By the time we walk up Main Street, there's already a long line at the ticket booth. Spike gestures for Margaux and me to step in front and buy our own 12¢ tickets while he and Fergie head off to load up on Milk Duds. By the time we get inside, there aren't four open seats in a row. Even in the dim light, I see Margaux's eyes flare up. Fergie spots two seats in the very front and claims he absolutely loves to sit with his head tilted back. He and Margaux start down the aisle while Spike and I drop into the last two seats in the very back row. I wave once to Margaux before the lights go out, and she gives me the finger.

At least it's a good movie, but it has some rather grown-up thoughts, I must say. Marilyn Monroe is gorgeous in every scene, and Tom Ewell is to die for. As the cheating Richard Sherman, Tom is supposed to be a musical highbrow, but when he says he'll teach Marilyn how to play Rachmaninoff's *Second Piano Concerto*, they end up playing *Chopsticks* instead. That part is a little disappointing.

The suggestions about sex are not surprising at all. That's what the story is about, after all. There's nothing even close to *real* sex, of course, but there are plenty of hints. When Tom tells Marilyn he's going to take her in his arms and kiss her, "very gently and very hard," I keep my face glued on the screen, as I don't want to look at Spike and read his feelings, and I certainly don't want him reading mine. Turns out, I probably should have been reading his. A few minutes later, in the scene where Marilyn starts to creep up the stairs with Tom, I feel a hand creep up under my sweater.

The sound of the back of my hand hitting Spike's face causes the people in front to turn back, and I smile sweetly, shrugging as if I have no idea where the noise came from. Meanwhile, Spike is cowering in the far corner of his seat, using his offending hand to dab at the blood dripping from his nose.

"Ohhhh, Angela," he moans in a pathetic half-honk, half-whisper. "Don't you know? Everybody does it."

"Guess what?" I hiss back. "Not *everybody*."

He holds onto his nose and pouts through the rest of the movie, and when we leave, he walks ahead and pays no attention at all to Fergie's description of how the reels are changed in the middle of the movie without causing interruption. I had hoped we might complete Margaux's first date with a stop at Mr. Conti's soda shop for a root beer, but nobody says a word, and we walk right by. I'm relieved when Margaux suggests the boys leave us at the

171

top of Union Street, and when we part, she grits her teeth and thanks Fergie for a good time. I don't say a word.

As we walk along by ourselves, I don't dare ask Margaux for a date report. Instead, I make small talk, and nod my head at several old men sitting on the steep wooden steps of the Lebanese Youth Club across the street, chatting away, smoking cigars. "How come there's never any youth at the youth club?" I ask, just for something to say.

"Same reason there's no women," Margaux shrugs. "Men are turds."

For once I agree with her and I seize the moment to tell her how Spike tried to deflower me right there in the back row of a dark theater. She exclaims "damn" and "turd" at least a half-dozen times during my account, and "good for you" at the end, when I tell her about my powerful backhand. We walk in silence the rest of the way home, and when we reach her kitchen door, she turns to face me and grabs both of my hands. "It's all my fault," she says, sadly. "I should have told you."

"Told me what?"

She answers with a question. "Haven't you wondered why Spike is not driving?"

"Assumed his car is in the shop."

"Bullshit," she says. "He doesn't have a license, that's why." She leans way into my face. "The judge took it away for a whole year."

Bells clang in my head. "Are you saying...?"

"Yup," she interrupts. "Spike's the one who hit your father."

I feel myself get a tiny bit lightheaded as she goes on with her confession. "I saw some scratches on the front fender of his car the night after the play, when he offered us a ride, and I told Bernie about it the day we proved Mr. M was innocent." There's more clanging in my head when I remember her walking on ahead after the headlight glass discovery, jabbering with Bernie. "Anyway," she rattles on, "you know that the night your father died, Spike missed the *Guys and Dolls* rehearsal because he was helping his father clean out at the Lockwood. Turns out that on the way home he drove up Front Street in the snow and clipped your father as he crossed the road. He should have reported it, but he was scared, and he didn't."

"He ought to have told *me*," I practically yell, "and why didn't *you* tell me when you found out? Am I the only one in Kennebec County who doesn't know the story?"

Margaux looks hurt. "Nobody knows. Spike's father pulled some strings and got him off with probation and a suspended license. Juvenile crimes aren't reported. Bernie didn't even tell *me* about it, and I'm the one who tipped him off. I found out from my father, who heard it from a friend at the Hathaway whose cousin works in City Hall. My father made me swear I wouldn't tell a soul, especially not you. I shouldn't have listened to him, and I'm sorry."

There's no use getting angry with Margaux; it's not her fault, and I decide to put the entire business on my long list of things that really don't matter. I tell her it isn't important how my father died as long as nobody blames Mr. M, and, in any case, I'm finished with Spike Moufette.

"About time," she declares, and then, as if we were trading 45-rpm records, she ups and offers to give Fergie to me. "You know you want him, anyway," she says, holding out her hands like she's making a gift. I feel a little foolish when I thank her.

Nineteen

Summer is a drag. Even though I've been elevated to the lofty position of head lifeguard at the shallow end of the pool, and I get to wear a snug T-shirt that says so, the thrill of the job has all but disappeared. Instead of feeling like one of those glamorous beach babes in the magazines, I've come to see myself as a prison guard for juvenile delinquents. One minute I want to kill the little brats; the next, I have to keep them from killing each other. There's nothing fun about it.

Fergie, God love him, is my salvation. He's happy working nights, tinkering with the machinery in the pressroom at the newspaper, and he spends the day with Margaux and me at the pool. I'm not sure when he sleeps, because most evenings he hangs out before work on the porch at my house, eating piles of chocolate chip cookies and making me laugh.

As for Spike, I haven't cast an eye on him since he got scratched during *The Seven Year Itch*. Margaux says she's spotted him once or twice, wandering around town like he was lost. I don't feel a bit sorry for him, and when I point out to Margaux that the girls have stopped swarming, she says she's not at all surprised. "Without the wheels, that bantam rooster's nothing more than a cow turd in a duck's ass haircut," she says, once again using a combination of animals to make her point.

Given Margaux's generally negative take on men, there's little wonder Fergie and I have found it impossible to get her a date, and by the end of the endless summer, we've just about given up. Now that school has started, I may suggest we try again, but in the meantime I've got a project of my own. Though it's still a while before graduation, I discover that most of my classmates are already thinking about what's next. Lots of them are looking around for jobs; a few say they'll go to college. Margaux is determined to become a nurse. Fergie wants to be an engineer. Gloria Bousam and Sheila Maroon will continue on for a while as off-stage Hot Box Girls and then get married as quickly as possible. I have no strategy whatsoever, but I've got to figure it out pretty soon.

Meanwhile, I've made up my mind to make the most of my senior year, and except for having to put up with the hopelessly childish freshmen, there's not much in my way. I can't say that I've become outrageously popular, but because of my stand-in performance in *Guys and Dolls,* at least now some people have started calling me by my first name, which is an improvement over a simple nod and certainly better than being snubbed altogether.

The piano miracle has also led to offers to play at a few small functions at places where I'd never have been invited if I couldn't provide the entertainment. Along the way, I've even been on the inside of some houses that I've only before seen from the street. There's something peculiar around here about going into someone else's house, anyway. You can be the best of buddies at school, but God forbid you would ever be invited into their homes. I don't think it's because you wouldn't be welcome, but it has more to do with the fact that lots of the parents can't speak English, and their kids are afraid you'll find out. None of it matters to me, but they could solve their problem if everybody wasn't so uptight about having to seem like Americans when they're Americans already.

My newfound fame has even begun to put a little extra money in my pocket. Some of it comes from unexpected places. When the pastor at The Second Baptist Church in the South End asked me to fill in on a Sunday, Mom said I shouldn't go anywhere near a Baptist church, but as soon as I told her I can get $5 for four hymns, she quickly changed her mind.

Most remarkably, the teachers are beginning to like me. Even Mrs. Bizier has been sticky sweet, sometimes making me want to throw up in the same spectacular fashion she did the night of my debut. Every couple of days she sidles up to me with her bracelets all a-jangle and invites me to practice on a school piano. I know it's not nice to be spiteful, but it feels good when I turn her down.

~

The first few months of the school year evaporate. Fergie takes me to the Homecoming Dance, and afterward we ride up Mayflower Hill and park by the pond. He never once suggests we get in the backseat, but he does give me a passionate kiss on the forehead before presenting me his class ring, which, he says, certifies we're going steady. I guess that's true, since there's no one else, but I don't wear the ring on a chain like most girls do, as I don't want to displace my silver dollar and I certainly don't want anybody to think we're "doing it," because we're not. He seems to understand.

Except for settling future plans and finding Margaux a boyfriend, everything goes swimmingly until an afternoon in early December when I head down to have a lesson with Mr. M. It's four o'clock, already dark, and I follow the lights from the woolen mill to navigate over the icy road to King Court. The only sound is the steady, familiar thumping of the looms, and I stop for a moment to listen and gaze across the river, where the giant smokestack is sending a misty white column straight up in the cold night air. To be sure, this place is never going to be listed as an escape place for tourists in the dead of winter, but it's a haven for me, and, best of all, at the end there's Mr. M's house, where I'm welcomed like a queen.

Today, however, the king is not at the door to greet me, and I gently push it open. The only light is from the tiny lamp on the table near the window, and Mr. M is fast asleep in his Morris chair. I speak his name softly, so as not to frighten him, and he opens his eyes. He barely smiles, and slowly shakes his head. Something's wrong, and it takes only a moment to figure it out.

"Where's Adagio?" I whisper, afraid to hear his answer.

"Oh, Angel," he says as he struggles to his feet, "she's gone." He puts his arms around me and cradles my head against his chest. The words tumble out. "Saleem drove us up to see the vet this morning. Doc said she was very old and sick, that she wasn't going to get better. It was so hard, but I couldn't let her suffer."

I can feel his body tremble, and my heart sinks. I don't know what to say. He loved that cat so much. She was the last tie to his beloved Jamilah, and a comfort in his loneliness. I can't imagine his sorrow, but I loved her, too, and I remember how she greeted me the night I came out of the storm and into this house, and think of how we laughed at her purring accompaniment when we played the piano. I hug him even tighter and tell him I'm sorry. "You should have told me," I say. "I would have gone with you." He says there was nothing I could do, and he didn't want me missing school.

We cling for a very long time, and then I ask if he's had anything to eat. He says there's stuffed grape leaves on the stove, and I offer to warm them as he goes back to his chair. While I tend the pan, careful not to break the leaves and spill the rice, a thought comes into my head and out of my mouth all at the same time. "I'm going to get you a new kitten."

"Oh, no, Angel. You mustn't do that. Cats live a long time. In case you haven't heard, they have nine lives." He makes the tiniest of grins. "A new cat would surely outlive me, and I couldn't bear the thought of leaving it behind." I push on, promising to care for his cat forever, but he holds up a hand to stop me. "I'm old, Angela. A cat is a lot of work if you do it right, and these days I do just about as much on purpose as I used to do by accident." He makes a bit bigger grin. "Besides, why do I need another cat when I've got an angel?"

In the days that follow, thoughts of Adagio haunt me. I knew she was old and sick, but in my mind I somehow foolishly placed the idea of her dying among the things that will never happen. I should have known better.

~

The week before Christmas, I return from school to find Mom waiting for me, all excited and waving a letter from Gabe. "He's coming home," she says, and then tells me we're going to have the most magnificent Christmas since the birth of Christ himself. She's already set candles on the windowsills and moved the furniture in the living room to make a space for the first real tree we've ever had. She claims she'll go and get it tomorrow, but when tomorrow comes she tells me she's changed her mind. Instead, she wants me to get it on Saturday, after lunch, and she gives me two dollars to buy it.

Mom's unusually precise instructions mystify me, but I go along, and Saturday morning I trudge up to Castonguay Square in front of City Hall where a man has been selling sweet-smelling firs all week. There aren't many left to choose from, but I notice a big one with a double top that's been cast aside. The man assures me that one of the tops will break off by the time I drag it home, and it'll be just fine. He offers it for a dollar, and I take it.

Holding the butt end and walking backwards, it takes me a while to navigate up Front Street. In front of St. Joseph, I find out the man was right. One of the tops snaps off on the curb and lands upright in the snow in front of the church. Mom would surely say it was a sign.

It's not hard to tell that the fat tree won't fit through the kitchen door, so I drag it around to the front and up the porch steps. I'm deep into my own thoughts as I tug the tree through the front door, and my mother's shout makes me jump and spin around.

"Surprise!"

I look, then blink my eyes. I can't quite believe what I see. Behind her, along the wall in the place she cleared for the tree, is a piano. A beautiful piano.

"Merry Christmas!"

Again, I jump. Mr. M is in the open doorway to the kitchen, arms crossed. I hadn't seen him, and I squeal in delight. He's smiling ear to ear, and he looks, for all the world, like Santa Claus.

It's not difficult to figure out what's happened. I'm not sure how or why, but I know that very second that I have my own piano, and I start to cry when I should be laughing, and then begin to sputter like the old Buick. "For me? It can't be! How come? Who?"

Mom is laughing and crying all at once. "Mr. Moussallem did it," she blubbers. "He came to the restaurant last week to tell me. Made me promise not to tell you. Al Corey's men delivered it today. That's why I sent you for a tree."

I'm still holding the stump, and let go of it to rush and give Mr. M a swarming hug. "Now, now," he says, the tears on his cheeks mixing with mine, "it's not new, mind you. Pre-war, in fact, but Baldwin is a good name, and it's in perfect shape."

"Liberace won't play anything but a Baldwin," Mom interjects, out of nowhere.

"I suspect Liberace doesn't use an Acrosonic spinet," Mr. M chuckles as we hold each other. "No place for the candelabras." He then tells me that when he went to buy us some sheet music at Al Corey's last week, he told Mr. Corey about me and about how I've managed to learn to play without having a piano of my own.

"Al said he'd heard all about you from Fred Petra, and that he'd let me have this trade-in for what it cost him, delivery included."

Suddenly, the mention of cost gives me a horrible thought, and I step back and stare into Mr. M's face. "The mayonnaise jar! You took the money from the mayonnaise jar, didn't you?"

"I don't need a TV," he says, confirming my suspicions. "There's more to life than watching talking heads in snowstorms." He takes my chin in his hand and lifts my face. "Besides," he says, pretending to be gruff, "talk of money doesn't mix with the business of giving."

The tree is still wedged in the front door, and the room is getting cold. Mom goes to wrestle with it, and I walk to the piano slowly, foolishly fearing a sudden move might make it disappear. I run my fingertips over the polished wood for a long minute before I sit down on the bench and gently play some simple scales. The sympathetic echoes of the rich low notes make me shiver, and I smile when the high notes ring like tiny crystal bells. I'm all by myself in heaven, and I don't want to leave.

Mom finally gets the tree inside, and when she slams the door I suddenly remember all the times that loud interruptions would silence my magic cardboard keyboard. I run upstairs to get it.

Mr. M lets out a gasp when I unfold the worn keyboard in front of him, and I realize he hasn't seen it since he first gave it to me, crisp and clean, nearly three years ago. The lines between the keys are smudged, and the painted paper is worn through to the cardboard along the middle octaves. "Oh, my," he says. "I'd say the Baldwin arrived in the nick of time."

"The Corrugated Steinway still works just fine," I assure him, folding it on the middle crease and placing it carefully under the piano bench.

~

Christmas is positively the best ever. On Christmas Eve we sit around like the cast from *The Adventures of Ozzie and Harriet* except, of course, Ozzie is missing. Mom is playing Harriet and rarely leaves the kitchen. Gabe is brother David and every bit as handsome. I'm Ricky, but instead of singing *The Christmas Song*, I play it on my new piano.

After an hour or two we can play and sing no more, and while we wait to leave for midnight Mass, Gabe entertains us with tales of life in the Army. He gets so wrapped up in describing the big rigs he's worked on that he seems not to notice Mom and I have our eyes glazed over, but we both perk up when he tells us he plans to re-up when his enlistment ends. Even more surprising than that, he tells us he's decided that he's not going to be a mechanic when he gets out, after all. "I think I'll use the GI Bill and learn something else," he says. "Who knows what I might become? Maybe a lawyer, like Mr. Shapiro."

Mom gapes at him like he's the Christ Child, and I begin to think how wonderful it is that he knows where he's headed in life. With all my heart, I wish the same were true for me.

1957

The simple, spinning Frisbee is a symbol of a fascination with all the things that go fast – on the airwaves and on the highways, in outer space and in the kitchens. Many will later say it's the best of times, but new obsessions don't come without cost, and there are growing hints it's time to pay. Carmakers make bigger fins, but sales drop by a third. Ford introduces the Edsel, and it doesn't help at all. The average worker can still make four grand a year and buy a home for twelve, but factories are geared to make more things than they can sell, and, here and there, shops and mills begin to close. Unemployment is on the rise; a bruising recession is on the way.

Predictions of a coming slump are largely ignored, but there's other startling news that can't be missed. Cops get radar, Elvis gets drafted, I Love Lucy *goes off the air, and the Dodgers abandon Brooklyn. The country is fascinated by the frantic race with the Soviet Union to dominate outer space, and Americans are stunned when the Russians put the first satellite into orbit. Unaccustomed to taking second place and still smarting from the stalemate in Korea, Americans are embarrassed. With unintended irony, the* Waterville Sentinel *publishes a photograph of Sputnik on page one, upside down.*

Young people are fascinated with movie stars and rock 'n' roll, but few think of going to college. Aspirations are worse for women, whose college numbers fall to a 30-year low. While they struggle with corsets and strive for pointy breasts, the culture urges them to stay home and have babies, or risk being "old maids" at the age of 24. Meanwhile, the Food and Drug Administration approves the Pill, for medicinal purposes only, and women with menstrual complaints visit their doctors in droves.

Three years after the Supreme Court outlaws school segregation, nine black students go to the Little Rock, Arkansas, high school, and an angry mob makes them withdraw. Governor Faubus calls the National Guard to support the segregationists, and President Eisenhower sends federal troops to enforce the law. Across the country, an entire generation of children, black and white, is left with scars.

In Maine, there's not much to integrate but the roads. The new highway bypass steals customers from the LL Bean store in Freeport, and they put up a parking lot to lure them back. Up the road in Waterville, merchants want more parking, too. An Urban Renewal project will soon pave over much of the old charm of Main Street.

Twenty

Fergie is plunked cross-legged on the lumpy sofa, doodling with a pencil. "How many cans in a case of soup?"

"Twenty-four."

"How many cases do you handle on a shift?"

"Ten or twelve."

"Call it eleven. Five days a week, right?"

"Look, if you don't mind, I'm trying to play the piano here. I don't have any music, and I'm working it out by ear." I start to hum again, but he looks hurt and makes me feel guilty. "OK," I give in, "five days a week, all year, except in the summer."

Margaux can't stand being left out. "And, don't forget, she does a lot more than stack soup cans." She turns to me. "And what's that song you're playing, anyway?"

I give up and turn away from the keys. If a stranger walked in they'd think for sure they were in a nuthouse. Mom is in the kitchen, muttering to God and praying the pipes won't freeze. Fergie's doing some weird calculation of soup cans, asking more questions than Bob Barker on *The Price is Right*; and Margaux is mutilating Oreos, pulling them apart, pressing the frosted sides together and throwing the blanks back in the bag.

I'd like to send all three packing, but they'd never go outside. It's the last day of December in what the *Sentinel* is claiming is the coldest Maine winter ever. Margaux copped her father's newspaper again this morning so she could show me a chart of yesterday's hourly temperatures alongside a photograph of a half-frozen man, wound up to his frosted eyebrows in a wool scarf, looking forlornly at a thermometer where the mercury is barely showing.

The cold doesn't bother me. I've spent the past week indoors, near the stove, playing my new piano. Most of the time I feel all warm and cozy, like Cinderella dancing in her glass slippers, but occasionally, like right now, I feel more like Alice in Wonderland. It's possible my condition has been brought on by kerosene fumes, since we're all buttoned up, but more likely the Alice feeling comes from spending too much time in close quarters with Tweedledum and Tweedledee, who persist in trying to lead me down one rabbit hole after another.

I take another leap into fantasyland when Tweedledee asks if I realize I've stacked up more than ten miles of soup cans over the past three years. Well, of course I don't; I've never even thought about it. "If you'd piled 'em all on top of one another," he goes on, "they'd reach up into outer space, and that's exactly where the Americans and the Russians are trying to go, right now."

Tweedledum is quick with the wet blanket. "Well, I certainly hope they're not trying to do it with soup cans, because they'll crash before they get up two feet."

Fergie makes a look like a baby who's bitten a pickle. Little wonder he's been working extra hard to help me find Margaux a boyfriend. She's been getting under his skin all vacation, starting every day when he drops by after lunch, claiming he just happened to be in the neighborhood, and she calls him a liar. Unfortunately, even double-teaming on the dating game hasn't worked. We've made at least a dozen good suggestions, but she's rejected every one. Worse than that, even when Fergie's right in the room, she makes fun of my dating campaign by calling my first attempt "a train wreck." Last night I went back through the looking glass and brought Moose LeGrand's name into the conversation, raving on about his many virtues, few of which I've actually witnessed. Margaux abruptly disqualified not just Moose but the entire football squad, claiming they're all dumber than hakes and smell a whole lot worse.

This afternoon, just as I'm beginning to think we might need to cast our nets into surrounding towns, Margaux makes a pre-emptive strike and not only admits she's on the prowl for a man, but also says she'll handle it all by herself. Then, just as if finding a boyfriend was like picking beans, she ups and names her victim: Edwin Tweedie.

Now, I'm not about to throw cold water on any sign that Margaux has a spark of romance, but really, Edwin Tweedie? He's a fine trumpet player, that's for sure, but after that, it's all downhill. To begin with, he's as stuck-up as Mrs. Bizier. He parades around school like he's Chet Baker on drugs, and hardly ever troubles himself to speak to ordinary, sober human beings. He wouldn't give Margaux a second glance if she did the Hoochie Coochie right in front of him. I'm tempted to suggest the banning of both football players and trumpeters, but there's no use. When Margaux has her mind made up, she's like Lola in *Damn Yankees* – whatever she wants, she gets.

It's already dark, and having given up on any further practicing of *Any Way You Want Me*, I remind my distractors it's time to pick up and head down to King Court. Last week, when I was trying to think of ways to cheer up Mr. M, I promised I'd bring him supper on New Year's Eve. What I didn't say, because I didn't know it at the time, was that Fergie and Margaux would be coming with me. It was Fergie's idea to make it a party, and the old maid invited herself. In fact, she offered to bring the blood pressure kit she got for Christmas and use it as part of the evening entertainment. It seems very odd to me, but Mr. M won't care. He knows Margaux's quirky, and anything that gets his mind off his beloved cat is bound to help.

I'm still thinking about Mr. M's delicate feelings as we stand shivering on his stoop. Fergie is holding a tray of kibbeh, and I have the baklava. Margaux is carrying her stupid blood pressure kit. "Listen up," I say, as we're about to go inside. "Don't you even *think* about mentioning the word *cat*.

Mr. M beams when he comes to the door and sees three faces instead of one, and then he frowns. "Haven't you young people got anything better to do on New Year's Eve?" He doesn't really want an answer, so I don't give one. "Oh, please come in," he says, grinning as we take the trays to the kitchen table, already set for two. "Goodness me," he laughs, "We'll have to eat in our laps. It'll be just fine."

"It'll be the cat's meow," Margaux pipes up brightly. If my eyes could shoot bullets, she'd be dead, and she knows it. "Sorry," she whispers, cupping her hand over her mouth. "Forgot."

With the things Mr. M has prepared and all the kibbeh we brought, it's more than an hour before we get to the baklava. We're spitting on our napkins and wiping the honey off our hands when Mr. M begins to reminisce about New Year's Eve celebrations in the old country, telling of family gatherings with fine food and fireworks he remembers from his youth. "It's the same the world over," he says, "except the food is different." He turns to Margaux, who's sitting next to me on the bench. "I imagine your people just love tourtière pie."

"I'm tellin' you," she comes back in a flash, "they think it's the ca…"

There's another cat reference coming, and I cut her off with a sharp jab of my elbow.

"Ouch!" she yelps. "It's the best."

The conversation rambles on long after the dishes are done. Mr. M is interested in what Fergie and Margaux have planned for next year, and Fergie says he's already applied to the university, and is waiting to hear. Margaux says she's set to go to Sisters Hospital School of Nursing, and of course that's all the excuse she needs to trot out her blood pressure kit, put the stethoscope in her ears, and begin a round of exams, starting with Mr. M. She gives me an odd look when she's done, and then declares him fit as a fiddle. She has a hard time to get Fergie's pulse and finally gives up, declaring that if he wanted to sleep through every winter, he could possibly live forever. I'm last. Margaux's catty remarks have sent my blood pressure sky high, and when she's finished, she solemnly pronounces that this is very likely to be my last New Year's Eve.

With the physicals out of the way, it's time for the real entertainment and I tell Mr. M we're about to have a live performance of *Any Way You Want Me*, with a surprise appearance of Fergie as Elvis. It's something Fergie and I cooked up; even Margaux doesn't know. I go to the piano, play an intro, and Fergie bends low, strums a fake guitar, and pretends he's singing to me:

> *I'll be strong as a mountain,*
> *Or weak as a willow tree,*
> *Any way you want me,*
> *That's how I will be.*

At the end, he bows almost to the floor, tosses his head, and runs his fingers through his hair. If he was a mite bigger and didn't have a zit blooming on his forehead, I swear he'd be a dead ringer for Elvis. Mr. M laughs and applauds, then tells us that the flip side of the record, *Love Me Tender*, is likely to be a much bigger hit.

Margaux doesn't disguise her disgust when I move on to classical music, and she sits there, bored to death, while I play a couple of pieces by Ludwig, Mr. M's favorite. He smiles through *Ode to Joy*, and sings along. I don't get to Brahms until ten o'clock, and I notice Mr. M slouching in his chair, his head bowing onto his chest. When I've finished *Good Evening, Good Night*, he's sound asleep. Margaux looks at him, winks at me, and grins. "Cat nap," she whispers in an evil sort of way. She's perfectly disgusting.

It's well past Mr. M's bedtime, and I go to rouse him so he'll know we're leaving. He starts to protest, then pats my hand, and I bend to kiss his forehead. "Happy New Year, Mr. M," I say. "I love you."

~

There's plenty of catching up to do on any first day back at school, and hardly anybody pays attention to the first bell. Several of us are milling in the corridor, just outside Mlle. Vachon's eight o'clock senior French class when, out of the corner of my eye, I see Mrs. Aldrich, bearing down on me.

"Oh, Angela," she gasps, "I've been looking for you." Then, with the entire world listening, she tells me I must come see her promptly after classes. Before I can ask why, she's disappeared, and Mlle. Vachon is madly whapping a ruler on her desk. "Vite! Vite!"

All day I'm left to wonder what my teacher-savior wants. She can't possibly know I have a real piano, much less that I've begun to fret that it might overtake me and cause another academic slump. Perhaps she's hired a Russian spy, or maybe Margaux is ratting on me ... for free.

My palms sweat while I wait for her to dismiss her homeroom class, filled with noisy, irritating freshmen who nearly knock me over when they finally bolt for the hallway like raccoons freed from a trap. I ease into the chair next to her desk, and I'm relieved to see she's wearing a big grin. It must be a good sign. "Angela, Angela," she says, scrambling in her handbag where she retrieves a sheet of folded paper, "just wait 'til you hear what I have to tell you." I wait. "Look here," she says. I lean to look, but she draws it back. "No, let me tell you." She then proceeds to flat out announce that she expects me to enter a music contest, coming up at the end of January.

I haven't heard about any music contest, and I'm not excited about going down another rabbit hole, but my confused face doesn't keep her from rambling on with the details. Seems the president of Colby is bent on building up the college's offerings in art and music. "He's a liberal arts man," she explains, "through and through," and then she goes on to explain he's recently hired new faculty and is looking for good students, especially in music. She tells me the local alumni club has gotten behind him and raised money for a year's tuition to be awarded to the best-qualified music student at Waterville High.

It's a lot to take in all at once, and I sit there like a dummy until she insists I must go see Mrs. Bizier at once, and sign up. *Does she truly think the woman who wouldn't let me play a school piano three years ago is about to let me enter a music contest where her own precious daughter is certain to be a contestant?* Mrs. Aldrich reads my face and is bobbing her head up and down. "Any senior with a B average and the recommendation of the principal can enter," she explains. "No other approvals are necessary." She reminds me my grades are far better than a B, and that she's already cleared things with Mr. Goode, who says he's most willing to recommend me. As for Mrs. Bizier, Mrs. Aldrich says it wouldn't be proper to have a contestant's mother involved in anything more than the signing up, and that the three contest judges all will be from Colby.

Obviously well satisfied with her pitch, the dear soul sits back and smiles. She's waiting for me to jump up and down and shout, but I can't, and I struggle for words to explain. "I don't think this is a very good idea," I tell her cautiously. "First of all, I can't possibly be the best music student in the entire school, and even if by some miracle I won and got the scholarship, I could never pay for the other three years." What I don't bother to explain is that ever since *Guys and Dolls* I've rather enjoyed being known around school as a good piano player, and I'm in no rush to risk it all by entering a contest that I'm bound to lose.

Mrs. Aldrich sags a little in her seat. She's so proud of having had a hand in getting me straightened out in my studies, and she's been my cheerleader in high places ever since. A rush of guilt makes me say I'll at least think it over, and then she brightens up and tells me I have one day before the signup deadline.

Having heard about the warrant Mrs. Aldrich issued to me in the morning, Margaux and Fergie are waiting for me in the hall when I leave, and I give them the news without any details. "She wants me to enter a music contest. The winner gets a one-year Colby scholarship."

Margaux smells a rat. "What's the catch?"

I shake my head. "There's no catch. It's just that it doesn't make a lot of sense. In the first place, I can't win, and even if I did, one year of college is like reading a quarter of a book."

Fergie doesn't agree. "Look here," he says, "tuition at Colby is worth about 800 bucks a year. That's a big deal, and you could live at home and not have to pay board and room. All you'd have to buy is a few books. Who knows what might happen after that?" Margaux is now vigorously nodding, but of course they both think I can play like Jo Ann Castle on *Lawrence Welk* and are forgetting what it would be like to need to take a job at the Lockwood after only one year of college.

When I get home, I discover Mom has also got her head in La La Land. Margaux is with me when I tell the story for the second time in an hour. "Well now," she says at the end, as if the matter was already settled. "I'll just go say a novena and ask St. Joseph to help."

Even Margaux is skeptical about *that* notion. "You know, don't you," she says to Mom, "Mother Perpetua at Mount Merici is Mrs. Bizier's sister. She'll have every Ursuline at the convent on their knees for her precious niece, you can bet on that."

Mom is still on the faith track. "It's three weeks before the contest," she says. "There's time enough for *two* novenas, and I'll

191

get Father Ataya in on it, as well." The reduction of the entire matter to a religious war between the Romans and the Maronites isn't helping, and I realize the truth of what I've felt all along. There's only one person who'll give me a straight answer, and I don't have a lot of time to dither.

After supper I go down to King Court by myself, running all the way to keep warm. Mr. M is huddled in his chair. A heavy blanket is pulled up around his shoulders, and he looks a bit like a friendly medieval gnome as he folds his hands and listens intently while I explain about the contest. I'm careful to stick to the facts until the very end, when I tell him about my dilemma. I even confess my private fear of stumbling in front of my newfound friends.

When I'm finished, I peer anxiously into his face, trying to read him as he stares at his folded hands, lost in thought. He doesn't say a word for a very long time. Finally, I break the silence. "You think it's a bad idea, don't you?"

My question startles him back to the present, and he jumps. "No, no, it's a splendid idea," he says. "I was just trying to think about what you might play."

Twenty-One

I'm still puzzling over Mr. M's abrupt conclusion in the matter of me and the contest when he pushes himself up from his chair, shuffles over to the piano, and begins to rummage through the scores under the bench. He's looking for Beethoven, I just know. Sure enough, within seconds he pulls out a dog-eared book of sonatas and flips through until he comes to Number 14, *The Moonlight*. He holds it out to me, beaming. "First movement," he says as if everything was already settled. "Perfect."

He and I have played Beethoven's sonatas before, but always from the easier versions in his wife's old lesson books. If he has his way, this time I'll play it alone and the way Ludwig wrote it, full of sharps, accented notes, and confusing accidentals. He sees me scowl. "Most anybody can poke out these notes," he says, "but the trick is to play it the way Beethoven intended. If you get it wrong, the audience is likely to fall asleep, but if you do it right, everybody, especially the judges, will be most impressed."

At the moment I'm not interested in impressing judges. What I'd really like to do is rewind the entire current scene, send Mr. M back to his Morris chair and rehearse for him the reservations that torment me. *What if I lose? What if I win?* I'm about to re-raise my objections when I catch the excited look on his kind face. He's grinning as if he's just discovered a lost treasure. I can't bear to disappoint him, and I give up. "Okay," I say with a groan, "I'll do it."

"Of course," he says. "And, you'll win, just wait and see."

The next day I go to school early. Mrs. Bizier is perched in her backstage office, lurking for early morning prey. Her back is to the door, and her ample rear end envelops the entire seat of her suffering chair. I fake a cough, and she struggles to turn around. "Well, good morning, Angela," she purrs, like the spider to the fly. "Have you come to find a time to practice on my piano?" It's not her damn piano, but I don't bother to say so. Neither do I tell her for the eighth time that I now have a piano of my own.

"I want to sign up for the Colby music contest," I say, fully expecting some instant, far-fetched objection. Instead, she cocks her head like she's hearing the wail of a distant train. "You?"

"Yes, me."

She re-centers her bottom on the seat. "Well then," she declares, "you will need a B average and the recommendation of Mr. Goode." I tell her I've got the average and Mrs. Aldrich claims I've got Mr. Goode, as well. She bristles at the very mention of Mrs. Aldrich, but she moves on. "May I ask what will you play, my dear?" I lie, and tell her I haven't any idea. "Well then, remember this will be your first time, and you should probably pick something quite simple." I feel my hair straighten, and I fight the urge to repeat her gagging performance on the night of *Guys and Dolls*.

There seem to be no papers to sign, so I'm thinking about escaping the web when curiosity gets the better of me, and I ask the names of the other contestants. She begins with the blood tie. "Well, there's Priscilla, of course," she says, and then, for no reason except to terrify me, explains her daughter has been in several of these contests and has won them all. There are two other contestants, at least so far: Edwin Tweedie with his trumpet, and Diane Buzzell, who will sing. Edwin is a given, but Diane is a surprise. The dear girl is terribly shy and can't say a single word without blushing, which, I happen to think, is possibly why she always stuns people with her beautiful soprano voice whenever she opens her mouth to sing.

I start for the door again, but Mrs. Bizier hauls me back with a jangle of bracelets. "By the way," she says, "this will be a most wonderful experience for you, but I must warn you that one rarely wins the first contest that one enters."

Now, she's made me mad. "Well," I say, cocking my head and twisting a loose curl with a finger, "*one* really never knows about these kinds of things, does *one?*"

The next morning there's a note on my desk saying contestants are to report to Mrs. Bizier's office to give the title of the piece we'll be playing and to draw a number out of a hat to determine the order of our performances. It also says there'll be a rehearsal in the auditorium at Colby the afternoon before the main event.

At lunchtime, I write out the title and hand it in: *The Moonlight, Piano Sonata No. 14 in C-sharp Minor, Op. 27, No. 2, Movement I. Ludwig van Beethoven.*

Mrs. Bizier looks shocked when she reads it. "Are you absolutely sure?"

"I'm sure. Where's the hat?"

Behind her is a list she's been making on the blackboard, and I can see the others have drawn ahead of me, making it pointless for me to pick a number, as there's only one left. When I tell her there's no need, she looks puzzled so I pluck out the four and hand it to her while I examine the roster. Priscilla is first, playing *I've Gotta Crow* from *Peter Pan.* I would have thought she'd pick something classical, like Chopin, but she probably got the same "keep it simple" advice from her mother and wasn't allowed to ignore it. Diane Buzzell is next. She's singing *I Could Have Danced All Night*, and everybody's going to love it because *My Fair Lady* is the current hit on Broadway, and the song is all the rage. Edwin Tweedie, up third, has picked another chart song, *Cherry Pink and*

Apple Blossom White, a very brave choice, if you ask me. The film *Underwater* is still in theaters and everybody's going to compare Edwin's effort to Prez Prado's trumpeter, Billy Regis, who plays the song better than anybody in the world. Of course that won't bother Edwin, who thinks he's better than Billy, anyway.

~

The next two weeks seem like one long visit in the moonlight with Ludwig. I practice on my Baldwin before I go to school and on Mr. M's Beckwith after work and into the evenings. Sometimes, in the middle of the night, I drag out my old Corrugated Steinway and tap away for hours. It's hard work, and Mr. M is tougher on me than he's ever been before. The sweet man who used to praise every piece I played and laugh at my mistakes, makes me stop every few measures and start again. Over and over, he tells me the music of Beethoven comes more from the heart than from the fingers, and I know it's true, but the fingers still have plenty of work to do. For some reason, perhaps to keep mere amateurs away from his work, Ludwig often makes you play the melody and the accompaniment with the same hand, and it's hard. On top of that, there's the business of finding the right techniques for the sustain pedal and a dozen other little adjustments that pile up so fast you feel like Lucy and Ethel in the chocolate factory.

As if I don't have enough to do, Margaux haunts me day and night about what I plan to wear and how I'll fix my hair. The hair part is easy – kinky, thick hair doesn't offer much in the way of arrangement options. I'll wash it, and she can trim it if she likes, but that's it. No flips, no parts, no braids, no bows, no nothing.

The decision on what to wear comes straight from heaven. Margaux has pawed the racks at the Salvation Army for two weeks without finding anything she thinks is suitable, but tonight I come home to find a big white box from Butler's Department Store on my pillow. When I open it, I don't quite believe what I see. It's the most gorgeous dress that God ever made.

Mom has done this, I can tell. The tag, with the price scratched out, is still hanging from a sleeve. The soft lavender color positively glows in the dim light of my room. The top has crispy narrow pleats with a small rounded collar, and the short sleeves are puffed just right. A matching belt cinches the waist, and the skirt flares out, but not too much. It's a dress for Cinderella's Ball, and altogether perfect for playing the piano. I shiver when I suddenly realize it's the first brand new dress I've ever had.

After a long admiring gaze, I hold it up in front of me and when I twirl around I notice Mom in the doorway, eyes shining and a grin on her face as big as I've ever seen. She's been standing there all along.

"Oh, Mom!" I cry out, much too loud for the moment. "Thank you, but you shouldn't have. We can't ..."

She cuts me off. "They let me open a charge," she says proudly. "It'll be paid off in no time."

~

When Saturday's rehearsal comes, I'm as ready as I'll ever be. Fergie has agreed to join me, to keep me calm he says, and Margaux is coming along too, which will likely erase his efforts.

My practice time is set for 3 o'clock, but Margaux insists on going early. She claims I'll need time to get settled, but I know that what she really wants is to run into Edwin Tweedie, who has the half-hour slot ahead of me.

The auditorium in Runnals Union is already set with chairs for tomorrow's contest, and we take seats in the back so as not to disturb Edwin, who's up on stage, blowing his heart out. His eyes are like walnuts, his cheeks are puffed round, and his mouth is puckered like the top of a milk bottle. I giggle at the array of circles, and it annoys Margaux, who is quick to assure me that if he gave up playing the trumpet for a week or so, his face would look entirely normal.

In real life, the auditorium is the women's gymnasium and, as Edwin slurs out the refrain of *Cherry Pink*, I notice that the sound ricochets back and forth a few times before it dies. The curtainless windows, paneled wainscoting, and empty metal chairs on the wooden basketball floor all team up to create the sound of a giant pinball machine. I mention it to Fergie, who assures me that tomorrow when the chairs are filled with people and their winter coats, everything will be just fine.

Edwin disappears behind the curtain the instant he finishes up, and Margaux suddenly pops out of her seat, hitches up the aisle, and vanishes a few steps behind him. "He's about to discover that Margaux's been stalking him," Fergie predicts with a sour face. "That'll be the end of it for her, and probably for us, too. We'll have to start hunting all over again."

The prediction is no more than out of Fergie's mouth when Edwin comes tearing back through the gap in the curtain, jumps off the stage, and races up the aisle toward us, cursing in a most unimaginative way and holding onto his left hand as if it was on fire. The instant he goes howling out the door, Margaux comes bobbing back up the aisle. "Well now," she gasps when she pulls up, out of breath, "I'm afraid you're gonna have to find me a new boyfriend."

I ask what happened.

"You don't want to know."

"Yes, I do."

"No, you don't."

"Simmer down. Just tell me."

"Well," she says, "I was being as nice as anybody could be, telling him how well he played, and all that. He seemed to enjoy it, but then I made the mistake of telling him that you were probably his only real competition."

"What'd he say?"

"You don't want to know."

"Yes, I do."

"He said he wasn't about to let any camel-riding desert monkey beat him."

"Shows what he knows," Fergie shrugs. "Lebanon doesn't have deserts, or monkeys or camels, either, for that matter."

I refocus. "So, what'd you do?"

"I called him a lard-eating frog and slammed the lid on his trumpet case," she says. "How was I supposed to know his hand was still in it?"

"Oh, my God," I say. "You're in big trouble."

"No, I'm not," she shrugs. "There's never been a boy who ever ratted on a girl who got the best of him."

"But, what if he can't play? They'll think I put you up to it."

Fergie is still clarifying. "A trumpet player doesn't need a left hand," he explains, "except to hold the horn."

By now, there's a lady up on the stage, calling my name. Margaux has already eaten a full five minutes of my practice time, but I don't really need it, and it all goes well. The college's Steinway grand has a rich, full tone and is freshly tuned. I make the most of it.

~

We spend most of Sunday morning in my room, primping. The contest isn't until three, and a clock moves like a turtle when you watch it. Worse than that, I have to sit perfectly still while Margaux fusses with my stubborn hair, complaining every minute. I've tried the dress on several times, and when I slip into it after lunch, I already know it fits perfectly. Once I'm all adjusted, I put the chain with Gabe's silver dollar under my dress, so it won't flop around when I play.

Mr. Mathieu has agreed to drive us all up the hill, but nobody's bothered to count. Mrs. Mathieu rides up front with him. Mom and I and Margaux and Fergie have to squeeze into the back. Mr.

Mathieu makes light of it, by observing that it's a good thing I don't play the tuba.

We pull up in front of Runnals Union at 2:30, and the auditorium is already nearly filled. The front row has been saved for the contestants and the judges, and several rows behind it are marked for families and special guests. I invited Mr. M to sit up front, but he said he wasn't keen about having to walk up the long aisle. Mr. Habib will bring him, he said, and they'll sit in the back. I look for him now, and when I can't find him in the crowd, the butterflies start to come. Dr. Bixler, a tall, gaunt man with a friendly face, starts things off with greetings from the college, thanking everybody for coming, and praising the alumni group for its hard work. The president then launches into a lengthy discussion of the philosophy of music, which I don't think anybody fully understands. Principal Goode is the master of ceremonies, and he doesn't mince words. "Priscilla Bizier on the piano," he clips without fanfare, "playing *I've Gotta Crow.*"

Priscilla looks somewhat silly in a sleeveless dress patterned with green leaves. It's easy to tell she's had it special made, to look like Mary Martin as Peter Pan. When her piece is over, Mrs. Bizier is the first to stand and clap. I can't tell whether those who join her are enthusiastic or embarrassed, but I get to my feet, in any case. She played without a flaw, and I'm pretty sure she's going to win.

Diane looks beautiful in a simple white sheath, and she sings like a bird. The only problem I can see is that she's singing *I Could Have Danced All Night* and, through the entire piece, her lips are the only things that move. I'm afraid the judges will expect more.

If there were a prize for best dressed, Edwin would win, hands down. He has on a handsome black suit with the creases down the front of his trousers ironed to a razor's edge. Every hair on his blond head has been safely glued in place, and he has chosen a bright red bow tie, clipped on with precision over his crisp white shirt. If it weren't for the Band-Aids on the knuckles of his left hand, he would be a picture of perfection. He does get a bit carried away with all the slurs and wailing, but he plays well, and the audience loves *Cherry Pink*. Maybe he'll beat Priscilla.

When it's my turn, Mr. Goode startles me when he skips over the details on the program: "Angela Jamal on the piano, playing Beethoven's *Moonlight Sonata*." That's it. No reference numbers, no nothing. I hesitate, then Margaux pokes me from behind.

I had imagined my walk onto the stage as being sort of a graceful sashay, but now I find I'm a wooden soldier. As I march stiffly up the steps, I can hear the people in the audience buzzing. The program has already gone on for nearly an hour. Maybe they're bored. I quickly arrange the music on the rack, reach to squeeze Gabe's silver dollar beneath my dress, take a deep breath, and gently bob my head to fix the beat.

The moment I raise my fingers above the keys, I begin thinking about my cardboard keyboard and the miracle of escaping into a world where there's nothing but the music. I go there now, and the notes come easily. In my trance, I concentrate on making the harmonies swim together, articulating carefully and, as best as my heart will let me, evoke the mysterious, melancholy mood.

I hold the final note until it evaporates in a wisp, and then bring myself back into the real time and place, and listen. Nothing. Not a sound. Maybe I actually have put them to sleep. It seems as if I wait a very long time, and then, suddenly, I hear the sound of scraping chairs and look out to see the audience rise up as one, waving, yelling, and clapping. In those few glorious moments, I let the tide of applause wash over me, and I realize Mr. M was right. I may not get the prize, but I have won, just the same.

By the time I get back to my seat, the judges have disappeared backstage, and the contestants sit in a row, waiting. Arrogant Edwin and the mute Diane are looking straight ahead. Priscilla is next to me, and I grit my teeth and generously congratulate her on her fine performance. "You did very well, too," she says, pleasing me before she adds, "considering it was your first time ever."

The few minutes before the judges return seem like an hour. When they get back in their seats the house lights go on, and Dr. Bixler appears on the stage. He compliments all four of us, then holds up a sheet of paper. "The scholarship winner and the newest member of the Colby class of 1961," he says, smiling broadly, "is Miss Angela Jamal."

My heart thumps nearly out of my chest as he beckons me onto the stage. I float up there in a daze, and he towers over me as he leans to shake my hand and present a certificate. I can't read it through the tears, and I don't hear a word of what he's saying. Instead, I stare out over the auditorium where everyone is once again standing and cheering. I spot Mom in the front row, yelling and twirling her beads like pompoms, and Margaux and Fergie who, miracle of miracles, are waltzing around their chairs in a lovers' embrace. Through the moving crowd, far in the back, I can see Mr. M, standing and bracing himself on the chair in front. I must go see him.

Mom, Fergie, and Margaux are waiting at the foot of the stage steps. I stop long enough to hug my dear mother, who's come all apart in the excitement, kiss Fergie and Margaux on their cheeks, and head up the long aisle through a gauntlet of teachers and friends reaching out and shouting congratulations as if I were a movie star.

Mr. M sees me coming and takes off his glasses, puts them in his shirt pocket, and holds out his arms. Tears stream down his face as he pulls me close. The warmth seems to melt me, and I begin to sob. "Oh, Angel, Angel, Angel," he repeats, over and over. "You did it. I just knew you would."

Twenty-Two

When I was 15, I thought I knew just about everything there was to know. Of course, I was wrong. Now that I'm nearly 18 and about all grown up, I realize that in the past three years I've picked up at least twice as much as I knew before, and one of the most useful things I've held on to is that life hardly ever turns out the way you think it will.

This spring is a perfect example. I imagined that when it came time to graduate, we seniors would be prancing around like queens and kings, receiving the praises of admiring subjects and sprinkling gifts of wisdom over the grateful masses. Instead, nobody's paying the least bit of attention to us at all, and we're bored stiff with high school and itching to move on.

It's hard to keep track of it all, but the boys seem headed in three directions. A few are going to college, but most will sign up with the Army or go off to Connecticut and make gobs of money building jet engines. As far as I can tell, very few girls are headed to college, but plenty of them are going ape over wedding plans. As for me, I haven't been able to get my mind off college since the day I won the scholarship. I've even stopped fussing about where the rest of the money will come from, as Mr. M tells me these things have a way of working themselves out, and I've come to believe him.

Thank goodness, some things don't change. Fergie is as sweet as ever, and while he sticks like glue, I don't care. He stops by most evenings and listens to me play the piano while he buries his nose in secondhand engineering books, often getting so excited by that stuff you'd think he was reading *Peyton Place*, instead.

Margaux hasn't changed much, either. She's still as distracting as ever. Right now, she's obsessed with all the medical insight she's managed to pick up without having yet spent a day in nursing school. Just yesterday, when Sheila Maroon's mother came limping out of Sittu's Bakery, Margaux diagnosed a case of gout from across the street. If that wasn't queer enough, she had the gall to tell the poor woman to go easy on the meat.

I'm afraid Margaux's medical fixation has even overtaken her search for a mate, as now she claims she'll wait until school starts and find herself a rich, young doctor. The plan seems sound enough, but her temporary vow of celibacy complicates planning for the Senior Prom. Fergie and I had hoped someone would take her off our hands, but instead, we have to compromise. She's agreed to attend the prom with the bachelor girls if Fergie promises to dance with her at least twice. I suppose that's better than me feeling guilty about her having to sit home alone, pouting.

The prom actually turns out to be a pleasant escape from the last dull days of classes. The gym has been transformed by strings of purple crepe looping over the basketball court, disguised and made slippery by clouds of white confetti. A huge glass ball hangs from the ceiling, slowly turning in the heat that rises from the clutching bodies below and making dots of colored light on everybody's faces. The chaperones hang out near the doors, front and back, pretending to be friendly while leaning in to check for alcohol.

I dance every number with Fergie except for the two he promised Margaux, which, for safety sake, I make certain are distance-keeping jitterbugs. The DJ is set up in full stereo, and he takes song requests from racks of records at least a mile long. There are two sets of three jitterbugs and a waltz before every break, when most of us head for the cookies and lemonade while the rest, including Spike Moufette, go outside to smoke. I saw the creep earlier, arriving in the passenger seat with Gloria Bousam behind the wheel of her father's Oldsmobile. He looked uncomfortable then, but now, after a few dances and several trips back to the car, he seems to be more at ease. In fact, he provides the high point of the evening. When Tab Hunter is about half through *Young Love*, Spike gets all heated up and lets his hands drift down onto Gloria's bottom. Mr. Fallon spots the violation, and as he runs onto the floor, he trips over the light cords and goes sprawling across the slick floor. The place goes bananas.

For the last waltz, Fergie requests *So Rare*, a song we've called our own since Jimmy Dorsey put it on the charts in January. We dance real close, testing the chaperones, while Fergie dreamily whispers the words into my ear:

> *You are perfection, you're my idea*
> *Of angels singing the "Ave Maria"*
> *For you're an angel, I'd breathe and live you*
> *With every beat of the heart that I give you*
> *So rare ... so rare*

Now, it's Fergie's turn to get carried away, although he behaves much better than Flash. "Oh Angela," he murmurs when the tune is over, "I'm so afraid you're going to forget me when you go to Colby." His face takes on the saddest look as he plods on with his nutty theory. "I just know you'll find some rich preppie and run off with him to New York, or someplace like that, and I'll never see you again." I can't help but giggle, and I make light of his fantasy by mocking Billy Holly. *That'll be the day*, I chime, *when I say goodbye*. We both have a good laugh, and I let my guard down and agree to take a spin up to Johnson Pond on the way home. I catch myself in time to warn him that there'll be no backseat bingo.

The rest of the school year disappears like the spring ice on the Kennebec. I'd expected a few extra drumbeats here and there, but the only really good thing that happens is that Gabe gets a pass and surprises us by coming home for graduation. Mom is in heaven, and I'm right up there with her. Life could be just about perfect if only Mr. M were feeling better. Margaux says it's his heart, and she's probably right. These days, he can barely move without getting out of breath, and we both feel terrible when he says he doesn't think he'll be able to attend commencement. I assure him we'll come down and replay the important parts for him when the ceremony is over.

Thanks to Gabe's graduation gift of a Brownie Hawkeye, I also promise Mr. M we'll get plenty of pictures, and over the next few days the magic camera gets a good workout. As soon as the graduation gowns are issued, we swish around in the driveway as if it was a wedding, posing in every possible combination. Fergie and I have gold cords to wear over our robes, signifying high honors, but I take mine off when I have my picture taken with Margaux, as I couldn't bear to hear her say one more time that she'd have one of those cords for herself if she hadn't had to spend so much time teaching me French.

As with other spring events, graduation itself falls short of expectations. Except for a great deal of marching up and down in segregated lines – girls in white, boys in purple – there isn't much to it. The featured speaker is a judge we've never heard of, and he drones on in the heat, well beyond everybody's attention span. By the time they're ready to hand out diplomas, most of us are soaking wet under our stifling nylon robes.

The minute the endless program is over, Margaux, Fergie and I scamper down to Head of Falls, gowns flowing, to give a full account to Mr. M and take pictures before it gets dark. Fergie gets a good one of Mr. M and me standing on the stoop, and before the week is out, I have it developed and give it to him. He hugs it to his chest and beams.

~

The following Monday I report to the North Street swimming pool for what I truly hope is my last summer as a lifeguard. Although I've been promoted to one of the tall chairs at the deep end, it's small consolation for a ten-week sentence in a zoo. The pool opens tomorrow, and we spend the morning practicing artificial respiration and going over the many Red Cross rules of safety we're called upon to enforce, even in the midst of anarchy.

After lunch, on the way to the bathhouse to change for a swim, I happen to see Bernie Nelson peering through the chain link gate, scanning up and down the sides of the pool. I shudder when I wave. It's not Bernie's fault, but he's become my boogeyman, scaring me half to death every time he shows up. My heart pounds when he spots me and calls me over.

There's none of the usual greeting. Something is wrong, and he blurts it out, right away. "It's Mr. Moussallem," he says, gesturing behind him toward the new Thayer Hospital, across the road, not far away. "I brought him there a few minutes ago. He's asking to see you. We need to hurry."

It doesn't take a minute get there, but it seems like an hour. Along the way, Bernie explains that Mr. Habib called the station to say he'd found Mr. M in a bad way and needing help. "I went as quickly as I could, but I just don't know," Bernie says, his voice trailing off.

I've never been on the inside of a hospital before. Everything seems oddly cold and white, even the grim-faced nurse who's guarding the door. She obviously knows Bernie and nods toward a room down the hall before she steps in front of me to ask if I'm related. Bernie whisks me past her, and only then turns back to answer. "Yes," he says abruptly, "she most certainly is."

I utter a small gasp when I enter the tiny room and see Mr. M lying on the narrow bed. His eyes are shut, and his face is expressionless and pale. A tube pulls at one corner of his mouth, and there are needles in his arms, attached to bags on metal stands beside the bed. A machine with flashing lights is on a stand nearby, eerily beeping the only sound in the room.

A nurse stands calmly on the other side, staring at the noisy machine. She looks up when I enter, and nods. "You must be the angel," she says, kindly. "He's been waiting for you."

I suck in my breath, bend down and take his hand. "It's me," I whisper. "I'm right here. It's okay." His eyelids flutter, then slowly open. His lips seem to make a smile, and his hand gives mine a tiny squeeze. He knows.

I stand rigid, having fearful thoughts and feeling helpless, when I notice something near his hand and lean to see. It's the graduation picture of Mr. M and me. Bernie sees me looking. "Made me go back into the house to get it," he says, softly.

I don't move for several minutes, desperately wishing there was something I could do, when the beeping sounds suddenly begin to skip, and Mr. M stirs, opens his eyes, and looks straight into my face. He's trying to say something. It has to do with the Beckwith, but the words are garbled, and I don't understand. He clears his throat and tries to speak again. This time, the words are crystal clear. "I love you, Angel." His words startle me and I want to climb onto the bed and give him a hug. I bend close and tell him I love him, too.

His mysterious, sudden revival makes me begin to think of miracles, but then the wretched machine suddenly stops beeping, and the silence is horrifying. I turn to face the nurse, who's come to take his wrist, and I watch in disbelief as she shakes her head, then turns to me. "I'm so very sorry," she says. "He's gone."

"Oh, no!" My mind whirls. "It can't be. You must do something. Please, help him." The nurse turns and gives Bernie a pleading look, and he comes and puts a hand on my shoulder as I sag onto the bed, bury my head on Mr. M's now quiet chest, and begin to sob.

After a minute or two, Bernie helps me to my feet so the nurse can do whatever nurses do, and I walk to the window in a daze. In the distance, at the very top of Mayflower Hill, I see the white tower of the college library, sticking out above the trees and gleaming in the afternoon sun. The view takes me to the coming fall, when I will begin an adventure there that would never be possible without Mr. M. He deserved to share that with me, but now he's gone. Life is not fair, not fair at all.

The nurse interrupts my thoughts and says it's time for me to go. I shrug her off. I can't leave Mr. M alone like this, but Bernie reminds me Mr. Habib is planning to bring Mom to the hospital after work, and we must spare them from finding out this way. Bernie says he'll take me home.

Mom is on the doorstep waiting, and she frowns when she sees the sergeant with me. "How is he?" she asks, cautiously. I'm afraid she might swoon when I tell her, but instead she walks down off the steps and wraps her arms tightly around me. It feels good, and I bury my head in her neck and let the sobs come, once again. "As much as I've prayed," she whispers, "I could never seem to protect you from the awful things. I'm so sorry." Now, she's crying as well, and in that moment I love her more than I have ever loved her before.

Bernie is fidgety, says he'll go find Mr. Habib. I thank him for his kindness, and when he leaves, Mom and I go and kneel by the window in the front room and begin the rosary.

Assalamu 'alayki yah Maryam, ya mumtalia namah, Arrabu ma'ki...

The Rosary in Arabic comes automatically, and my mind drifts as I gaze onto the busy street. Cars are going up and down, and people are on the sidewalk, carrying lunch pails, cheerfully greeting one another as they pass. It's as if nothing has changed at all, even though the world has turned itself completely upside down. I don't understand.

We finish a decade, and I get to my feet. Mom would go another round or two with the beads, but I tell her I have to leave. "Mr. M said something about the Beckwith piano," I explain, "but I don't know what he meant. I have to go and see."

I wave back at Mom as I cross the street, then walk slowly into the darkness of the tunnel under the tracks. When I return to the sunshine, I pause to take in the familiar sights and sounds of Head of Falls – the clanging Iron Works, the throbbing woolen mill, the narrow lanes embraced by the tight rows of graying tenements and warehouses. Farther on, I see the setting sun reflect off the fast water above the dam, dappling the long brick walls of the paper mill across the river.

I must have come this way a thousand times, but today is different. Always before, I've been eager to arrive on King Court, to the place of refuge where I found love and laughter, and lessons of life and music. Now, it's all disappeared in an instant, and my destination is nothing more than an old, vacant house.

Mr. M once told me he'd hidden a house key under an overturned plant pot on the stoop. We laughed at his poor attempt to fool a burglar, but none of it ever mattered. The house was never locked, and it isn't now. I take a deep breath and walk straight in. My heart lifts just a bit at the familiar smell of Mr. M and his Old Spice, but seeing the empty Morris chair plummets me back to sadness. I don't want to stay here long, and I move quickly to the piano and raise the lid. There, resting on the keys, is a folded note. Mr. M's handwriting was always hard to make out, but I learned to decipher his scrawls from the hundreds of notes he made on the margins of my scores. When I sit down to read, I make out every word.

Dear Angela,

When you read this, I will be gone. I am sorry because I should have prepared you, but we had better things to talk about. I would have told you that it's okay to grieve, as I am doing at the thought of leaving you, but you mustn't let your sadness become despair. I know, because I lost all hope when Jamilah died, and then, in the darkest moment of a terrible storm, an angel appeared on my doorstep and brought the kind of joy I never thought I'd see again. Shed your tears, but then move on. There will be more storms ahead, and you will weather them all with your courage, the joy of music, and the lessons of our friendship that will never die.

While I own little of any value, all of it is yours. Go and see Mr. Shapiro. He has my instructions, and he will guide you. The house is not worth much, but there's enough to see you through Colby, and the old Buick will keep you from having to hitch rides up and down the hill. And please, find a child much like yourself, with not much money and a big love of music, and make the Beckwith a gift from you and me.

Think of me often, dear Angel, and when you do, I promise I'll come to you in ways that matter most.

All my love,
Mr. M

I read the note once more, then fold it carefully and put it in my pocket. My dearest friend is gone, but he's helping me still. I reach to close the lid, and then decide to make one more gift to him, and I sit back down to play the old piano for the last time. *Für Elise.* His favorite.

The sun has set, but I don't need the light. With my eyes closed, I am once again playing on the old cardboard keyboard, and the house is filled with joyful music. A gentle gust of warm spring air swings open the door behind me, and in this moment I feel Mr. M sitting here beside me, and I know I hear the angels sing.

Epilogue

Blocked by stones and overgrown with brush, the narrow cut beneath the railroad tracks on Front Street can still be found, but beyond it, the tiny ghetto called Head of Falls has completely disappeared, razed in an Urban Renewal project of the mid-1970s. All that remains to mark the once teeming place is the wire cable Two-Cent Bridge, restored and open to all who are tempted to walk the swaying span over the Kennebec.

The Syrian-Lebanese immigration that began here at the end of the 19th century has all but stopped, and while descendants of those who first settled along the riverbank still live close by, most have scattered through all parts of town. Together, they contribute in uncounted ways to the richness of the culture, character, and the cuisine of the entire community.

Readers should know that the story of the Angel and Mr. M is not made of pure whimsy, for the Lebanese-Americans, who share the many virtues common to immigrants of all nations, have an extra measure of the loving generosity that leads them to reach out and sacrifice in order to enrich the lives of children and make their dreams come true.

Acknowledgements

I am grateful for my own memories of coming of age in the time and place of this book, but I could not remember it all, and although it is a delicate matter to name names and risk hurt feelings, there are some I must salute. First are three friends who scoured every chapter: Michael Donihue, economist, pig farmer, and literary cheerleader; and Fred Letourneau and Charles Ferguson, both earnest copy editors, proofreaders and, to my good fortune, musicians. I also want to thank Wally Buschmann, my pro bono attorney in writing on matters of the law; Ann Beverage, a local historian who knows where good things are buried in City Hall; and Stana Short McLeod, who once managed the popular *Facebook* page for those who share a love for Waterville. I am also indebted to a number of people who contributed bits and pieces, often without even knowing: Meg Bernier Boyd, Osborne Ellis, Francis Hallee, Theresa Ani George, Jim Meehan, Marie Paradis, Wayne Pelletier, Claudette Bard Rancourt, and Catherine George Vaughan. Finally, but with no less fervor, I am grateful to Pat Newell, the kind and wise publisher at North Country Press; and my wife Barbara, who encourages me to write. I also planned to thank my Golden Retriever Benjamin, but I can't because he persists in nudging my elbow with his nose, causing typos.

Other books by

EARL SMITH

Fiction

The Dam Committee
More Dam Trouble

History

Mayflower Hill, A History of Colby College
With the Help of Friends, A History of the Colby Art Museum

CPSIA information can be obtained
at www.ICGtesting.com
Printed in the USA
BVOW08s1303141116
467798BV00001B/7/P